47 men

by robin maguire

47 Men

Robin Maguire

© 2015 Robin Maguire, ALL RIGHTS RESERVED
ISBN-13: 978-0-9906081-0-3 (Paperback edition)
ISBN-13: 978-0-9906081-1-0 (eBook edition)

Library of Congress Control Number:
2015941656

Acanto Press
Los Angeles, CA. 90049
Please direct queries to robintmaguire@gmail.com

47 Men is a work of fiction. The events and persons are imagined. Any resemblance to actual events, or to persons, live or dead, is purely coincidence.

For Marc and Joan,
Hailey, Piper, Gracie & Ramsey

Why people don't accept love as it is, full of agonies and extasies, a *misterious* force that keeps the universe together? But no, even for love there is a need for explanations....

Paulo Coelho (in response to the 1/5 of a second to fall in love data - from his blog dated 11/18/10)

Forty-seven.
Forty-seven men.

Jupiter Campbell had slept with forty-six men.
Her goal had been fifty.

Forty-seven.
Forty-seven stopped her in her tracks.

He had orange hair and a bloody lip
when she first laid eyes on him.

Forty-six was three weeks ago, a mortician from The Cedar Hills Cemetery in Hartford, Connecticut. They fornicated in a coffin on display in the mortuary. Jupiter selected the most expensive one, The Angel Wing; with a pink shirr crepe interior. It was luscious. Benedict was not. She wondered if he had put a curse on her.

With only four to go and feeling slightly desperate, Jupiter resorted to calling her friend, Guillaume, who lived in New Haven. His boyfriend was a divine Hispanic boy called Estaban. She figured between the two of them there had to be at least one straight man they were lusting after. Guillaume called her back with detailed directions to a barn behind the Conoco Filling Station on South Main and a code word: menudo. Apparently, the strapping Estaban generated his income by running the only cock-fighting operation in the greater Connecticut region and forty-seven was going to be in attendance.

TEN (10) DAYS

(10) Days
Gestation period for cimex lectularius
commonly known as a Bed Bug.

(10) Days
Waiting period after the purchase of
a handgun in California.

(10) Days
Vipassana Meditation: ten-day course for self-
transformation through self-observation.

(10) Days
1950s, the Pentagon conducted a study to
determine behavior at different stages of starvation.
After ten days without food, ninety percent of
people will steal, pillage, and kill for food.

(10) Days
Number of days remaining for Jupiter Campbell
to actualize her objective of fifty men.

SOUTH MAIN STREET
New Haven, Connecticut

J upiter hooked the eyelet bra that matched her panties and sat down at her dressing table. Behind her in the mirror, a large orange cat called Charlie Tomato watched her every movement.

"You know Charles; I think this is going to be a good one." She said as she wrapped her neon blonde hair into a twist, threading a red chopstick through the knot, applied a little blush and a swipe of mascara.

"Don't look at me like that, Charlie," Jupiter stood up and pulled a pair of white pants over her skinny legs. "I'm close Charlie, it's almost over."

Charlie Tomato turned away, meowed loudly and jumped off the bed.

"No judgment Charles, it's not cool. Besides, no one asked for your opinion." She slipped her arms into the sleeves of a white gauzy top and buttoned it before fishing a white shoe from under the bed then walking around in circles looking for the mate.

"Dammit Chuck, you made me lose my shoe." Jupiter yelled in the direction of where the cat had been.

"Oh right," Jupiter remembered and ran to the kitchen, "I used it to kill a spider."

The white shoe sat alone on the counter in an otherwise pristine kitchen. Jupiter slipped it on her shapely foot accented with tangerine toenail polish, opened a can of cat food and dumped it into the orange bowl at her feet. Charlie Tomato returned pronto.

"I know you love me," she said as she twirled around.

She picked up the cat and kissed him on the nose, "You'll always be my number one Charles."

Charlie flattened his ears and made an unfriendly sound so Jupiter dropped him to the floor, removed her purse and keys from labeled hooks by the front door and headed off in search of forty-seven.

Jupiter sat behind the wheel of her mother's Mercedes 280 zinging along I-91 when the highway lit up like stripes on the American flag. The three-hour trip turned into five-and-a-half and by the time she arrived at the fire-engine-red door, password ready, the fight was over.

She went in anyway. The door squealed as it opened; revealing a dirt floor with what looked like a boxing ring in the center. A puddle of blood marred the square and a naked light bulb hung from an unfinished beam in the ceiling. Jupiter caught sight of a dark lump near the edge of the ring. She stepped closer and heard the distinct sound of a man's voice. He had ice- blue eyes and a nest of orange hair. His lip was bleeding and in his lap was a pulsating, bloody cock. He continued to talk.

Oh, please don't…

Don't die…

Fuckin' bird…

I know you're only half mine but I love you bird.

Preston fucking Pickett…

What the fuck was I thinking?

"Rooster, I'll give you an extra thousand bucks. Just take the bird to New Haven."

Fuckin' New Haven.

Fuck. You're our money bird. You can't die. He's gonna kill me. Fuck.

Why did I say yes? I'm a photographer for fuck's sake. I have four sisters. What do I know about cockfights? Preston fucking Pickett, why'd I let you send me outta New Orleans for this?

What am I supposed to do, bird? Blood's squirting all over. Are there chicken vets? Fuck I wish I had a brother… Ahhhhh bird, you're gurgling.

What am I gonna say? Dude Farfalle won, our bird fucking won. I have twenty grand man...but...

Our bird's in adios park...

The cock's dead.

The cock visibly flinched in his arms.

Oh sorry, I didn't mean to scare you. What can I do for you?

Do I bring you back?

Fuck I need a drink. Right now, man: Jack and Coke. Fuck.

"Is it over?" Jupiter's voice blurted into the still air.

"What?" The man's voice cracked.

"The fight?" Jupiter moved in closer.

"He's dyin'," He stated plainly.

Somehow his stating the obvious was endearing.

"I'm sorry," Jupiter said earnestly.

"But he won," He said with bravado, his bloody fingers trying to console the injured bird.

"Well, congratulations then, I guess," Jupiter said feeling uncomfortable with the way he was staring at her.

"He was the best cock..." His voice trailed off as the edge of Jupiter's smile tried to contain itself.

"Why are you here?" The man asked, his southern drawl falling softly from his bloody lip.

"Forty-seven." Jupiter blurted out.

"Forty-seven what?"

Jupiter's mind raced. Three weeks of down time had given her the opportunity to do some research. Forty-seven is the quintessential random number of the universe, a mosquito has forty-seven teeth; forty-seven bones of the "Lucy" skeleton were unearthed in 1974; there are forty-seven states that actually matter, the forty-seventh President might be Hispanic or a woman; a forty-seven sided polygon is called a tetracontakaiheptagon;

there are forty-seven ways to cook an egg; the atomic weight of Titanium is 47; the country code for Norway is forty- seven; the "47 Society" actually exists. And forty-seven men.

How do you explain forty-seven men?

"You're bleeding," Jupiter said attempting to redirect.

"It's him," The man returned.

"No, from your lip," Jupiter motioned to her own lip.

He wiped his lip on the sleeve of his white T-shirt. His blood smeared into the seam.

"He clawed me... after he won... what's forty-seven?"

Jupiter studied this pile of a man sitting in the dirt, covered in blood and thought for a moment, what the fuck... maybe I should just tell him. Then her father flashed into her mind.

Her father had not spoken for the better part of two years and in a bizarre and pathetic attempt to shock him out of his zombie-like state, Jupiter had made a commitment to random sex.

Fifty as a number seemed slightly obscene while still being manageable. She had calculated that over the course of a one-year period she would have to have sex with a different guy once a week, giving herself a two-week vacation. At first this hadn't posed much of a problem; Jupiter was the particularly beautiful product of her parents. Platinum locks, chestnut skin, long limbs and green eyes that conjured notions of the Emerald City. Phillip DuPont, an architecture student, was number one even though they were boyfriend and girlfriend at the time she'd made this commitment. He had walked in on number two, Thor, a nude model from Jupiter's life-drawing class. Three through eight were on the hockey team and nine through twelve were from the psych department during a sleep study. She went through the fraternities but word got out and in a bizarre twist of fate the Delta Tau Deltas and the Sigma Chis of Dartmouth College decided that they didn't want to be *used* by Jupiter Campbell.

After number sixteen, the Hanover Fire Chief, Phillip DuPont (number one) tried to reason with her.

"Jupiter, people are talking about you. The things they're saying... well they're—"

"Phil...lip, we broke up. I'm not your responsibility."

"But it's not safe what you're doing. You need to stop."

"Phillip, you're sweet to care."

"Don't dismiss me. I know what you're doing."

"No, Philly, you have no idea."

"You're sadly textbook: stage two on the Kübler-Ross grief scale. You're stuck in anger."

"Keep it to yourself, Philly; I don't need the psychobabble. Besides it's kind of empowering getting to be the one in charge. A whole new world of female dominance."

"Jesus, Jupiter, you have to stop this."

"Nope, it's the ultimate freedom, no commitment, no B.S., just get it and go."

"You sound like a dude who—,"

Jupiter kissed him on the cheek and waved behind her as she left him mid-sentence.

Jupiter's mother, Ruth Ann Campbell, had been on vacation in Palm Beach, Florida with her husband of twenty-two years and Jupiter's father, Russell. Ruth Ann wearing spanky new Lilly Pulitzer from head to toe was crossing swanky Worth Avenue holding Russell's hand.

According to reports, she dropped something "shiny" and reached down to retrieve it. Russell stepped ahead of her and reeled around just as a JFK Ambulance bound for The Good Samaritan Hospital collided with Ruth Ann.

"She flew up in the air like a rag doll and then splattered all over the ground," Chief Nigel Bakker of Battalion Two said, quoting her father, as he gave Jupiter the news. Russell was in shock. It was February. Jupiter had forged to the airport in her North Face down jacket and gamey Sorrels and flew to West Palm Beach, Florida.

The Battalion Chief met Jupiter at the hospital morgue. Russell, slouched in a molded plastic chair, was entirely catatonic.

"So, are you named for the city?" the Chief asked, trying anything to delay the inevitable.

"What?" Jupiter said as she blew past him and yelled over her shoulder, "No, my father is a scientist."

When the Chief caught up to her, tapping foot and vicious back-and-forth doorknob turning, he put his hand on her shoulder.

"Hang on here for a minute." He said, trying ever so hard to prepare her for a sight no one should ever see.

"Hang on?" Jupiter said turning to face him. "I just lost the one person I can't live without. So please sir, let's just get on with it."

Ruth Ann's body lay on a metal table covered with a blue sheet, which the chief pulled back briskly. No amount of caution could have prepared Jupiter for the viewing. Ruth Ann's face looked like it had been dragged along I-80 going at a hundred-and-twenty miles an hour. The Chief's arm jerked at the sight of her and the sheet slipped exposing the top of Ruth Ann's breast. Jupiter threw her hand down with a thwack onto the sheet so he wouldn't see her mother's nakedness.

"Sorry Mommy."

The absurd words echoed against the acid-green tiles. Jupiter held her breath and reached for her mother's frail right eyelid. She pulled it back to reveal the luscious green orb that had, in the miracle of DNA, been passed down the gene pool to Jupiter.

"Forty-seven what?" The man staring at her repeated.

"What are you going to do with the bird?" Jupiter dodged him again.

"I don't know."

"It's suffering." She moved in closer. The sleeve of her white gauze shirt brushed the top of his head. "What's its name?" she asked as she sat down in the dirt in her white pants.

47 men

"Farfalle," he said, watching curiously as her white shoes tapped in the dirt. "What's your name?" he said still watching her feet.

"Jupiter."

"Uranus," he replied without looking up.

Jupiter punched him in the arm.

"What's your name?"

"Rooster." He said rubbing his arm.

"Cock–a–doodle. Doo." Jupiter started to laugh. The sound of her own laughter surprised her.

"Never heard that one before," he said but looked at her and cracked a smile.

Jupiter reached out to pet the dying cock.

"You need to do something," she advised.

"I know, but what?" he said, studying the quiver in her fingers as she removed her hand from the bird.

Jupiter paused for a moment, then reached in, grabbed the animal by its throat and with deft precision broke its neck. The sharp crack echoed through the still barn and then silence. Rooster looked at her dumbfounded.

"Why in the hell did you do that?"

"He was suffering."

"Well, I hope you're not busy."

"Why?"

"Because, Miss named after a planet, you're coming with me to tell Preston Pickett that you murdered our bird."

"I euthanized him," Jupiter corrected.

"I don't care what you call it." He stared into her green eyes trying to find a clue. "You killed our bird."

"Fine, but only if I drive," Jupiter said.

"Why did you do that?" Rooster asked again, shaking his head.

Jupiter looked at him, the stubble of his beard, the pouty lower lip and the crystal blue eyes that seared right through her.

"I don't know," she said quietly.

Then she got up off the ground and extended her slender hand. Rooster, in his blood soaked clothing, grabbed it and holding the bird in one arm, stood up and followed Jupiter outside. There were two cars in the dirt parking lot, her own tan Mercedes 280 with delicate lines and a chocolate cloth top, and a Ford Pinto station wagon, light blue with wood paneling.

"Nice car," Rooster remarked.

"My mom's," Jupiter whispered.

She brushed off her bottom, opened the trunk and produced a crusty floral beach towel.

"You can wrap him in this," she offered.

"I have a cage," Rooster said.

"No cage."

Rooster looked at her then shrugged and Jupiter watched him delicately wrap the bird in the towel and gently place it in the trunk. After that he turned and walked to the Pinto. He was taller than she'd thought six-one or two and handsome but in a way she wasn't used to.

Then she had a genius idea. Maybe this was it, the dead bird, the blood; maybe this was the shock that would snap her father out of his catatonic state.

"Do you have other clothes?" she asked.

"Whatever you want, princess," he said as he opened the hatchback and an avalanche of belongings fell in the dirt.

"Shit," Rooster boomed.

He retrieved a huge Japanese paintbrush and hurled it toward the driver's seat, then fished out a rumpled Oxford cloth shirt, pulling his bloody white T-shirt off over his head. Jupiter stared at his bare torso, the definition of his butterscotch-colored back, the curve of his ass where the top of his jeans met his skin. The shirt came down like a curtain at the end

15

of Act One. Rooster half buttoned his shirt and lifted the strap of a camera around his neck. Finally, he grabbed an old leather bag that captured Jupiter's interest.

"Where'd you get that?" she inquired.

"Great-grandfather," Rooster answered and slammed the hatchback shut.

Jupiter slipped into the driver's seat of the pristine car.

"Jesus, anyone ever use this car?" he asked as he got in and shut the door.

"Not for a while," she said, and added, "I have to stop to check on my dad before we go, is that okay?"

"Where's your dad?"

"New Canaan. It's on the way,"

"You don't even know where we're going,"

"Somewhere south," she mused.

"How do you know that?"

"Because Preston Pickett is not from Maine."

Jupiter turned the key in the ignition and as the engine sprang to life with a mellow rumble, Rooster tuned his undivided attention to the driver and smiled.

"Nice," he said.

OENOKE RIDGE ROAD
New Canaan, Connecticut

R ooster hauled an ancient Leica out of the leather satchel, sat sideways with his back up against the car door, and started taking pictures, first of his fingers.

"Two cameras? Wait, what are you doing?"

"Documenting."

In one brief movement the lens of his camera was in her face, clicking, one after another.

"Hey, that's not fair. I wasn't ready."

"That's the point."

Then he returned to his own body, now holding his bloody hand directly under the lens and very carefully pressing the shutter down. She continued to drive but glanced at him, trying to anticipate his next move. Finally, Jupiter gave up and turned her head away from him. They drove in silence except for the clicking of his shutter.

"How'd you know how to do that?" Rooster asked looking at her through the viewfinder.

"What?"

click

"Kill my bird."

click

"My father."

click

"Why?" he asked, still peering at her through the lens.

click

"In kindergarten, we hatched baby chicks and I wanted to keep all of them."

"Why?" he peeked out from behind the camera.

"Only child."

"So?"

"So... they made noise."

"That's strange." He put the camera down in his lap and watched her.

"Then they got too big so they had to go outside, but they laid eggs so my dad let them stay."

"Stay?"

"He liked the eggs. But if one ever stopped laying eggs we had to kill it and cook it. I was supposed to be learning about the food chain."

"But weren't they your pets?"

"Yep," Jupiter said, not looking at him.

She stared out the window and tried to get the chicks out of her head, instead her father's image popped in. She had begun an unfortunate ritual of visualizing how the encounter designed to rouse her father from his catatonic state might play out.

I walk slowly into his library. I saunter over to where he's sitting in his big leather chair.

"You know Daddy; I have selected mother's coffin and urn. The coffin is called the Angel Wing. But Daddy the URN, I just don't know what to do, too many choices. Apparently you can bring in your own vessel but Daddy, the reason I am here..." I pause for effect and then say ever so sweetly...

"Daddy, do you know what I did?"

Then he looks down at me on the rug by his feet.

"I had sex; you know, actual intercourse, with fifty men. Fifty Daddy, the big five-oh. I didn't even know some of their names." I laugh.

Then he grabs hold of my chin and begins to laugh and it reminds me of the way he laughed when he taught me to ride a bike. He ran alongside my wavering two-wheeler with its pink sparkle banana seat and pink-and-white streamers flying from the handlebars. A white fence stood confidently to my right I reached out, grabbed a post and the bike came to a dead stop. Daddy kept running and finally stopped twenty feet beyond me. He put his hands on his hips "Jupiter June," and then the same laugh... which continues but then becomes kind of hysterical. Then he says,

"Jupiter, you are such a liar. Good joke though. Go and tell Willy to get dinner ready. Your mother should be home soon."

"SHE'S DEAD," I scream at him, "AND I DON'T KNOW IF SHE WANTED TO BE CREMATED OR BURIED. I NEED TO KNOW."

"Where are the houses?" Rooster asked.

There were acres of white fences and long driveways with no houses in sight. Jupiter drove faster and finally turned into one. The tires crackled over the rocks in the gravel driveway.

Rooster turned his lens to Jupiter and clicked off two shots.

"Don't!" she snapped.

A house finally appeared. It was gray stone and looked like a boy's boarding school in the English countryside.

"Damn," Rooster murmured.

Jupiter parked the car and started to get out but turned back to him.

"Follow me and don't ask any questions."

Jupiter went to the trunk and pulled the bird out of its careful wrapping.

"Jesus Christ, what are you doing?"

"I'll explain later."

She approached the massive door, opened it and left the key in the lock. Rooster followed behind her. The foyer looked like the Metropolitan Museum of Art.

"Hurry," she begged.

Jupiter dashed through the barrel-vaulted corridor and up two flights of Italian marble steps to a long dark landing. Rooster clung to the polished

19
47 men

walnut banister awestruck by the magnitude of the art collection mounted on the walls. Jupiter broke for a moment, like a child faking a tantrum.

"You have to keep up with me," she demanded.

"Didn't get the playbook," Rooster said annoyed.

Jupiter pushed open a set of double doors.

The setting sun pierced the room with a ray of light falling directly on Russell in a tall wing-backed leather chair, his blue eyes watery from the strain, blinking hard to see the interruption. Jupiter hovered in front of him holding the bird she'd killed. Rooster caught up just as she gently placed the bloody beast into her father's corduroy lap. Then she kneeled in front of him and whispered, "Daddy, you have to help it. The bird is dying. You have to save the bird. Daddy, please!"

When her father did not respond, Jupiter laid her head on top of the dead bird in defeat.

"Jupiter sweetie, he's had a good day today, ate a whole plate of my cinnamon buns," a woman's voice said out of the shadows as the sun set.

The room was quiet except for Jupiter's soft crying. A cherubic black woman stepped forward and put her enormous hand on top of Jupiter's back and Rooster watched as the fight drained out of Jupiter's body.

"Come on now, get up from there. Not doing you a bit a good. What's your name, son? Get over here and help me."

"Rooster."

"Well then Rooster, you pick up that dead thing and I'll take the baby. Don't worry; she'll be back to normal in a couple hours."

"What's your name?" Rooster's Southern drawl made the woman smile.

"They call me Willy, short for Wilhelmina. Come on now, no time for chit chat."

Willy moved Russell's heavy hand and picked up Jupiter. Her face was half covered in wet blood.

"Jesus," Rooster said taken aback.

"Rooster," Willy said firmly.

He picked Farfalle up out of Russell's lap and tried to brush the blood away.

"No use there," Willy said.

Rooster followed behind Willy, who carried Jupiter like a baby. He got to the door, turned back and looked at Russell with his lap full of blood sitting in the purple twilight.

"This place isn't good for her till he comes to. Best you go," Willy said over her shoulder.

"Go where?" Rooster said to no one.

Willy maneuvered down the corridor and out the front door to the Mercedes 280.

"Oh honey, you're the one who took the car," Willy sighed heavily. "You are just like your daddy; can't talk about a thing but always the dramatic gesture." Her eyes shot to Rooster, "She can't drive, sugar, you're gonna have to. You can drive, can't you?"

"Yeah," Rooster said trying his best to reassure her but not entirely sure why.

"Take her home with you."

"Uh... I don't know..."

"You gonna take care of my girl, Rooster."

Something in her voice tapped into the Southern gentleman ingrained in his soul and contrary to his better judgment he could not say no and Willy knew it.

Willy placed Jupiter in the front seat. Rooster watched through the driver's side window as she held Jupiter's little white face in her big black hands, "He loves you baby girl, he's gonna come out of it." she said and kissed Jupiter on the forehead. Jupiter's fingers moved slightly as if grasping for something and her legs looked uncomfortable crammed up against the console. How the fuck had he gotten himself into this situation?

Willy shut the car door and summoned him.

"Come on in the house; let's get you some nourishment for the road."

21

47 men

"What about her?" He asked looking at her body all jacked up in the front seat.

"She's not going anywhere," Willy said walking into the house, not looking back.

Willy's hips swayed as Rooster followed her toward the kitchen. She reminded him of Mabel who had worked in his momma's house for the past twenty years. Willy pulled out a wood stool for him to sit on and went to the refrigerator.

"Where you from?" she asked with her head in the fridge.

"New Orleans, how 'bout you?"

"Momma was from Hattiesburg, Mississippi. Then she was taken up north. I was born in Boston."

"But your accent?"

"I know," she chuckled, "my momma taught me how to talk or maybe it's just something in your soul, Rooster. How 'bout some fried chicken drumsticks and I got a few biscuits left."

"Sounds great," Rooster said, realizing he hadn't eaten since breakfast.

Willy packed everything into a brown paper bag.

"Are you sure she's gonna be okay?" Rooster asked.

"Sugar, he's been like this for some time. She keeps trying all these crazy stunts; seems like the more she tries the worse he gets."

"How long has he been this way?"

"Almost two years."

"Is she crazy?"

"No, no, not to worry." Willy said, moving a little faster.

Willy got a piece of paper and wrote in perfect script her full name and telephone number. "Now, you take this and if you have any trouble you call me, hear?"

"Yes ma'am," he said taking possession of the bag of food.

They walked out to the car and Willy tried to hand him a roll of bills.

"Please, take this."

Rooster shook his head, "No ma'am," He did not wait for an answer but got in the car and settled into the driver's seat. Willy went to Jupiter's door and opened it. Leaning in, she whispered, "Be good."

Jupiter whispered back "Can you call Phillip to feed the cat for me?"

Willy nodded, shut the door and patted the roof of the car. Rooster drove slowly back over the crackling driveway. The click of his camera's shutter made him turn. Jupiter held the Leica in front of his face. She peered at him from behind it. She pulled it away and winked at him.

NINE (9) DAYS

(9) Days
For serial killer and cannibal Albert Fish to consume
the body of ten-year-old Grace Budd.

(9) Days
For Satan to fall from Heaven.

(9) Days
The reign of Queen of England, Lady Jane Grey
"The Nine Days' Queen" July 1553. She was imprisoned
and finally beheaded in February 1554.

(9) Days
All that remains for Jupiter Campbell to get with the
program and consummate L (the Roman numeral for fifty).

INTERSTATE 485
Outer S toward Spartanburg

"Fuck."

"What?" Jupiter's groggy voice cracked.

"Sorry, did I say that out loud?" Rooster said looking at her.

"Yeah," Jupiter yawned hard, "Why'd you say it?"

"Forgot the damn bird on the driveway."

"He's dead," she stated plainly.

"I wanted to bury him."

She yawned again, "Sorry about before."

Rooster didn't say a word.

"I... it's just, he's been like that since my mother died. I read that shock is the only thing that snaps them out of it."

"What does he have?"

"Nothing, there's no medical reason for it," she said softly.

Rooster didn't say anything.

Jupiter was quiet.

He stared out the side window into blackness. Her head finally hit the glass window with a thud. She was asleep.

Rooster shimmied the camera from Jupiter's grasp and held it as far away from her as he could. Every five minutes or so he clicked off a picture. She slept like an Angora kitten and he drove exceedingly fast, snacking on drumsticks and butter biscuits, until the sun cracked over the horizon to greet him upon his return to the Big Easy.

GARDEN DISTRICT
New Orleans, Louisiana

Jupiter Campbell woke to the drawl of women familiar with each other's company. She lifted up the pink coverlet and matching floral sheet and surveyed herself. Yellow cotton nightgown, blood still caked to the underside of her wrist, and slowly the image of her father and sound of the click of the camera's shutter came back to her. She mashed her head into the feather pillow, wishing she could erase the bloody screaming performance that played in her mind like a bad movie. How had she done all of that in front of him? The smell of the pillow brought her back from the rancid images to the Downy fabric softener she'd only learned of when she went to college. Jupiter didn't move, just inhaled the pillow.

She began to pick out the voices. One, soft, older, probably his mother: the other, faster and more staccato and finally Rooster's, right as rain.

"Is she up yet?" He sounded annoyed.

"Hey Roo, Leila said to tell you she's happy you finally brought home a girl, even if she was a bloody mess. She was starting to think you and Preston were lovers."

"Shut up, Dar."

"Where'd you come from anyway?"

"Connecticut," Rooster answered.

"Why on God's Acre were you all the way up there?" his momma asked, "You're not running those damn birds again are you?"

"Will y'all keep an eye on her? I gotta go." Rooster said ignoring the question.

"Sure sweetie, we'll see to her. What's her name again?"

"Jupiter."

"Such a strange name. Go on, we'll take care of your *friend*," Momma whispered. "Just might have to give her a nickname is all."

"You do that Momma. Just be a little careful, she's kinda prickly."

Jupiter shot up from her cozy little bed and started to say *I am not* and then stopped herself.

"What do you mean prickly?"

"You'll see."

"You're kinda making her sound like a rabid dog." The young voice said.

"Not a bad comparison."

Jupiter bristled again and this time a sound came out. She threw her hand over her own mouth.

"Darwin Boudreaux, you stop that, it's that damn Preston Pickett. I don't want that sweet girl to think I raised a hoodlum."

"Momma, she's not sweet... she's—I don't know what the hell she is... hardly know the girl."

"Rooster Boudreaux," the young voice said in imitation of her Momma's voice, "You will not talk that way in my house."

"Darling, don't you make fun."

Jupiter heard keys jingling and then the steady pounding of Rooster's boots on the floor. She heard the car door slam and the engine of a truck rev into the thick southern air. Jupiter pulled the covers back over her yellow nightie, mashed her head back into the soft feather pillow and closed her eyes. She wasn't sure how she would venture out of the small dark pink room and she wasn't sure she wanted to.

EIGHT (8) DAYS

(8) Days
The duration of the Jewish celebration Hanukkah
also known as the Festival of Lights.

(8) Days
The length of time a human can survive without water
at a temperature of eighty-five degrees Fahrenheit.

(8) Days
"Eight Days a Week" a song written by Paul
McCartney and John Lennon in 1969.

(8) Days
The brit milah, "covenant of circumcision" is a
Jewish religious circumcision ceremony performed
on an eight-day-old male infant by a mohel.

(8) Days
The sum of days Jupiter Campbell has left to
complete her task. "Be the ball, Jupiter."

COLISEUM STREET
New Orleans, Louisiana.

Honking and yelling finally roused Jupiter from the depths of her sleep cocoon. She bolted upright, confused for a moment as to her where-abouts. Then she heard a young man's voice hooting and hollering.

"Rooster Boudreaux, get your ass out here and give me my money. Woooo-hooooo!"

"Preston Pickett, will you shut that trap o'yours, we have a house guest and she is sleeping."

"Sorry Missus Boudreaux. But it's four o'clock in the afternoon."

"They had a long drive."

"Who did? Does our Rooster have a lady friend stayin' with y'all?"

"Well, actually, yes, but no shenanigans from you, young man. His sis-ters are enough of a burden for any man to carry. He doesn't need you piling on. You hear?"

"Yes, ma'am. Is he here?"

"No, he's down at the studio getting ready for the show. So don't go down there either."

"Alright, I'll come back, what time?"

"Why don't you come back for supper? I'm making Granny's fried. Seven o'clock. Now get on outta here you loud thing."

"What's her name?"

"None a your beeswax. Git."

Jupiter laughed and pulled back the covers. *None of your beeswax.* She hadn't heard that since second grade. She sat up and rubbed the sleep out of her eyes. Finally she stood but dizzying stars forced her back down to the edge of the bed. She saw a pile of clothing with her name on it sitting by the door and wondered how she hadn't heard the door open and close. She got up slowly this time and picked up the pile; white shorts, a navy striped T-shirt, white Keds and a little note saying *Hope they fit* with a smiley face. She put everything on and studied herself in the mirror. Then she went into the bathroom, splashed some water on her face and swirled some around in her mouth and spit. She looked for toothpaste but no such luck. She smoothed her hair down and walked to the door, putting her ear to the pink painted surface.

When she was convinced no one was there, she twisted the knob and the ancient thing creaked open.

"That you, sugar?"

Ugh, she thought, hoping to have a few moments alone in the house to get her bearings.

"Uh... yeah..." her voice squawked.

"Come on in here and let me get a look at you."

Jupiter tiptoed toward a sweet little sun porch. She touched her head and tried to smooth her hair again. She ran her tongue across her teeth; they felt like they were wearing little wooly sweaters. She peered into the room tentatively. Mrs. Boudreaux was sitting in a pale pink velvet chair reading the *Times-Picayune* with her slippered feet propped up on a matching foot-stool. She was wearing a floral apron and her auburn hair was pinned up in a twist at the back of her head. Her cotton-candy-colored reading glasses were perched on the end of her nose assisting her emerald-green eyes that reminded Jupiter of her own mother's eyes.

"Oh good, you found the clothes, Dar picked them out. They fit okay?" She said sitting up and removing the glasses to get a better look at Jupiter.

"Yeah, perfect, thank you." she said standing awkwardly and fidgeting with the outside right leg of the shorts.

"Well, I must say you look much better than you did when you arrived. You hungry?"

31

"A little. I'm so sorry we woke you." Jupiter was blushing hard at the memory of not just being covered in blood, but giving this woman a five AM wake-up call to boot.

Mrs. Boudreaux put her glasses up on her head and swung her little legs around to the floor.

"Don't worry sugar. Come on; let's get you something to eat, you must be starving."

Jupiter followed her to the kitchen like a Retriever puppy. She sat down on one of the stools in the yellow kitchen that matched her own yellow hair.

"Well sweetie, what would you like? I'm makin' fried chicken for dinner and that's not far off so how about a little tuna salad, or maybe a fresh-baked cookie?"

"A cookie sounds... perfect." Jupiter looked around the kitchen. It didn't look like anyone was making anything; with the exception of a glass cake plate housing a pyramid of perfectly baked golden biscuits. The sight made her mouth water. The kitchen smelled like warm cinnamon and browning butter.

"How 'bout some sweet tea to go with?" Mrs. Boudreaux said with her back to Jupiter, reaching into the upper cabinet to retrieve two glasses.

"Sure. But what's sweet tea?"

"You certainly are a Yankee aren't you?"

Jupiter laughed. "Yeah, I guess I am."

"We drink sweet tea by the gallon down here, you're gonna love it. Honey, where'd Rooster say y'all are from?" she asked pouring the caramel brown liquid into the ice-filled glasses.

"Connecticut." Jupiter said.

"Have you lived there your whole life?"

"Pretty much. Went to New Hampshire for college. I didn't get down to the South much except for when my mother died." Jupiter almost tipped off her stool, shocked at her mouth for uttering those words.

"Oh darlin', I am so sorry. What happened?"

Mrs. Boudreaux picked out a floral china plate with pink roses and gold trim for the cookies.

"She was hit by an ambulance." Jupiter said quietly.

"Sweet Jesus." Mrs. Boudreaux turned around and looked at her.

"I had to go identify her body and get my father."

"All by yourself?" she asked incredulous.

"Yeah..." Jupiter tried to go on but a huge lump sat in the back of her throat. Tears started to pool in the corners of her eyes and her heart felt like someone was squeezing it with their bare hands.

"You come on here," Mrs. Boudreaux said witnessing Jupiter's anguish. She crossed the kitchen and embraced her, rocked her back and forth. "Not fair what God serves up sometimes, is it?"

"No, I... miss her." Jupiter said in a muffled voice, her head smashed into Mrs. Boudreaux's bosom, which smelled deliciously like cinnamon sugar. Ordinarily Jupiter would never have accepted such an open display of affection or publically shed tears. But her body collapsed under the soft touch of a mother's hand on her back and suddenly tears, which had never come before, arrived in a flood. Mrs. Boudreaux held her until they dried up and when Jupiter was finally quiet Mrs. Boudreaux unwrapped her arms and squeezed Jupiter's shoulders.

"I'm so sorry." Jupiter said mortally embarrassed by her outburst.

"Don't be silly, it's important to let that go. You're gonna be just fine. But sugar, we have to come up with a sweet name for you cuz I keep looking at your pretty face and wondering why your momma named her baby girl such a thing?"

"My father named me." Jupiter said now feeling terribly awkward in Mrs. Boudreaux's grasp.

"Shoulda known."

"He hasn't talked since she died."

"He'll come to." Mrs. Boudreaux pulled five sheets out of a Kleenex holder and handed Jupiter the white wad.

33
47 men

Jupiter returned to the island of her stool.

"You know, that is so funny, the exact same thing happened in my family when I was just a girl." Mrs. Boudreaux said offering her another cookie knowing, like she did with her son, when it was necessary to pull back.

Jupiter blew her nose.

"Thank you, what same thing?" Jupiter asked grabbing the gooey chocolate chip cookie from the plate.

Mrs. Boudreaux added a few more cookies and joined Jupiter on the stools.

"I really shouldn't eat these but they're my momma's recipe and I just can resist." She said breaking off a piece of cookie and popping it in her mouth.

Jupiter bit into the soft moist center. Suddenly, she could taste what she was eating, all butterscotchy with a hint of chocolate.

"Yum." Jupiter said.

Mrs. Boudreaux nodded and settled in, "Let me tell you a little story, might give you some hope. One of my mother's cousins lost his wife. They were real fancy, rich side of the family, not that we were poor but they, well, it was grand livin' is what it was. So cousin Luther and his wife, Merryweather packed their trunks and set off for a real African safari."

Jupiter sipped her sweet tea with rapt attention.

"Luther'd married a trust-fund girl and hadn't worked a day since the wedding. He was real fat and I thought he better be careful or he'd end up a fine supper for a lion. Well, wouldn't ya know, coupla weeks later, Momma got a telegram. It wasn't at all what we expected."

Mrs. Boudreaux took another bite of her cookie and a sip of tea and continued.

MERRYWEATHER TRAPPED IN JAWS OF A LION STOP
TRIED TO SAVE HER STOP LUTHER'S FACE MANGLED
STOP SOMEONE MUST RETRIEVE LUTHER STOP
CAN'T TRAVEL ALONE STOP **TANGANYIKA TOURS
AND SAFARIS LTD.**

"Well, Momma and Daddy Bear decided Momma would be the one. I thought my momma was the bravest woman in the world to go all by herself to Africa. She sent one telegram.

IT IS DISASTROUS STOP WORSE THAN IMAGINED STOP MISS YOU TERRIBLY STOP KISSES.

"I stole it and put it under my pillow 'cause I thought it had actually been in Africa. Well Momma came home with Ole Luther and Merryweather in a pine box, what was left anyway. We were all spooked by Uncle Luther. If you looked at him from the right, he looked pretty okay, but from the left... his eye, having been practically ripped out, was dangling from the socket and part of his cheek and jaw were gone. More tea?"

"Sure." Jupiter said.

Mrs. Boudreaux poured from the pitcher on the counter and continued.

"Well, three *years* went by and Luther didn't say a word. He'd sit at the dinner table with a huge white Panama hat dipped way down so you could only see the right side of his face. Took to wearin' it all the time, even in the house and Granny'd shout from across the table, 'Luther you take that damn hat off in this house.' Granny was blind as a bat, so we'd all pipe in and say; 'No, no Granny, that's the way now,' cuz none of us kids wanted to see that soppy side of his face. And do you know what finally snapped him outta the *state*?"

Jupiter shook her head.

"A white kitten. His youngest daughter had it playing around at his feet and he leaned over and said 'What's your kitty cat's name?' We asked him why he didn't talk. He said he didn't really know but didn't much remember any of the last three years. After that he told us what happened to Merryweather in a real dramatic radio voice, 'We were in the bush, fishing, Merryweather was behind me. Out of nowhere I heard her scream. Turned to see a lion on top of her, tearing away at her neck. Ran toward the huge cat with my fishing pole, he leaped at me from a hundred yards away with his mouth open. His canines ripped into the flesh of my cheek. I felt a tremendous burning, another gouge and then my eye went dark. The guide told me the lion left me and returned to chew on Merryweather some more. When I woke up," he said, "I was in the hospital with a vague recollection of the events, half a face and a dead Merryweather. It was all most peculiar.'"

The front door slammed shut and Jupiter jumped.

"It's just Rooster, baby." Mrs. Boudreaux said patting Jupiter's arm as she got up off of the stool.

"So you're finally up then?" Rooster's voice boomed through the house. "Momma, what're you going on about?"

"Oh nothing, just talking," she said mischievously and winked at Jupiter.

"How you feelin'?" Rooster said, turning his attention to Jupiter.

"Better, thanks," her eyes shot toward the ground, hoping to hide the fact that she'd been crying.

"Sweetie, why don't you take Jupiter outside and show her around. I need to get dinner going."

Rooster grabbed her hand, which surprised both of them and walked her outside to the palatial front porch.

TRINITY EPISCOPAL SCHOOL
New Orleans, Louisiana.

T he screen door thwaped behind them and bounced. A little black nose poked out, and popped back in just before it closed tight. The fragrance of honeysuckle flavored the air and the sun shot long across the front lawn. There was a white wooden porch swing and a tire hanging from a thick rope out of the biggest Live Oak tree Jupiter had ever seen. Rooster plopped on the porch swing and patted the seat next to him. She complied. He pushed them back and forth with the toes of his boots.

"When I was six, the fire department had to get me outta that tree."

"Really?"

"Yep. Wanted to see if I could make it to the top and I got stuck. Momma was in the house playin' the piano so she couldn't hear me... so, I closed my eyes and hummed along."

"Who finally found you?"

"Dahlia came walking home with a boy. I was real quiet till they got right under me. I yelled, 'Help,' and scared the daylights out of them. Dahlia started swearin'. 'Jesus Christ, YOU little piss ant, I can't believe you're up there spyin' on me!'" Rooster said imitating his sister voice.

"Which one is she?"

"Third. Finally, Momma came out and yelled, 'Rooster Boudreaux you're late for supper.' I said 'Momma, I'm up here' and she started screaming, 'Don't you dare move, Rooster Boudreaux, what on God's green earth are you doing up there?' She called my daddy and he said call the fire department. Hook and ladder came howlin' round the corner and the whole neighborhood ended up in our front yard." He said pointing out to the lawn. "I'd been up there so long I couldn't move. Fireman's up on his ladder beggin' me to let go. Finally Dahlia screamed, 'You little chicken shit, let go of the tree.' I grabbed his coat sleeve and slipped a little. The crowd screamed as he got me back. I was a legend in the first grade."

"I don't think I've ever been a legend."

"You still got time." He said smiling.

"Running out of it."

Rooster stood up and shuffled his paint-covered work boots. Jupiter remained in the swing wearing his sister's hand-me-downs. She was feeling far more comfortable than normally acceptable on the Jupiter Campbell scale of intimacy. Her scale was as follows: *zero*, where she maintained her consistent personal best of a lack of intimacy, to ten. Ten had previously been reserved for her mother. No one had moved above zero since her mother's passing and presently she was creeping into the two range with Rooster and may have even reached a seven with Mrs. Boudreaux.

"Wanna go for a bike ride?" Rooster said, snapping her out of her calculations.

"Sure," she said, "I haven't ridden a bike in a while though."

He sauntered across a rolling lawn to a huge hunter green garage with a pair of matching wooden doors and pulled them open. Inside, a ride-on-lawnmower and gardening supplies obscured a mint condition Model-T on blocks at the back. Jupiter pushed past him.

"Oh my God, whose car is this? My dad would love this car," she said, smoothing her hand over the shiny racing-green paint.

"That was Mr. Boudreaux's pride and joy. We joked he loved that car more than he loved us."

Jupiter climbed in the front seat and pressed on the horn and a sick duck sound shouted from under the hood. She started to laugh.

"Why'd you put it on blocks?"

"Made her too sad. So I put it in here, only place I still remember him, cause of the smell." Rooster hopped into the passenger seat, closed his eyes and took a huge whiff.

"He smoked his pipe in here, smelled like a pine tree. When I was a kid, I'd come lie on the floor and draw while he tinkered." He patted the side of the car, "I miss him."

"I miss her," Jupiter said, shooting up to five on the intimacy scale.

"He shot all those ducks," he said pointing up, changing the subject.

A craggy shelf built about six and a half feet up and all the way around the room housed what must have been Mr. Boudreaux's proudest achievement. Every foot and a half rested a taxidermy duck, probably seventy-five in all, covered in a gummy layer of dust, their former color trying its best not to be forgotten.

"Holy shit," Jupiter said as she assessed the death-filled room. "Why did you freak out so bad about the bird then?"

"Let's just say I had a bad experience."

"What happened?"

"Don't really want to say," Rooster said turning his body slightly away from hers.

"It's okay," Jupiter said putting her hand gently on his shoulder, "You can tell me."

Rooster waited for a minute and decided to oblige, not looking at her.

"He took me hunting, I was eight, didn't want to go, but he wanted to go *huntin' with his boy*. So up at four, had some Egg McMuffins and met up with his huntin' buddies. I'd only shot a BB gun before but now I had a real shotgun in my hands. It was all cool 'til that black V of arcs hit the sky. The guys started shooting. My dad yelled to me, 'Shoot, now.' I fired the gun and it kicked me back into the grass. The duck careened like an arrow dive-bombing toward me. He told me to get up and follow the dog, so I did. I spotted the writhing bloody bird; the dog ran to it and tried to get it in his mouth. I pushed the dog out of the way and got hold of the duck. It was flapping and bleeding and I'm saying sorry to the bird. One of the huntin' buddies comes up behind me, tells me I'm acting like a girl and I should get a sack. He yanked the bird outta my hands and wrung its neck. Dad came up, I'm crying and all bloody and he thinks I'm shot cuz I'm cryin'," Rooster paused, his head down, eyes in his lap. "When they figured out I was just cryin' that was the worst part."

"I'm sorry I killed your bird," Jupiter said very quietly.

"You saved me some money," Rooster looked up at her and cracked a smile.

"What?"

"Oh I'd a found a vet, spent a bucketa money to save a bird Preston's just gonna kill next week. So I owe you one."

"He's coming for dinner and he wants his money."

Rooster rolled his eyes at Jupiter and pointed to a pile of rusty cruisers.

"Bikes are over there."

"Do they work?" Jupiter asked, walking toward them to survey.

"Mr. Boudreaux called it *a functional state of decay*." Rooster grabbed a rusty red one off of the stack. He squeezed the tire. "See, perfect."

Jupiter picked out a yellow bike and wheeled it into the twilight. Rooster followed with a blue one.

Rooster jumped on the bike and yelled, "Follow me." Jupiter got on and tentatively peddled behind him. He sped up and after a few blocks screamed, "That's where I went to elementary school." Then Rooster pulled a small camera out of his pocket and started taking pictures of Jupiter on her bike, up really close and then far away.

"Let's go see it," Jupiter said, riding her bike back toward the entrance to Trinity Episcopal School. Rooster piled his rusty bike on top of hers and followed her to the playground.

Jupiter made a beeline toward the monkey bars.

"My favorite class, Miss Hogue," Rooster yelled pointing toward a classroom.

"I used to be able to skip two bars," Jupiter said with blind focus. She steadied herself on the ladder preparing to show off her superior playground skills. Her skinny light brown arm swung out and grabbed the metal above her, her legs bent at the knee so as not touch the black rubber mat with her feet. She skipped the next two bars with ease and then her hand slipped and she landed hard on her knees.

"Ow." She stood up and brushed off the black rubber granules imbedded into her knees.

"How'd your mom die?" Rooster asked attempting to be blasé.

Jupiter didn't respond and went back around to try again. Rooster took the hint, walked toward the swings and jumped on one, swinging his legs straight through. In seconds he was flying over the playground. He pulled the camera to his eye and began taking shots from his changing relation-ship with the ground. He heard Jupiter thump again. "You better not take a picture of me," she said, now sitting on the black rubber mat, defeated by the bars.

"Maybe you should try the swing."

Jupiter walked over and sat in the swing next to him, going the opposite direction.

"Let me just take some of your feet. They look cool coming at me."

"Nothing else," she warned.

"Can't promise that kind of accuracy." Rooster said, eye in the viewfinder.

Click – the bend of her knee.

"What did she look like?"

Click – the edge of Delilah's dirty white Ked.

"Who?" Rooster replied attempting to hold the camera still while moving.

Click – missed it.

"Miss Hogue."

Click – dirty laces, pink sky.

"Didn't think you were listening."

Click – upturned edge of green eye.

Jupiter smiled. "It's a curse. So?"

Click – teeth.

41
47 men

"Red beehive and once she wore white go-go boots to school. Caused quite a stir."

Click – hand clenched on metal chain.

"Go-go boots?"

Click – bluish and pink sky.

"Yep."

Click – white blonde hair flying.

"Are you sure it wasn't the short skirt that went with them?"

Click – pink sky.

"You know," he paused. "I wonder if that wasn't a walk of shame?"

Click – black rubber mat with white shoes.

"A what?" Jupiter asked naively.

Click – ear blurry.

"Next morning, clothes from the night before—sometimes have to wear 'em all day."

Click – bent elbow, blonde arm fuzz

"How do you know?"

Click – metal triangle, black rubber seat, white shorts.

"Walk of shame was a Boudreaux family favorite. One would come in and the other would say, 'Oh my God... DID you JUST get HOME???' Momma with her bionic hearing would come in wielding a wooden spoon, smack the offender and tell 'em they were grounded."

Click – lips.

"Is that why you never brought girls home?"

Click – fuchsia sky.

"Yes ma'am."

Click – shoulder.

"Smart."

Click – fuchsia sky.

"Did you ever bring anyone home?" Rooster asked.

Click – silhouette of Jupiter flying through the air jumping from the swing

Her feet bumped hard against the rubber mat as she landed, making black marks on the toes of Delilah's shoes. She returned to the swing and sat motionless.

"My family's not like yours," Jupiter said.

Rooster pumped himself higher, "All families are screwed up."

"I guess."

Rooster went higher.

"Did you see your dad dead?" Jupiter asked with her eyes to the ground.

"He was still warm," Rooster said as he sped through the air, "He didn't look so bad."

"My mom looked like a gray crayon with a bloody tip."

"Did you touch her?" Rooster asked.

"They pulled away the sheet, her face was so mangled, all I could do was look at her hand. I held it, felt like the underbelly of a dissected frog." She said looking up at his silhouette in the swing.

"And then I..." Jupiter was now bounding past six on the intimacy scale edging toward seven, having never revealed the information she was about to tell. Rooster flew past her again. "I asked the guy if I could have a minute. I opened her eyelid. Her eye was still bright green, it looked like a marble."

"Like yours?"

"Huh?" Jupiter wasn't listening; she was reliving the moment in her mind.

Rooster stopped swinging. He came to rest right beside Jupiter, their feet parallel.

"How did she die?"

"In Palm Beach, crossing the street, she dropped her wedding ring. She always played with it. An ambulance on the way to the hospital with a heart attack victim killed her."

The dong of a dinner bell floated through the air and Mrs. Boudreaux's voice faintly calling out stopped Jupiter. Rooster didn't move a muscle.

"She was the only person who ever really saw me." She said swallowing the end of her sentence. Then she jumped off the swing and walked off the edge of the black mat.

"We better go," she said, walking purposefully toward their pile of bikes.

Rooster remained in the swing, eye focused into the lens of his camera. He watched her small shoulders as she picked up his bike and leaned it against the concrete wall so it wouldn't fall. He watched her get on hers.

Click – girl on bike in twilight.

Jupiter rode straight back, didn't look over her shoulder even once, but she could hear the squealing of Rooster's pedals behind her. Why had she said that to him? Eight was dipping into dangerous territory she thought to herself.

She had only gotten to ten once when she was thirteen. One of the fathers she babysat for had stuck his fat furry tongue down her throat before he gave her the four dollars an hour his pretty wife had promised. It happened twice and on the third time, Jupiter bit down as hard as she could. He'd slapped her across the face and had tried to yell but his damaged tongue wouldn't let him.

Jupiter and Ruth Ann Campbell were in the kitchen with Willy and Mirabelle bustling around them when her mother asked why she wasn't babysitting for the Debarges anymore; Jupiter decided it was time for full disclosure. Livid, Ruth Ann picked up the telephone and called Mrs. Debarge, who said they were both liars. When asked about the bite out of her husband's tongue, Mrs. Debarge replied it had happened chewing on a piece of steak.

"Really?" Ruth Ann said, starting to laugh.

It grew into a regular old belly laugh, which made Jupiter laugh too, and pretty soon Willy and Mirabelle joined in. Ruth Ann left the receiver sitting on the counter and let Mrs. Debarge hear all of their laughter.

"Mommy, I couldn't live without you."

Ruth Ann wrapped her arms around Jupiter and kissed the top of her head. "Baby girl, I couldn't live without you either."

It was a perfect ten.

PORCHES
Boudreaux Home, Coliseum Street

Jupiter rested her bike against the wall and took in the Boudreaux compound. It was the quintessential southern mansion—gigantic porch, high ceilings and the requisite musty scent from *the rainy season*. Returning to Rooster's home, Jupiter was struck by the majesty of the architecture and the resplendent landscape, which she'd obviously missed upon her arrival.

Rooster leaned his bike against hers and brushed a piece of the black rubber mat from her cheek.

"Ready?" Rooster asked, pointing to the front porch filled with people, cocktails and the hum of Southern women.

Everyone was all squeezed in together on chintz sofas in front of a coffee table loaded with cabbage roses, Mint Julep glasses and platters of delicious morsels. The footstool of a dog lay under the table waiting for scraps.

"Well, finally," Mrs. Boudreaux said. "I thought I'd lost you two to the Quarter. Alright, darlin' girl, let's introduce you around. This is my sister June Bug and her husband Darryl. They live in Baton Rouge and Darryl sells used cars."

June Bug was rail thin with long auburn curls cascading down her back. White apparently was the color of choice this evening as she and Darryl both sported it from head to toe. Darryl looked like he'd been a linebacker in college. He had a thick head of brown hair parted hard on the left side and combed across his forehead in a greasy mass.

"Uh, uh, uh Rosie... I am a purveyor of previously owned vehicles," Darryl interrupted shaking his finger at her.

Then June Bug interrupted him. "Where y'all from?"

"Connecticut," Jupiter said politely, rubbing her palm nervously down the leg of her shorts.

"Never been there," June Bug said, giving Jupiter the once-over. According to Rooster, June Bug, Mrs. Boudreaux's youngest sister, had no children of her own, so the fact that June and Rooster were both the youngest of five created a special kinship between them.

"What exactly are your intentions with my nephew?" June Bug's eyeballs scorched through the top layer of Jupiter's skin.

The question was ignored by everyone save Jupiter, who looked at the ground and felt the familiar rush of color arriving at her cheeks. Thankfully, Mrs. Boudreaux pushed her along the line of family members, the cadence of Rosie's speech reaching warp speed.

"Now this is Rooster's sister, Delilah, and her husband, Corbin." Delilah shone like a radiant jewel, clearly the female star of the family. Jet-black hair, bright red lips and the same ice-blue eyes as Rooster. No one ever noticed Corbin. "And these are my darling grandchildren, Conner..."

"Hey," said a droning twelve-year-old with pimples a-plenty.

"Candace..."

"Nice to meet you, ma'am," said a sweet ten-year-old with perfect brown braids decorated with ribbons.

"And Christian..."

"Nooooooooooooooooooooo, I don't want to meet you," the five-year-old screamed.

"Hey there mister, that's my friend, you be nice," Rooster said, and Jupiter blushed again.

"And you met Dar earlier. Oh no, wait, you didn't...this is Darling," Mrs. Boudreaux said.

"Hey, nice to meet you. Glad the clothes fit," Darling said smiling.

Darling was just that—cherubic with auburn hair that matched her mother's, the kind of girl who wanted to go through life never bringing attention to herself.

"Yeah, thank you..." Jupiter started to say, putting her hand out awkwardly to shake Darling's hand.

"And this is—" Mrs. Boudreaux began as a man jaunted up the steps calling out.

"I AM the one, the only Preston Pickett, and you are a fantastically enchanting young lady."

Jupiter turned to see a freshly showered, strikingly handsome man, six foot two or three, slim with dark hair, wearing a perfectly tailored gray suit, blue shirt no tie.

Preston grabbed her hand with both of his and looked into her eyes.

"Damn girl, you got some green eyes, dontcha. Lucky for you, we got a cocktail to match those eyes."

"Oh my God! Preston, you make me want to vomit," Delilah said making a puking motion.

Mrs. Boudreaux turned to Jupiter and whispered, "They dated for a bit. It ended badly."

"A cocktail from Preston Pickett must never be turned down. It's a house rule, follow me," Rooster said grabbing her arm and meandering his way through several rooms to a mahogany bar that must have been the pride and joy of Mr. Boudreaux.

"Okay y'all. Let the master in. I have been serving cocktails from behind *this* bar since I was thirteen years old," Preston said pushing his way through.

"Benefit of being the youngest in a family of girls," Rooster explained to Jupiter.

"Hi, I'm Jupiter," she said reaching across the bar to shake his hand, "I'm sorry about your bird."

"Wait... just... one... little minute here." Preston said pulling his hand away, his voice turning dark and icy. "YOU'RE the one who killed Farfalle?"

Jupiter froze, shocked by his quick turn of emotion.

"Sugar, can you come in here and help an old woman out. I need an extra set of hands," Mrs. Boudreaux called as she rounded the corner of the bar.

Jupiter moved in the direction of Mrs. Boudreaux's voice.

"I can't believe YOU killed our bird." Preston said bitterly to Jupiter's back and then tried to recover, turning back to Rooster.

"Brother man, that is one H-O-T piece of ass but why the fuck did she kill our bird?" his voice filled with venom.

Rooster shook his head, "No idea."

"She's not your usual speed Boudreaux. She's a little too clean."

"Rooster, I need you too." Mrs. Boudreaux yelled out.

Rooster rolled his eyes to Preston and moseyed past him toward the kitchen. Mrs. Boudreaux held a bucket of oysters and Jupiter followed carrying the oyster platter.

"I completely forgot about the oysters, will y'all go on out and shuck'em while we get everything else ready? I just don't know where my head is."

"Yes ma'am." He said taking the bucket from his mother.

Jupiter followed him out to the back porch, the screen door smacked shut behind her. He dropped the bucket on the top step and sat down beside it. Jupiter stood above him awkwardly holding the platter.

"Sit," he said.

They sat side by side on the steps with a view out to the mammoth-sized backyard. Rooster yanked on a glove, then pulled his oyster knife and an oyster out of the bucket and began to expertly shuck it.

"Is he mad?" Jupiter regarded him seriously.

"Yep and holds a grudge."

"Is there anything I can do?"

"Ignore him, but be warned he might get nasty."

"Great."

Rooster slid the thinnest part of the knife under the edge of the shell. The knife jerked slightly and the oyster popped open. He moved the point across the top edge of the membrane and underneath the oyster, freeing the fresh meat from its shell and producing a perfect specimen.

"Wow, where did you learn that?"

"Mr. Tyrone. He worked here weekends; day job was in the Quarter at Felix's. He had this special needle thing."

"Can you teach me?"

"Sure, put on the glove. This is an oyster knife." Rooster held it up to her face. "Has a real sharp point on the end, be careful of it slipping. It'll go straight through your hand."

He fingered the point of the knife. Then he readied the position of the oyster and she copied him.

"Now see the hinge, you kinda wiggle in, up and down and then a turning motion, like pulling out a loose tooth. You work at it and wiggle it around and pop it comes out. Very satisfying."

Jupiter fought with the oyster and finally got it open. She tried to emulate Rooster's moves and mangled it. She showed it to him, disappointed.

"Try it again." He handed her another craggy shell and looked down at the oyster in his hands. He began to speak quickly without breathing, something in his tone made her stop her jimmying and look at him.

"My daddy was having an affair when he died. I caught him." He paused and then continued almost in a whisper, "I was in Baton Rouge interviewing for staff photographer position at the *Advocate*. I was walking down the street and saw him havin' lunch at some café, kissing a young girl in broad daylight... If I'd been five minutes later, I mighta missed the whole thing."

Jupiter, stunned by this sudden burst of honesty, took a moment to react. She brushed a strand of hair away from her eyes with the side of her shoulder.

"Did he see you?" she whispered, not looking directly at him and still holding the half shucked oyster in her bare hand.

"Yeah, but pretended he didn't. I just stood there and stared at him. Finally, he couldn't take it and they left. I told him he had to tell Momma by Saturday or I'd do it for him. He had a heart attack on Friday night and died. If I'd never seen him, he might still be alive."

Jupiter sat frozen on the step, unable to find her voice.

47 men

"I feel like it's my fault."

"It's not your fault." Jupiter said quickly, wracking her brain for a reason why on earth he would be telling her this. No one ever told her anything... or maybe they did, she thought, maybe she just never listened properly before... But why now and why him? She wiped her hand on the side of her shorts, the oyster shell was dripping water into her palm, tickling and annoying her simultaneously.

Rooster continued shucking with his head down. She looked at the back of his neck. It was pearly white, unlike the rest of his light brown skin. She wanted to touch it gently, tell him everything was going to be okay. But she couldn't move and she'd forgotten to breathe. God, why does this boy make me feel so much, she thought. She sucked in a huge gulp of air, which made him look in her direction, compelling her to say something into his solemn blue eyes.

"That really sucks," was all she could muster but was grateful any words came out of her mouth at all. Relieved she took another breath.

Rooster looked at her and laughed.

"Yeah, it really does." He said shaking his head, "I have no idea why I just told you that."

Neither do I, she thought. All those men she'd been with... she tried to remember one thing any of the previous forty-six had said to her. But nothing... not a thing came to mind. All she could remember was Phillip DuPont looking down at her in bed with the art class model telling her she was shameful. But it didn't really count because he'd actually been her boy-friend at the time.

Not a single sentence in a whole year of her life.

Rooster stood up like a free man, his movement knocking her out of her stupor. He looked out over the yard and stretched his arms above his head.

"I've never told anyone that before."

"Really?" Jupiter said staring at him, moderately terrified. "Uh, how do you feel?" she asked quietly not really wanting to know.

"Actually... I feel pretty good."

She breathed in again and stood up next to him, her oyster still in one hand and the knife in the other. Rooster leaned in to kiss her just as she began to step down off of the porch,

"Are those grave stones out there?" she said as they awkwardly collided, her head bumping into his shoulder.

"Yep," Rooster said trying to regroup.

Jupiter blushed and kept walking. As she got to the headstones and surveyed the names she turned and called to him,

"Why do they all say Ed Peterson?"

"She names all the cats Ed Peterson, then it's like they never really died."

"How many are here?"

"Twelve maybe?"

Jupiter stood for a moment looking at all of the curious shapes and sizes of the headstones and then walked back to Rooster on the porch. She sat down on the bottom step and looked up at him.

"Does she know about your dad and the girl?"

"Hell, no."

"Are you two about done?" Mrs. Boudreaux asked through the screen door, and Jupiter almost jumped out of her skin.

"Yep, Momma, we sure are."

Rooster gave Jupiter a brief death stare and stood up with the full platter of oysters in hand.

"Can you put those on the buffet Roo and go on and check everyone's cocktails for me?" Mrs. Boudreaux asked.

FORMAL DINING ROOM
Boudreaux home

The palatial dining room was festooned with three gargantuan crystal chandeliers and two antique gold mirrors. Rooster and Preston entered carrying wine and cocktails adorned with mint sprigs.

"Bring that over here," Mrs. Boudreaux said motioning to Preston who was carrying the wine bottle. "Now I apologize for the simple cooking; Mabel and Mary Grace are off on Sundays, the Day of the Lord and all."

Enormous platters of food filled the table. A pile of the best-looking fried chicken Jupiter had ever smelled, creamy mashed potatoes with a lob of butter pooled in the center, a bowl of some kind of a green leafy thing, the mouth-watering biscuits, homemade peach jam, white gravy and the fresh oysters. Jupiter's mouth salivated as she waited to be seated.

"Y'all just plunk down wherever."

Rooster and Jupiter were stationed half way down the table directly across from June Bug and Darryl.

"Okay now, let's drink a toast to y'all for coming out and bringing a little life to this old house." Mrs. Boudreaux said.

Their glasses clinked and Preston rose from his seat.

"Oh, sit down," Delilah said, under her breath.

Preston held a Mint Julep in one hand and a glass of wine in the other. "I'd like to propose a toast to you Mrs. B.; to the best mother I have ever known. I love you more than my folks. And this is the BEST fried chicken I have ever had."

"I'll drink to that," Five-year-old Christian raised his Shirley Temple. The table erupted in laughter.

"How long you stayin' down here with Rooster?" June Bug asked, staring directly across the table at Jupiter.

"As long as she wants," Mrs. Boudreaux offered ignoring June as she replied, "You hear me sweetie? I can always use company in this big ole house. Besides, they're all tired of my stories."

Jupiter played with a hangnail on the side of her thumb, under her napkin, under the table. She fixed her gaze on the heaping plate of food in front of her, attempting to divert June Bug's prosecution.

"Well, how do YOU feel about that Rooster?" June Bug leaned in toward him, a strand of auburn falling down into her face.

Delilah blurted out, "Have ya'll ever been to Jazz fest? You have to stay for that."

"You hate Jazz Fest," Corbin said.

"I know, but I hate everything. She might like it." Delilah smiled at Jupiter and Jupiter smiled back.

"What's your name again? It's so odd?" June Bug continued her pursuit, as she tucked the loose strand behind her ear.

Jupiter felt the sentence hit her in the solar plexus like a dagger skewering straight through her guts. Mrs. Boudreaux jumped in and diverted.

"June Bug, you remember that time at Jazz Fest? After Percy Beebe's funeral?"

"Don't you *dare* tell that story. It's not nice to Darryl," June Bug said, finally looking toward her sister.

"Oh, it was a hundred years ago. What does he care," Mrs. Boudreaux said.

Jupiter sat back in her chair relieved, Rooster leaned forward, Darryl rolled his eyes at no one, Rosie Boudreaux smiled and began. "So... there we all were, like twenty of us. We'd just had this funeral and it was *terrible* because Percy died in a plane crash so it was *real* unexpected. Was he married to Eliza or were they just engaged?"

53
47 men

"Engaged," June Bug whispered. "You remember, her momma made her send back all of the wedding gifts. We were tryin' to cheer her up."

"Oh right. Well, we were all pretty young but June Bug here was the youngest. She was a *drama major at Tulane University*," Mrs. Boudreaux made quotation marks with her hands. "So it was the day after the funeral AND Jazz fest so *everyone* was in town. We met up at the Columns, beautiful old hotel with a big wide porch and just the perfect breeze blowing along St. Charles Avenue." She said looking at Jupiter. "We were all sittin' on the porch drinkin' Mint Juleps." Mrs. Boudreaux held up the half empty Mint Julep glass from the table. "And this crop of young men mosey on out from the bar. Four of the best-looking fellas I'd ever seen, all done up for a wedding, lookin' like some niiiiiiiiice sherbet on a hot afternoon. They sat down next to us and I'm pinchin' June Bug and she's pinchin' me back. They tell us they're in town for a weddin', in from *Shreveport*, best friend's marryin' a girl from New Orleans and *did we happen to know her*. Did we know her?" Mrs. Boudreaux asked June Bug.

"Not too well. She was younger than me and was – *with child*." June Bug said making a pregnant belly motion.

"Right, right. So June Bug's across the table wearing a white Marilyn Monroe dress, lookin' all sassy molassy and I say out loud to everyone, 'Our Miss June is going to do a monologue from a Tennessee Williams play right here, right now on this very porch.' Well, the boys from *Shreveport* start clappin' for June. She got right up there, introduced herself, stole one of Bennie Price's cigarillos and lit it up. She started in on the monologue, leaning up against the huge white pillar with her leg up and smoking that cigarillo. The boys from *Shreveport* started whistling and June Bug just stayed in character—that's the way to say it, right?"

June Bug nodded.

"So Junie spins over and picks the most handsome one of the bunch, delivers the rest of that monologue lookin' deep into his *EYES*. When she finished, the crowd *ERUPTED* into applause. THEN... the boys bought a few *bottles* of champagne for her," Mrs. Boudreaux smiled. "And a little while later who do I see standing by the pillar in the garden with that young fella all in a thither? Well, it's none other than MY little June Bug. So he asks her to come to the weddin' as his *date*."

"That's how I knew about the baby," June whispered.

"So she goes and in a white dress, of all things."

"At least *I* shoulda been wearin' white."

"*June*, that's not nice. So she goes with this fella—what was his name?"

"Winston," June answered, with that Darryl got up, asked if anyone else needed a cocktail and left.

"*Winston* turns out, happened to be the great grandson of a tire manufacturing family, *drippin'* with dollars. They have a marvelous time and he starts comin' around like a dog in heat. Well, *then* he sets a meetin' with our Daddy, without even askin' June, asks permission for her hand in marriage. Would you have married him?"

"I don't know," June said.

Mrs. Boudreaux kept on, "Well Daddy spilled the beans before the poor guy even had the chance to ask. And Miss June over there was so mad he didn't ask *her* first that she stopped answering his calls. He was devastated by you. You know that, don't you?"

"Did you sleep with him?" Rooster said to her quietly.

"Well damn straight she did. Why else would he want to hold on to her so bad? Musta been good too," Preston piped in.

Darryl returned with a fresh Mint Julep. The entire table silent, turned and stared at him.

"What, y'all? It's only my second," Darryl said defending himself.

June Bug rose from the table, flipped her hair dramatically and skulked off. Mrs. Boudreaux made eyes at all of them and followed June Bug out to the kitchen.

"Hey, what do you say we play a game of I've never?" Preston belted out.

"You start, big hitter," Delilah countered.

Jupiter watched June Bug turn the corner with Rosie following closely behind her. She glanced around the table to see if anyone else was watching them. They were not. She found this disconcerting somehow, but couldn't pinpoint why.

"Fine, I've never French kissed my younger brother," Preston said looking Delilah straight in the eye.

Delilah pulled a handful of ice cubes out of her glass and threw them at Preston's head. The clear cube flying through her line of vision brought Jupiter back from her thoughts. She looked over at Rooster, he did not look back.

"I'm not playin' if you're gonna pull that shit, Pickett," Delilah shouted with her hands on her hips.

"What's going on in there?" Mrs. Boudreaux called from the kitchen.

"Nothin', Mrs. B., just playin' a little game out here is all," Preston answered. "Rooster, you start."

"No," Rooster said.

"I'll start," Darryl said. "I've never slept with three people in the same day."

Preston put the glass to his lips, as did Jupiter, Delilah and Corbin.

"Jesus Christ, I sure as shit missed out," Darryl said looking at the group of drinkers.

"I've never gotten crabs," Delilah said quickly because Rooster was looking at her trying to calculate who the three guys were. Everyone else at the table drank.

"Delilah, you're such a liar, you've had crabs," Preston ribbed.

"Don't you start with me—" Delilah started to say.

"I've never had sex on a rock," Corbin said interrupting her.

Everyone else drank.

"What's the matter, Cor, don'tcha like a little nature?" Darryl teased.

"Who'd you have sex on a rock with?" Corbin asked Delilah.

"You don't want to know," she said quietly.

"Me," Preston announced.

"Be right back." Preston left Corbin staring at Delilah.

"I told you." She said.

"Little late," Corbin said, slightly pissed.

Rooster was next.

"I've never slept with a Mardi Gras Queen."

Darryl and Corbin chugged heartily. Preston came back with an arm-ful of Shiner's and passed them out. Jupiter sat back in her chair with her knees up, arms wrapped around them, fresh beer in hand... watching, enjoying being one with the people. She took a swig of beer and glanced in Rooster's direction. The creases by the corners of his eyes turned up. There was a twinkle and a sort of freedom emanating from him, which made her smile, think about having sex with him on a rock and subsequently blush.

"What was it?" Preston said.

"Just drink, you've done it," Delilah said.

"Well alrighty then," Preston chugged half of a beer.

"Who was it?" Rooster asked with a chuckle.

"Who was what?" Preston said looking around wondering what he drank to.

"The guy you slept with?"

"Hey hey hey, the Pickett only likes the pussy. No foreign objects in the out hole." He winked at Delilah. The crowd laughed and Preston's eyes narrowed in on Jupiter,

"Your turn, sugar."

She put her legs down and looked around at the table full of eyes staring at her.

"Ummm, I've never had sex on a plane." She said relieved she had come up with something benign.

Every single one of them drank.

"No way, in that tiny bathroom?" Jupiter said looking at Delilah.

"Afraid so," she said, squeezing Corbin's arm. "Daddy was still alive and he told Corbin he'd kill him if he found out we were doin' it. We had to fly to Tallahassee to Corbin's grandma's funeral and I was stayin' in the same room with his little sister. So we did it on the plane and in the bathroom at the funeral parlor. Remember that Igor guy came and banged on the door?"

Corbin smiled at her.

"First class," Darryl said. "In the seat."

"In front of everyone?" Jupiter asked.

"It was a night flight," Darryl tried to explain.

"Me too, but in coach," Rooster said.

"How?" Jupiter questioned sitting up in her chair.

"Sat on my lap," Rooster replied.

"Ohhh... smart," Jupiter said.

"The galley," Preston said.

"Bull shit you did," Rooster said, staring him down.

Preston cracked and started laughing. "You're right. It was in that damn bathroom and my ass hit the hot water faucet burned the shit outta of the boys, screamed like a girl. The Stew came bangin' on the door asking if everything was alright, and we both answered. Then she said, 'Get out of there immediately.' Alrighty, my turn." He said watching Jupiter like a hawk. "I've never had sex with five people in the same day." He had thrown down the gauntlet.

Everyone looked around at each other. Delilah reached for her beer.

"Oh Christ," Corbin said.

"Ha! I'm just playin' with you," Delilah said and kissed him on the lips.

Jupiter pondered for a moment. Should she or shouldn't she? Intimacy scale screamed no. But she had already told him the seven. This seemed more in the five to six range. She wasn't going to tell about the forty-six... but the day when the visiting Maryland Terrapins lacrosse team had annihilated the Big Green, Jupiter had been a one-woman victory party. She'd racked up 33, 34, 35, 36 and 37. She lifted the beer to her lips and...

"Holy Christ girl, did y'all get gang raped?" Darryl yelled.

"Oh my God," Jupiter said. "I didn't mean to drink," lying, because she suddenly felt far less brave than she had moments before.

Preston smiled and nodded at her as he took a pull off of his beer.

"You're a man whore," Delilah declared.

Jupiter's hand fell onto Rooster's leg just as June Bug sauntered back into the dining room. She looked to see if Mrs. Boudreaux was behind June Bug but she wasn't. She didn't know what to do with her hand that now sat lamely on Rooster's thigh.

No one acknowledged June's entrance. She walked up next to Darryl and picked up his beer from the table.

"Hey baby," Darryl said not looking at her.

She put the amber glass to her lips and swallowed the entire contents in one gulp. She delicately replaced the bottle, emitted a small burp, said excuse me and left the room. Jupiter looked around, no reaction from the crowd.

"Preston has a list," Rooster reported, loudly.

"Are you kidding me?" Delilah moaned. "What number am I, you old pig?" Delilah asked.

Jupiter remembered her hand. She looked to see if Preston was watching. He wasn't paying attention so she gripped her fingers a little tighter. Rooster's leg was strong and warm under her grasp.

"You don't count. I didn't even put you on there."

"What's that supposed to mean?" Delilah's icy tone signaled war. Rooster grabbed Jupiter's hand from his leg and pulled her back from the edge of the table.

With the finesse of a leopard, Delilah picked up her beer bottle and flung it across the entire dining room right at Preston's head. He ducked at the last second and the bottle hit the hand-painted Chinoiserie wallpaper and shattered. With that Mrs. Boudreaux came running. June Bug lagged behind, her eyes red and glazed over.

47 men

"What on earth is going on in here?" Mrs. Boudreaux with her hands on her hips looked around the room for the culprit.

"It was Delilah," Preston reported.

"Delilah go get the broom and Preston, I think it's 'bout time you run on home before Delilah decides to slit your throat with that broken bottle."

"Yes ma'am, will do. Thank you for a wonderful evening."

Preston bent way down to give Mrs. Boudreaux a kiss on the cheek and she smacked him on the rear in return. He patted Corbin and Darryl on the back, glared at Jupiter, said "G'night, Belle Gunness" just as Delilah came at him swinging the broom.

"Goodnight y'all, I had a lovely time." He ran down the hallway and they heard the huge front door slam behind him.

"Honestly Delilah, why do you let him get to you the way he does?" Mrs. Boudreaux asked exasperated.

June Bug deposited herself down next to Rooster, intentionally interrupting the handholding. She pulled out a pack of Parliaments. Her hand shook as she removed the cylinder from the pack. Rooster slipped the matchbook out of the cellophane, struck the match and held the flame to her face. She sucked hard into the flame and finally it lit. Rooster wet his fingers in his mouth, placed them on either side of flame, and pressed them together snuffing it out with a sizzle. Jupiter watched intently, wondering if it hurt. Then she studied June Bug's profile as she inhaled deeply, the heavy creases in her upper lip, the coarse texture of her skin and the steel gray circles under her cloudy eyes.

"Hey, hey there, I thought we were stopping with the cancer sticks Junie," Darryl said, obviously pissed.

"Darryl honey, can you go stick your head outside and make sure that Christian didn't get himself stuck up in that tree?"

"It's dark."

"*I know it's dark*," Mrs. Boudreaux said annoyed. "*That's why I want you to check.* They've been awful quiet."

Darryl got up and muttered to himself and left looking back over his shoulder.

"Y'all, Darryl and Junie are havin' some troubles," Mrs. Boudreaux whispered and patted June's knee. "So, Junie's gonna take a little time and stay here with us. Isn't that great?"

No one responded, Jupiter shifted uncomfortably in her chair and looked at Rooster who glared at his mother.

Jupiter looked across the table at June Bug in a halo of smoke, pale and sullen as she sucked on the last of her cigarette. The hollow look in her eyes seemed vaguely familiar. Jupiter watched her puny arm trying to get its shaky fingers to her mouth to suck out the last bits of nicotine. The appendage reminded Jupiter oddly of her own. Conversation batted around the table, logistics and what not, June Bug stared deeply into space not listening to any of it. Jupiter was transfixed, drinking in every movement of this woman.

Her eyelids dropped over her eyeballs but slowly, the interval abnormal. Her mouth sort of chewed, but there was nothing in it. A second cigarette, now burned down to the bitter end, was about to singe her fingers. Jupiter waited to see the pain hit her face. But it didn't. When she thought she could smell the skin burning, Darryl finally pulled it out of her hand and mashed it out. He looked at his wife and then directly into Jupiter's eyes and shook his head. She smiled at him and awkwardly looked away. Was that how I did it, she thought, lost myself in tendrils of black smoke?

Jupiter excused herself quietly from the table. She went to the little pink bedroom behind the kitchen and climbed into the safety of the double bed with tiny pink flowers on it. She did not go to the bathroom, brush her teeth or wash her face. She did not want to see herself in the mirror, didn't want to have to look into her own eyes. Her head sunk into the down feathers with the soft cotton case and she starred up at the white ceiling feeling untethered.

Jupiter woke up in the middle of the night with Rooster lying next to her wearing all of his clothes. She listened to his soft breathing and watched his chest move up and down with his breath. He lay on his side with his back to her; Jupiter filled her body into the shape behind his, keeping her arms at her sides. She inhaled his neck, Dove soap and a little bit of salt. She thought about what his skin would taste like on her tongue, she looked for an open patch of skin within reach, nothing without moving. She held her breath and threaded her fingers through the belt loop in his jeans. She pressed her knees up against the back of his and finally letting go of her breath tried to sync with his. She got a little bolder and ran her hand down the side of his leg, following his strong bare arm to his hand. She laced her fingers in between his. His palm was soft with circles of calluses; his thick fingers responded, holding on to hers, such an easy fit. Fit, she thought, tonight for a moment she fit, with him, with his family it was a fullness she had never known. She squeezed his hand again and thought of her minute and hollow family. There was no music of voices, no joy, no repartee. There was thought and conjecture, rules and planning. Her father had been stern with both Jupiter and her mother. He did not laugh with her, he was never spontaneous. He was methodical and calculated. She inhaled Rooster again, soap, photo chemicals, salt and something sweet. What could that be, she wondered, shampoo, lotion, maybe June Bug's perfume? Rooster stirred and Jupiter froze. When his breathing returned to its steady pattern, she inhaled him again. The sweet smell seemed to be gone. Then she thought about his father smelling like pipe tobacco and she tried to think of what her father smelled of. Desperately, she tried to remember if she had ever smelled him. A cologne, a room, a mint, shaving cream, his chair or a place, like the front seat of the Model-T where she might remember his scent. It seemed to her that her father was devoid of smell... sadness overwhelmed her, back to the hollow place and back to her mission...

I walk into his office; it's morning and the golden light fills his room. I think this must have been a very pleasant place to work in the mornings. I am wearing my mother's pale pink Lanz nightgown from when she was in college. He sits in his big brown high-backed chair looking out at nothing, per usual.

"You know Daddy; I am looking into cryopreservation for Mommy. It is the preservation of humans in liquid nitrogen post mortem, but I'm sure you already know that. It's all the rage in Hollywood. There is a company in Arizona that does it. There is an initial fee of one hundred and fifty thousand dollars and then a five hundred dollar annual fee. It seems fairly reasonable if you do a cost analysis against the family tomb. Remember when you took me to the tombs at Père Lachaise Cemetery in Paris? I was thinking of something perhaps like Oscar Wilde's. Remember it was the one will the lipstick kisses and the castrated winged angel standing guard. I was thinking something like that might be nice and speaking of kissing. I have been doing quite a lot of kissing lately as well as fornicating and I seem to be having some issues with my vagina. I think it might be falling out because I have had sex with fifty—count 'em—fifty men... this year alone. Man, was I busy. Do you think a vagina can actually fall out? Mommy's not here so I thought you might be able to help me out with this." My father stands up out of his chair and slaps me so hard across the face that I start to cry. Then he yells,

"What in the name of God are you talking about? What is the MATTER with you? Have you gone MAD? Your mother and I did not raise a floozy. What is the matter with you Jupiter? Ruth Ann get in here, please come talk some sense into your daughter."

"RUTH ANN is DEAD!" I yell back at him.

SEVEN (7) DAYS

(7) Days
The amount of time it takes, once acclimated
to the altitude, to ascent Mount Everest.

(7) Days
To receive the results from HIV antibody
screening test (ELISA).

(7) Days
Shiva-formal period of mourning observed
after the funeral of a close relative in the
Jewish tradition, know as "sitting Shiva".

(7) Days
Lucky seven days remain for Jupiter Campbell to get to fifty.

DOUBLE BED
First Floor, Delilah's Room

"Oh my God, y'all, get in here! Look at them! They are so damn cute!" Jupiter opened her eyes. She was wrapped in Rooster's arms.

"They're lying here all cuddly in *THEIR CLOTHES*! You two are too much," Dar said with her shower-wet hair and navy blue dress on.

Rooster did not move a muscle. Dar left to give her report to a live audience.

"Sorry about that," Rooster said, his voice gravelly with the morning.

"It's okay."

"Not too much privacy in this house." He said and lightly kissed the back of her neck. It sent shivers through her entire body and she spoke quickly, hoping he hadn't felt her shudder.

"Honestly, it's okay. How's your aunt?"

"Crazy."

"What do you mean?"

"Long story," Rooster whispered into her neck.

"Tell me," Jupiter whispered. She felt him take a deep breath.

"Bipolar. Does this every couple of years. Momma makes excuses and tells stories like last night but leaves out the bad parts. She was actually on a three-day bender. The Winston guy, June Bug took him around the side of the building and gave him a blowjob. It's the reason I started taking pictures, Momma's stories never seemed to add up to the truth. Pictures don't lie."

Rooster suddenly stopped talking, like he'd hit his own ten. Jupiter was quiet and put her hand gently over his.

"Will you show me your pictures?"

"Sure."

Jupiter patted his hand and slowly got up out of bed, feeling like he might need a moment alone. She went into the small pink bathroom and shut the door quietly behind her. She opened the medicine cabinet to look for toothpaste. There was an ancient tube of Crest with the end rolled up. She opened the flip cap; there was crusty white all around the outside. She squeezed some into the bowl of the sink and took a finger full of the freshest part. She closed the cabinet door and watched herself brushing her teeth with her finger. She looked different, odd almost, like happy or calm but something she had never seen on her own face before. She kept looking into the mirror like somehow her reflection might talk back and give her an answer.

"Maybe..." she said to her reflection "I don't need to finish this, maybe I could just stay here for a while."

"What?" Rooster called out to her.

"Nothing," Jupiter said as she watched herself turn beet red.

ATTIC
Boudreaux home, Coliseum Street

T he attic was long and narrow, blue indoor-outdoor carpet on the floor and white wood slats on a pitched roof, which provided a home to thousands of photographs. It was a ceiling of people and smiles and frowns and bits of nature and stormy skies and Rooster's life.

"So, I have to go to my studio for a bit. Will you be okay here?"

Jupiter looked at him, his messy hair and twinkly blue eyes and smiled. "Sure, I'm good."

"Cool." Rooster laughed at Jupiter sprawled out in the middle of the floor surrounded by boxes of photographs.

Still in her clothes from the day before and with bare feet, Jupiter lay on her back and stared at the ceiling like she was looking at a starry sky. The huge tree in the front yard, limbs like arms climbing out of the picture right at her. A smiling photo in front of a Christmas tree, Mom, Dad and all five kids in matching outfits. Rooster about seven, Dar next to Mom, Delilah next to Dad, Daphne and Dahlia next to each other but off by themselves. Mr. and Mrs. Boudreaux have their arms around each other; Rooster is nestled tight between them. A headstone from the graveyard.

"Did you know the graveyards here are above ground because the water table's too high. When they flood real bad, bones float through the streets," Rooster told her matter of factly.

Jupiter tried to make out the name on the headstone from her vantage point, Mary something but she couldn't see the rest.

An old man's hand. Jupiter wondered if it was Rooster's grandpa who told the boy Winston not to marry his daughter. Would her father ever do something like that to her? Tell her beloved that she had slept with forty-six men and that he couldn't recommend Jupiter to be of sound mind or body. She squeezed her eyes shut.

Her eyes opened to a picture of three small black boys with bright white teeth wearing suits with thin black ties, their heads hanging out of a window on a bus. "That looks like it's from the fifties." She raised her legs above her head and looked at her toes with the pictures as a landscape behind them. She had her mother's toes; just beyond her left big toe she saw an eight by ten picture of two smiling women, from perhaps the mid-sixties. Bright red lipstick, one wore a Pucci scarf tied around her head with long auburn hair down past her shoulders. The other was in a white Marilyn Monroe dress with mahogany colored hair but the same eyes. Jupiter put her legs down and stared at the picture from her back on the blue carpet. The women were resplendent, so intoxicating that Jupiter could not take her eyes off of them. Mrs. Boudreaux was more beautiful than June Bug. But June stood a few inches taller and had a body that could stop traffic. Their arms curved around each other and they were holding cocktails. June smoked, her eyes looked past the camera. Mrs. Boudreaux's eyes gleamed right into the lens. Must have been Mr. Boudreaux taking the picture. They stood on the porch of this very house. Jupiter moved in really close to investigate the picture. She walked along slowly looking for more, trying to find a picture of the man who wanted to marry June Bug. Mountains, deserts, cars, cocks— twenty or thirty of them, families laughing at picnics, toasting glasses, smiling on the beach. She returned to the floor and spilled the contents of the biggest box all over the blue carpet. There were hundreds of pictures of bits of people, noses, arms, legs, hands, breasts, fingers, genitals, tongues, teeth, ears, hips, belly buttons, hair, nostrils. Every piece of a person but not a whole one in the lot. She left them and went to the next box in hot pursuit of the picture of June Bug's beau. She poured the photos from the second box in another pile. This one had bits of nature, trees, flowers, rivers, rocks, fish, barnacles, starfish, sea anemones, snails, cockroaches, black dog noses, whiskers, paws. She ventured to the next box and tipped it over. Faces and families and smiles and babies. She lay down on her stomach in front of the pile and slowly waded through them, observing each one trying to figure out who the people were, and which babies were which based on the ages. Baptisms, birthdays, parties. Then she reached the old ones where the paper was a little yellowed and the babies had not been born yet. Jupiter rolled over on her back and holding a professional photo of Rooster's parents above her head, just to take them in. Mrs. Boudreaux's skin was a little browner than in the other photos and the twinkle in her eye was perhaps a little more pronounced. Her strapless cocktail dress was in the perfect shade of pink and his white dinner jacket, slicked hair and gleaming pearly whites completed the picture.

"Wow." Jupiter held the picture and rolled to her side on top of all of the other photos and stared hard at it, so beautiful together, somewhere tropical probably, like the Bahamas. Her eyes were feeling droopy but she blinked hard to keep focused.

Rooster was suddenly above her. His curly hair fell in a crazy halo around his face and shadowed his eyes. His shining bone white teeth were held by a grin that made her feel like Sleeping Beauty being awakened by the prince, she smiled at the stupidity of this notion. Rooster pulled up the fabric of his jeans at his thighs and kneeled down next to her. She pressed the back of her head in to the carpet and followed his eyes. The reddish lashes fluttered and then his eyes locked on to hers. The irises were clear at the edges and cloudy in the centers, she wondered what that meant as he bent his head slowly to her mouth. He smelled like Christmas trees and cigarette smoke. She wanted to watch his eyes as his lips touched hers softly but she couldn't see them anymore. His tongue delicately made its way into her mouth. It was warm and smooth and soft, he tasted vaguely minty and her tongue wrapped around his, a velvety mixture of their mouths circled and teased, first soft and then more forceful their desire pushing up from their insides. Jupiter arched her body up to his, holding the loops of his jeans and nothing else.

Rooster slid his arm underneath the small of her back, his meaty hand just under the edge of her shirt, gently pressing her pelvis up and into him. This push gave her permission to let her hands explore his body. She wrapped her arms around his neck, running her fingers through the soft curls at the nape of his neck. Her mouth wanted his again but he let her head drop back and leaned over her, kissing the skin along her neck following the line of her throat, his tongue tasting the soft flesh behind her ear lobe. She shivered and giggled pulling away unable to handle the intensity. She brought her hands back to his brawny arms feeling the bundles of taught muscles and then the bones of his shoulder blades. She leaned her face into his chest inhaling the sweet smell of laundry detergent. Her hands continued to survey his body, reaching underneath the fabric of his T-shirt to feel his skin. He was smooth and his muscles flexed lightly under Jupiter's touch, she traced the vertebrae down to the base of his spine where she gently threaded her fingers through a downy patch of hair and pressed her pelvis firmly against him. She could feel him hard through the fabric of his jeans. She wanted to touch him, feel all of it but instead she moved her hips in a circle, feeling his stiffness bold against her stomach. Her fingers made their way to the top of his jeans and she slid her hands inside to feel the bare cheeks of his ass. There were fine hairs covering his skin and the shape was round and firm. She grabbed handfuls of him and pulled his ass against her, back and forth. He moaned softly into her mouth, the hot breath, the guttural sound originating in his groin made her pelvis tingle, she could feel the wetness at the edges. He pulled away to slow himself. Then he delicately unbuttoned Jupiter's shirt looking into her eager eyes as he did. His gaze moved to her bare chest and the curves of her breasts. He reached inside the fabric and gently cupped the right breast as his head moved confidently to the left one, his mouth finding its way to her soft pink nipple. He lightly circled the swollen raised edge then flicked the top of it. Her body flinched and he laughed softly and did it again.

Rooster's hand continued to unbutton while his mouth toyed with her. He pulled the edges of her shirt to the side and paused for a second. She smiled and reached her hand out and touched the outline of him through his jeans. Her desire was like nothing she had ever felt; to her core every cell in her body was electrified. He smiled watching her body arch in response to him. He gently caressed her inner thighs, running his fingers tantalizingly

71

close. He teased her a bit longer and finally let his hand trickle across her smooth stomach and make its way down, finally slipping his fingers inside of her, delicately pressing back and forth until he had her at the edge of the cliff, safe to finally jump and fall; she heard her voice scream out as her body released her, tumbling down shudder after shudder through her insides. She tore at the button on his jeans wanting him now with ferocity and he wriggled free exposing his largess. She looked at the whole of him, strong, erect and quite serious as he lowered himself on top of her. The weight of him pressing down on her, in and out in quick succession and when she thought she couldn't take it anymore he thrust himself deeper inside of her, she gasped and dug hard into his back with her hands. She savored the friction of his motion, the weight of his body, the feeling of him trying to slow, to stop himself. She heard her voice, low and strong, making sounds she didn't know she was capable of and his rumbling response in return. He paused and peered into her eyes, like he was trying to catalog the moment forever in his brain. His eyes were glassy and full. Jupiter had never felt this, had never really wanted a man. Sex had been so clinical up to this point, and now she was awash in something that words were incapable of describing. His pace quickened his breathing rapid and hers elevated in sync. She watched his torso stiffen and she closed her eyes and experienced the sensation of him inside of her, feeling parts of herself she didn't know existed. He groaned, his arms collapsing as he rested the full weight of his body on top of her. Jupiter could feel their hearts pounding against each other under the surface of their skin. She wrapped her arms around the strength of his back, not wanting to let him go. They lay quiet, neither moving nor speaking so as not to break the intensity. Finally, when he felt like he was crushing her he nuzzled his head into her ear and whispered, "That was amazing." His breath was like butter; he kissed her earlobe and gently sucked at the edge of it. Her body felt like it was levitating above the ground; she thought this must be the state of bliss that people spoke of.

"Jupiter, wake up," Rooster's voice jiggled her from sleep.

maguire

Jupiter's body jumped and her eyes blinked opened with a start. She bolted upright, looking around, slightly confused. Rooster peeled a photo off of her cheek.

"You okay?"

"Yeah, I must have fallen asleep."

"Yeah, the drool's usually a pretty good indicator." She wiped her mouth on her sleeve.

"You were talking."

"Dreaming."

"About what?"

Jupiter blushed. "I don't remember."

"You're red."

"It's hot."

"What happened up here?" Rooster said surveying the piles of photos.

"I was trying to find June Bug's beau, the one who wanted to marry her."

"Oh, there's one in here somewhere. Lemme look." Rooster started to pick through the pile of yellowed photos. She watched him move, his firm body through his pale blue T-shirt. She flushed at the thought of her dream, the taste of his mouth, his skin; she shook her head to snap herself back.

"Why do you take so many pictures of pieces of things? Why are there no wholes?" Jupiter asked looking at top of the pile with the snail antennae, and the other with a woman's ear, trying hard not to look at him.

He continued his search, "I wanted to figure out the pieces so I could make sense of the whole."

"If you don't see the whole, how can you ever understand how the pieces fit together?"

"Look at the wholes here." He held up a picture of his sisters. "You don't know anything from the wholes. It's only when you look at the parts that you ever understand anyone." He finally looked at her and touched her cheek with the back of his hand. "Parts are definitely more interesting."

Jupiter blushed again. Rooster returned to his stack.

47 men

"Your parents were so—"

"You picked my favorite picture of them. Look at the wrinkles by my dad's eyes..."

"But look at your mom. She's... she's... I can't even describe it. Maybe, dazzling and I don't think I've ever used that word before."

Rooster looked at the picture for a long time. "Yep, dazzling is the perfect word." He handed it back and returned to hunting.

"Here it is," Rooster announced. He held out a black-and-white three by five picture with Kodak typed on the side and May 1967 next to it. A dark haired young man with a heavy side part in a tuxedo stood next to June Bug in her Marilyn Monroe dress. Jupiter took the picture and held it up next to the Boudreaux's.

"Nice, but not dazzling." She held it up so he could compare them.

"Nope." He took the snap shot back. "It's hard to imagine she was ever like this."

"He should have just let her get married."

"I don't know about that."

"RROOOOOSSSSSTTTTTTEEEEEERRRRRRR! Where are y'all?"

"Up here, Momma," Rooster called down.

Her heels clicked on the steep winding steps up to the attic. "What are y'all doing up here?" Her voice preceded her arrival. She peaked around the corner, "Lord Almighty what's going on up here?" She said breathing hard.

"Just givin' Jupiter an education about parts and the Boudreaux's!"

"Heavens, I haven't been up here in years." She walked to Jupiter. "Which one are you lookin' at?" Jupiter turned the picture toward her.

"Oh my Gawd, that's our honeymoon. We were in Bermuda, about to have dinner at the captain's table." Mrs. Boudreaux, fresh from the garden club, snuggled in next to Jupiter in her St. John knit suit. She kicked off her navy Ferragamos and started leafing through the piles with them.

"Rooooooooster," Preston yelled in a high-pitched girl's voice.

"Oh shit, I forgot, Preston wants us to drive with him to Henderson for a fight. Do you want to go?"

"Oh Lord, honey, you can't take her to the cockfights. It's just not right."

"Oh come on, Momma, she hasn't taken a shower for a couple of days. She'll fit right in."

Jupiter smelled her armpit. "Do I smell?"

"Something awful," Rooster teased.

Preston, now in the house, was yelling, "Y'all get yer asses out here. We have a fight to git to. *Gone-a-Fowl* has a date with destiny."

"Are you game?" Rooster asked.

Jupiter winked at Mrs. Boudreaux.

"Rooster, go get her some pants from Dar's room then. I don't want those jackals looking at those pretty legs," Mrs. Boudreaux said, "Leave this, I'll clean it up." She picked up the picture of June and Winston. "Nice to see June Bug smiling, isn't it?"

Rooster was already down the stairs. Jupiter turned, "She looks better smiling."

"Don't we all," Mrs. Boudreaux said looking at the picture of the young couple on their honeymoon.

I-10 HENDERSON EXIT
St. Martin Parish

The trio boarded Preston's brand spanking new black Toyota Tundra with four cages in the truck bed.

They drove to St. Martin Parish, about 120 miles to the west of New Orleans. Preston peeled off the I-10 at the Henderson exit; drove up to Peggy's Lounge and then along a gravel road to two metal warehouses. Preston parked on the grass field to the right and yelled to a guy named Chopper who had a matching truck, three cocks, and a mean set of pork chops growing down his cheeks.

"Yo Pick, who you got today?" Chopper bellowed.

"Four best. Gonna whoop your ass, my friend," Preston said.

"Hey Roo," Chopper greeted Rooster.

"'sup Chop."

"Not much. Lickin' died last week. Sucked. Fuckin' Joey, put somethin' fuckin' illegal on his gaff. Bled like a stuffed pig." Chopper said, clearly upset by the death of his prize bird. "He was a fuckin' Albany. I coulda bred him for Christ's sake. Fuck." He grabbed his pork chop and pulled on it hard. "I'm going in. Seen Dale yet?"

"Nope. See ya inside," Rooster replied.

"Nice filly you got there, Roo," Chopper said, eyeballing Jupiter and pulling on his chop again.

Rooster looked at his shoes and didn't say a word.

"Hop outta there, kids. Rooster, grab Gone-a-Fowl. He's goin' first. I gotta get in there, get on the board," Preston said, putting on his cap with *Gone-a-Fowl* emblazoned in gold.

"This is weird," Jupiter said with no emotion.

"But it can pay pretty well." Rooster said, getting the bird ready.

"Like how much?"

"Depends if you win."

"What's a dag?" Jupiter stood in the bed of the truck looming down over the cocks.

"A gaff?"

"Yeah that."

"It's a spike they attach to the bird's leg. Object is to get the other bird in the soft underbelly below the wing. Some guys use blades but Preston likes the gaffs. They can poke out an eye, maim a leg or wing but not as deadly. Then he can still breed 'em."

"How do you breed them?" Jupiter's hands rested on her hips as she continued to stare at the cages below her. The birds chortled and fluffed themselves like they knew they were getting ready for the ring. "How much does it cost?"

"Hundred and fifty dollars a bird and twenty bucks to get in. And other stuff cost money but Preston does all that shit."

A couple guys in lumberjack shirts hooted at Jupiter. Without even looking in their direction, she aimed her middle finger right at their heads. Rooster watched.

"Whoa, you got some skills, filly."

Ignoring him Jupiter asked, "How many birds can fight in a night?"

"As many as you can afford and time will allow."

"Is there like a *King* of cockfighting?"

"Dale, but he's had a bunch die lately. Joey's been cheating, sounds like."

"How do you make money?"

"Gambling, sister."

"Why do they fight?"

"Bred for it, instinct."

"Is that why they use the blades?"

"No, that's to draw blood. The people love the blood. I don't watch the birds I watch the crowd, try to tell who's winning by their reactions."

"If you don't watch, why do you come?" Jupiter asked, still staring at the birds.

"Habit."

"Liar."

"Yep." Rooster looked down at his feet again.

Jupiter stared at the cages and then moved back to him. "The ducks?" she said loudly and her eyes returned to the cocks.

Rooster held Gone-a-Fowl like a baby. "Gotta get him to the cock house."

"Cock house? How can you all say this stuff without laughing? You've got to admit there's something funny about two men saying *my cock is gonna kick your cock's ass*. Where's the cock ring?" Jupiter noticed he was not amused. "Okay, where's the cock *house*?"

"I'll show you, come on."

She hopped down from the back of the truck and started walking toward the metal door.

"Wrong way." Rooster turned the other direction. They entered the second metal building, with air conditioning and stalls for each of the fighting birds. "Are you kidding me? This is nicer than jail." Jupiter noted.

"How do you know?"

"Know what?"

"About jail?"

"Just do."

"How?" Rooster pushed.

"Spent a couple days there." Jupiter blushed.

"And?"

"And nothing."

"I'm not taking you in 'til you tell me."

"I can go in without you," Jupiter retorted.

"Where's your money?"

Jupiter perched on the edge of a wooden bench. She tried to smooth her hair, which she hadn't bothered to brush since she arrived.

"Public intoxication."

"For a couple of days?"

"I was in a fountain. We were pretending to be Roman statues. You know, like the Trevi Fountain in Rome. Me and my friends, Phoebe and Jason, it was our final project for Art History. We covered ourselves in white paint and Phillip DuPont took pictures. We had a whole plan; only Jason thought it would be funny if he gave me and Phoebe Ecstasy. So we went to the fountain... in the middle of Hanover... during daylight hours. We were just supposed to jump in, take the pictures and get out. But the water was so nice we stayed... and the paint was water based and pretty soon we were naked and the three of us were all holding each other, trying to do statuesque poses and then... Jason got a boner and there were kids and they saw everything. Then I grabbed Jason's boner for shock value and we fell on each other in a pile and they thought we were actually having sex. But we definitely weren't because we were laughing too hard. The Hanover police came and Phillip DuPont ran because he was a DuPont. Phoebe's dad gave a bunch of money to the police and Jason and I went to the pokey. I wouldn't call my dad so I stayed in jail."

"Why didn't DuPont get you out?"

"Political aspirations. Didn't want a Jupiter in his past, kinda sounds like a black hooker."

"He said that?"

"No, I did. Here's the thing about my name, your mom, for example, can't even call me by my name. You can't either really. When you say it, it gets caught in the middle of your mouth like you think you might be saying it wrong, or like you're trying to figure out a way to shorten it. It's like a psychological experiment. The ones who say *JEW – pi – ter* outright like that, I never like them. They're usually assholes. The ones who can't say it at all, they're usually my friends. No one has ever been as blunt as your mom, it was very refreshing. I hate my name, really. Phillip said it was distinctive. And I said, 'For a hooker.' One must be very careful with the names chosen for children. They mark you for life."

"So what are you marked as?"

"Odd," Jupiter stated.

"You threw me off with the black hooker. I would have gone with the waifish kid who grew up on a commune with eighteen brothers and sisters, not really sure who your father is. Open prescription for medical marijuana, aspiring to graduate from Berklee College of Music, though never applied. Married to an organic farmer at fifteen, living off the land. Have a tribe of kids that never bathe and nurse them all until they're seven or eight years old. And when they're done on your teat, you'll make butter outta your breast milk and sell it at a huge premium."

"That's disgusting."

Preston rounded the corner yelling, got really close to Jupiter and blew a party horn directly in her ear.

"Will you two lovebirds get a move on? My baby's got a fight. Let's go, let's go, let's go!"

They walked in just as Preston's number was called. Rooster followed him toward the ring and Jupiter scampered to keep up. Rooster reached back for her hand and pulled her up next to him. Jupiter heard a whistle blow and the birds went at each other like an exquisite flamenco dance and then suddenly Jupiter saw a gush of blood coming from Preston's beautiful cock's wounded neck.

"Fuck you! Fuck you, Joey," Preston was screaming.

Preston grabbed a gaff from his back pocket. Joey held his prize bird above his head and danced in circles in the dirt as Gone-a-Fowl tipped over into a lake of its own blood. In the dust cloud, Preston shadowed Joey and in one stealthy move Preston stabbed Joey's cock in the neck. "Fuck you, Joey, fuckin' cheat." Preston swung across with a right hook that cracked into Joey's cheekbone. Jupiter screamed. Rooster grabbed her pulling her toward the door. Bodies piled in the middle of the dirt pit and writhed where the birds had just been. Old men threw dollar bills on the backs of the fighting men and Rooster pulled harder at Jupiter. She couldn't take her eyes off the mayhem. A skinny meth-head kid ran up the side of the wall and flew on top of the pile.

"I gotta get you outta here."

His pleading eyes made her legs move toward the door but her neck cranked around trying to see if she could spot Preston in the pile.

"What about Preston?" she said as Rooster started a slow gallop toward the truck.

He pulled a hide-a-key magnet from the back bumper and yelled, "Get in! We'll go around back and see if he comes out."

The truck was moving before Jupiter could get the door shut. A few guys ran toward the truck so Rooster floored it right at them. They spread like chickens and the tires burrowed into the dirt as he cranked the wheel toward the back of the hall. The lights hit a bloody Preston yelling, "Come on, come on, come on!" Rooster slowed and Preston heaved himself and the dead bird into the back with the other cages knocking around him. He hit the side of the cab three times hard. Rooster hauled ass out of the parking lot just as Joey ran out with a gun and started shooting in the direction of Preston's truck. Rooster threw Jupiter's head down toward the seat. Preston stood up.

"Fuck YOU, Joey! Good fuckin' luck killing' me." He jumped up and down flipping Joey the bird with both hands.

"Preston, fuckin' sit down," Rooster yelled out. Jupiter watched Preston through the back window. He kneeled down and she watched him pick up his bird and smear blood across its chest as he petted it. He pulled apart the edges of the wound. Blood gurgled out and he wiped it away trying to find the end of the bloody hole.

"What's he doing?" Rooster barked.

"Nothing, holding the bird," Jupiter replied. "Why?"

"Sometimes he does weird shit," Rooster said.

81

47 men

"Like what?"

"We need to bury the bird as soon as we get far enough away."

"Oh my God he's suck—oh my God that's so gross." Jupiter put her head in her lap. "Oh my God, ohhhhhhhhhhh." She shook her head trying to wipe the image out of her head.

"Yeah, that," Rooster didn't turn around but pounded his fist against the window. "HEY, cut that out."

They drove for a long time in the quiet; Jupiter stayed still with her head in her lap.

"Is it over?" she asked.

Rooster peered in the rearview mirror; Preston was no longer in view. "I don't know. We need to get to a bar."

"Why?"

"You sure ask *why* a lot."

Rooster sped up. Jupiter heard the engine rev and she pushed her head firmly against the glove compartment, still afraid to look up. She felt the truck circle an on-ramp and then accelerate again. The *click-click-click* of the blinker and then the slope of the off ramp, the turn from asphalt to gravel to dirt to pavement again.

"We're here," Rooster yelled, jumping out of the truck before Jupiter could see where she was and before she could see Preston.

"Clean up." Rooster threw a towel at his head.

"Why'd ya have to do that?"

Preston wiped his face. He pulled out his wallet and threw it to Rooster.

"Get a room, would you?"

MAGNOLIA INN
St. Martin Parish, Louisiana

There were two levels of rooms with parking in front at the Magnolia Inn. The white neon light of a flower glowed half lit and resembled a penis jutting into the night sky with only the letters Ma_n ia lit up. The restaurant bar called the Petal sat on the other side of the horseshoe. A few teenagers smoked cigarettes and kicked at the gravel by the bar's entrance.

Jupiter kept her head down so as to avoid seeing Preston. Rooster's feet crackled across the gravel.

"Here, 207." Rooster threw the key at Preston's head.

"Hey, hey, hey... easy there *mon coeur*." Preston grabbed a bag and the dead bird.

"Go bury it first," Rooster demanded.

"Settle down there, Roo."

"Fuck you, Preston."

"Go buy yourself dinner and a cocktail. I'll be there in a shake."

Preston ambled to the side of the building that opened out into darkness. Rooster waited for him to disappear into the black. He leaned into the cab of the truck. "He's gone. You want to get a drink?"

Jupiter pulled the handle and gently pushed the door open. She quietly joined Rooster and they crossed the horseshoe to the Petal. Rooster pulled open the red leather door with a diamond shaped window to reveal a bustling pack of older folks having dinner and imbibing at the bar; a generally jovial crowd, save for a group of brooding teens in the corner booth.

47 men

"Y'all sit anywhere you like," called out a woman with a buttercup-colored beehive, cone shaped double D's, skintight pink leggings and clear-heeled stilettos.

"Sure are a pretty little thing, aren't you? Looks like you could use a good meal. Burt back there—hey Burt, I'm talking 'bout you sweets—cooks a mean strip."

"Thank you," Jupiter said and smiled.

"My name's Penny. I'll be right over." She handed menus to Rooster and shooed them toward a large red booth in the opposite corner from the teens. They slid in and sat close to each other facing out. Rooster cracked open the menu.

"So what do you feel like?"

"Can we talk about...?"

"Can we not?" He asked.

Jupiter starred into her menu, not seeing a word.

"What can I do you for?" Penny said interrupting the silence. Penny wore a turquoise synthetic shirt and big white plastic jewelry. Jupiter smiled again in spite of herself.

"I'll have Burt's famous strip and a beer and a shot of tequila," Rooster said.

"Baked potato or rice and Thousand, Italian or Ranch?" Penny said writing on her pad.

"Baked. Thousand."

"Can I have the same but with Ranch," Jupiter asked.

"Just like peas and carrots, that's what you are." Penny pinched Rooster's cheek. "Be right back with the drinks. Buuuuurt got a couple of lovebirds out here, just like us baby."

A bellow from the kitchen echoed through the room. "Lucky man, Miss Penny, that what I am." And then he sang "A Lucky Man." The crowd at the bar clapped and Penny beamed.

She brought the cocktails on a red metal tray. "He's got a real nice voice, my Burt, dontcha think? Here you go kids. Enjoy each other, you hear me? Don't find love like this but once." Penny said wandering off.

Jupiter picked up the shot glass. "Here's to you saving my life."

Rooster tapped her glass lightly. They drank and he handed her a lime, took a swig off of his Budweiser and leaned back into the red Naugahyde. Jupiter leaned into him and they sat.

Quiet. Still. Penny brought two more shots, winking as she set them down. They ate. Thousand. Ranch. Penny delivered two more Budweiser's. Strip, baked, sour cream, chives. Then Penny brought Preston, who was showered, clean clothes, hair combed. Quiet. Still.

"Boy says he was lookin' for you. Looks like he could use a good meal. Burt, sweetie, need another strip! You like potatoes or rice, darling?"

Preston didn't answer.

"Potatoes," Rooster said. Preston sat awkwardly next to Rooster. "And a shot and a beer."

"Want another?" Penny said quietly.

Rooster nodded.

"You okay, bud?" Rooster asked, patting Preston's hand.

Preston nodded, not looking at either of them.

Rooster raised his glass. "To Gone–a-Fowl, may he rest in peace."

"To Gone-a-Fowl," Jupiter said.

Preston raised his glass and poured the golden tequila down his throat. Jupiter handed him a lime. He took it but just held it in his hand. It was quiet for what was to Jupiter a sufficient amount of time.

"Why do you do this if it makes you sad?"

Rooster kicked her under the table.

"Oww."

Rooster rolled his eyes; Preston's were aimed at the table.

"Don't right know. Guess I like takin' care of 'em. Makes something matter."

85

47 men

"But they all get hurt or die," Jupiter said to no one.

"Never had a pet, did ya?" Preston said. "Wait, scratch that. You had pets. Just never had to take care of them yourself." The edge in Preston's voice shut her up.

"Did you put the others in the room?" Rooster said attempting to change the subject.

"Yeah," Preston said, taking bites of his salad.

Penny brought three more shots.

"You tryin' to get us drunk," Rooster said with a bit of a smile.

"No, sweetie, y'all just seem a little sad."

"You're a real peach, Penny." Penny patted him on the head.

"We're staying tonight." Preston said.

"Sure," Rooster said, looking at Jupiter, "Whatever you want."

SECOND FLOOR
Room 207, Magnolia Inn

They took their beers and walked across the parking lot up the concrete stairs to Room 207. Preston's gaze fixed on the crack of darkness beyond the building. He shoved the door open. There were two full-sized beds with gold, burgundy and rust velveteen striped bedspreads and gold shag carpet. The cocks were lined up in a row with beige towels covering their cages. They rustled at the sound of the three of them entering the room.

"I have to go pee," Jupiter announced.

The bathroom's florescent light made the gold look puce. Jupiter ventured in further to see the matching sink, toilet and tub. The bathroom had been reorganized by Preston, everything in a specific spot. He had toothbrushes, one for each of them with toothpaste already carefully applied. His Dopp kit sat neatly on the shelf. She sat on the toilet and as her flow of pee started she timed the unzipping of his bag. It was like someone's anal mother had packed it. His personal effects were all in their proper compartments. Jupiter had no personal effects. She quickly zipped it back and replaced it in the exact location she found it.

Jupiter unpeeled a thin bar of white soap and pulled off her pants. She turned on the bathtub and stood in the warm water trying to wash her feet. Realizing how drunk she actually was, she decided to balance on the narrow edge of the tub, trying not to fall in. She dried her feet and opened the door. "Can I use this toothbrush?" she asked holding the pink one.

"It's for you," Preston said without looking up.

Sports Center blared and Preston lay supine on top of the velveteen coverlet next to his cocks. Rooster, curled in a ball, was on the other bed.

Jupiter came out of the bathroom with clean teeth in her underwear and T-shirt asked, "Where should I go?"

Rooster patted the spot next to him. She took the velveteen coverlet off her side and pulled back the cardboard sheets. She surveyed before she advanced.

"It's okay, I already checked the beds," Preston said from across the room.

Jupiter got in bed and rolled toward Rooster's back when the first hiccup reverberated against the thin motel walls.

Rooster twisted around. When it happened again he smirked. She held her breath but the birds started to cluck in time to her hics.

"I'm so sorry you guys," Jupiter said getting out of bed, searching for a glass.

Hic – cluck – hic – cluck – hic – cluck.

Rooster watched her pick up a glass and drink from it backwards and upside down. Water spilled down her leg as she came back up for air.

"See they're *hic*," *cluck*, "gone."

"You need a paper bag," Preston said with authority.

"Do you have one?"

"No," Preston said.

"No, you need sugar. Eat a spoonful of sugar or get one of those packs," Rooster offered.

"There's one *hic*," *cluck*, "in the bathroom with the coffee thing," Jupiter said. The birds' cacophony filled the room and Preston kicked the cage.

"Shut up y'all!"

Jupiter returned with the pack of sugar. "Okay now what?"

"Open it and pour it into the back of your throat," Rooster instructed.

She opened it and attempted to pour it into her mouth but it spilled all over her face. Then she got the giggles on top of the hiccups and soon she was crying from laughing so hard. Rooster caught the giggles too and even grumpy Preston cracked a smile.

Jupiter fell on the bed right on top of Rooster in a frenzy of arms and legs trying to pretend they didn't want to touch. She squealed and one of the cocks squawked back. They finally came apart, each on their own side on the bed.

"See, I told you the sugar would work," Rooster said. Preston rolled over, his back to them.

"Roo hit the lights would ya?"

"Sure."

Rooster snapped the switch but a weird florescent light glowed from the bathroom into Jupiter's eyes.

"Goodnight," Rooster said as he hugged his side of the bed.

"Goodnight," Jupiter replied.

Preston didn't say a word.

Jupiter tried to fall asleep by listening to their breathing but the flickering light in the bathroom taunted her. She flipped onto her back and watched the crack of light flutter against the cottage cheese ceiling.

"You awake," Rooster whispered.

"Yeah," Jupiter said.

"Sorry about that, with him... earlier," Rooster nodded in the direction of Preston.

"It's okay. It was just a little weird."

"Yeah," Rooster said as he punched the pillow. "I hate bad pillows."

"I felt bad for him," Jupiter said, not letting him change the subject.

"My momma thinks he's bad. I just think he's sad."

"Hey," Preston yelled. "I know you're talkin' about me so would y'all shut the F up."

"Sorry man," Rooster said as Preston heaved his body toward the wall.

"Good job," Rooster whispered.

"Thank you," Jupiter whispered back.

"Will you two SHUT UP and go to SLEEP?"

Rooster winked at Jupiter and pressed his head into the pillow. She faced him and smiled. He smiled back and they grinned at each other for a long time. Finally when Preston started to snore, Rooster leaned in and kissed Jupiter softly on lips. She kissed him back. Yearning for this moment, Jupiter pulled him toward her and reached down to touch him, her force of habit greedily taking over. Rooster grabbed her hand before any contact could be made. He shook his head.

"What?" Jupiter whispered.

Rooster smiled at her and touched her face lightly.

"Not here, not like this," he whispered back.

Jupiter, embarrassed and humiliated, pulled away.

"It's not that I don't want to, just not here with him." He gestured toward Preston.

Rooster tried to bring her back from the dark place she'd gone to, but he couldn't because she wouldn't. She'd returned to her father again...

I walk into his office, it's afternoon and Willy is in there with him, chatting up a storm. Telling stories about when she was just a young thing comin' to work for Mr. Russell and Mrs. Ruth Ann and how she just loved working for them and then when I was born it was like God answered her prayers. Willy hears me come in but does not see me.

"Jupiter, sweetie we need to take care of your momma. It's just not right. She needs to be buried."

Without skipping a beat, I answer.

"I've been thinking about a Viking funeral with a pyre. I did some pricing on a Viking long boat, the real thing is impossibly expensive but we can have a life-size replica built. I am sourcing out boat builders as we speak. Then we would just need to choose what body of water would be best. Dad, you'll need to weigh in on that. We have to hire some archers to shoot the flaming arrows to ignite the boat. I think with your and Mom's Nordic heritage, this could really be the way to go... Speaking of lighting things on fire... I just have to tell you that I have been quite industrious in the art of... let's just call it bed lighting. I have lit up the beds of the

great states of New Hampshire and Connecticut, tallying up some fifty hombres in all."

Willy turns around and looks at me.

"What did you just say to me?"

"I slept with fifty dudes, all shapes and sizes."

"What kind of girl does that? Where is my Jupiter?"

Willy pushes me back with all of her force. I fly backward unable to keep my balance.

"What have you done with my baby girl?"

Then my father stands up, I am on my ass on the ground. He looks down at me pathetically.

"Now come on Wilhelmina, there's got to be something we can do to re-virginize her. You have to have some kind of voodoo or Baptist magic you can perform."

Willy is so shocked my father is standing that she falls to the ground as well, unable to speak.

"Come on now Willy, snap to, go get Ruth Ann so she can help us with this mess."

"She's dead, RUSSELL, mort, gone, adios, bye bye," I yell at him.

SIX (6) DAYS

(6) Days
"For in six days the Lord made heaven and earth,
the sea and all that is in them." Exodus 20:11.

(6) Days
A Plutonian day, in Earth days, is six
days and nine hours long.

(6) Days
Olympic gold medalist Michael Phelps's key to success:
his six-days-a-week training regime and 12,000-calorie
daily diet, six times the intake of a normal adult male.

(6) Days
The Six-Day War, 1967 – Israel gained control
of the Sinai Peninsula, the Gaza Strip, the West
Bank, East Jerusalem and Golan Heights.

(6) Days
After the fertilization of the human egg, it takes
six days for implantation to take place.

(6) Days
Jupiter Campbell has 144 hours to rack
up four more men to get fifty.

TEXACO STATION
I-10, Grosse Tete

"Time to go, up and at 'em, let's go go go!" Preston shouted, fully dressed, regrouped and standing over the bed.

Jupiter bolted up right and looked around. Rooster wasn't there.

"He went to get coffee. I gotta get back."

"Uh... yeah, I'll just be a second," Jupiter said patting her hair down.

"See ya out there," Preston turned on his heel and was gone.

She stood slowly, the room was empty. Her brain thumped against the inside of her cranium.

Jupiter surveyed her bloodshot eyes in the gold bathroom. She brushed her teeth with the pink toothbrush especially laid out again with the toothpaste already on it. Her clothes sat folded on the lid of the toilet. She shook her head and thought her brain might pour like salt out of her ear. She lowered slowly to the gold toilet and attempted to dress herself. She heard a light tap on the door.

"You okay?" Rooster asked.

"Yeah." Her voice cracked. "I'll be right out."

"Okay. I'll wait by the car," he whispered at the door.

She heard the motel room door close. She stood up as the vomit crested at the back of her throat. She tried to get the toilet lid open but was unsuccessful. Jupiter looked at herself in the mirror. Tears dripped out of her eyes, snot hung from her nose, pieces of dinner from the night before clung to her chin. The floor was covered with the rest of it. She washed her mouth out with water, watching herself as she did it. She blew her nose with a washcloth. More dinner remnants. She draped a worn beige towel over the vomit pile and looked back at the mirror as if she didn't know the person she saw. She touched her lips and ran her fingers across her eyebrows. They were identical to her mother's—pale, almost non-existent with lashes black, long, curling toward the place brows should have been. Her eyes filled with tears and throw up suddenly filled the sink. Another light tap on the door.

"Are you sure you're okay? Can I get you anything?"

Jupiter tried to spit out the rest of the vomit before she spoke.

"Uh yeah. Schweppes."

"What?" Rooster asked.

"Ginger ale," she said and sat down on the floor.

"Okay. I'll be right back," he said.

The golden linoleum was cool. She nestled her head on the edge of the tub away from the toilet and saw an errant pubic hair in her line of vision. Jupiter closed her eyes and tried to think about ginger ale. Her mother believed ginger ale to be the cure-all for any childhood ailment. For chicken pox it was ginger ale; for heartbreak, a ginger ale; bee sting... ginger ale. She would serve it in a pink crystal goblet with winter scenes etched into the glass. Ruth Ann would put Jupiter's age in ice cubes in with the sparkly liquid. When Jupiter's father was away on business, Ruth Ann always used the special occasion pink goblets pouring champagne into hers and ginger ale into Jupiter's. She told Jupiter it was important to celebrate "just us girls." Men would come and go but they would always have each other. She would kiss Jupiter on the forehead and tell her she didn't know what she would do without her. She would smile a smile that only worked on one side of her mouth. Jupiter rolled over onto her back careful to avoid the barf towel, swallowing the bile/saliva combination that eked its way up the back of her throat. She made a deal with God that if she didn't throw up anymore she would never drink again. She'd made this deal with God before in a similar bathroom. Same ceiling. Same linoleum. Same light. Same vile, shitty, humiliated feeling.

Jupiter swallowed hard two more times and then had to sit up because the bathroom had started to spin. Sweat beaded on her top lip and she swallowed seven more times, marveling at the amount of secretion emitted prior to vomiting. But the bile had an agenda all its own. She heard a strange noise come from her throat as she leaned toward the toilet and a green milky fluid flew from her mouth. She prayed again, this time that Rooster was nowhere in the vicinity. But she heard him rustle by the door as she cleared her throat.

"I got it. I'll just leave it by the door. I got you a cup with ice too in case you want it. I told Preston to go. He was real jumpy and I figured you weren't ready to travel yet."

"How will we get back?"

"We'll figure somethin' out. Just try to drink a little. I'll be back."

Jupiter heard the door close and his footsteps pad down the walkway. She waited for a bit and mustering her strength, leaned to the doorknob to turn it, her hand shaking as she did. A tiny pink flower sat next to the green can and the Styrofoam cup of ice. There was a smiley face drawn in blue ballpoint pen in the side of the cup. She poured the golden liquid over the ice and while it wasn't the pink goblet, her fingers traced the pattern of the drawing just as she would have on her special glass. It tasted delicious as it traveled down her raw throat and into her belly. She took another sip and prayed one more time, this time thinking about her mother.

"Why did you take my mom?" Jupiter said aloud, quietly.

"I wanted to know that," Rooster said, sitting on the shag carpet somewhere outside the bathroom door.

Jupiter jumped. She took another little sip and tried to clear her throat.

"Did you ever find out?" Jupiter asked.

"No," he said.

"It isn't fair," she said.

"No, it's fucked," he said.

"What do you miss the most?" Jupiter asked.

"He used to come sit on my bed every night. He would make me tell him one special thing that happened during the day. Thought it was stupid when I was a kid. I'd tell him, 'Nothin' special happened.' Then he'd open the window and point at a star, tell me it was special because both our eyes saw the same star, at the same time, made us joined. When I got older he still came in, sat chewin' on his pipe, he wouldn't ask anymore, he'd just sit there. I miss the smell of him chewing on that unlit pipe."

Jupiter leaned against the bathtub taking tiny sips of Schweppes and listening to Rooster's voice lilting through the door. She held the green metal can at her temple. He was quiet for a while. On the intimacy scale, silence that did not have to be filled ranked at about an eight point five for Jupiter.

"What do you miss?" he asked finally, leaning against the doorjamb now, knees into his chest.

"Forgetting," she said and then paused, "when there's no one there to remind you that you forgot something, you can't forget anymore."

"Never thought of that."

"I liked when she came running out to the car with my lunch bag flying through the air like it was a priceless body part being medi-vaced to save someone's life."

"What'd she make?"

"Oh, she didn't make it. It was just the look in her eye running down the driveway in her pink nightie, my dad's navy blue coat and some kind of Wellington boots from the mudroom. She'd kind of giggle as she handed it to me through the window."

Rooster smiled at the thought of a Jupiter-like woman running in gigantic yellow rubber boots.

"You're smiling," she said through the door.

"How'd you know?" Rooster asked.

"Want some ginger ale?"

"Does it have barf on it?"

"No, but the bathroom does," Jupiter replied surveying her surroundings. "Do I need to clean it up?"

"No," he said, "but why don't you come out of there."

"I'll try."

Jupiter moved very slowly holding her foam cup and the can. She caught a glimpse of herself in the mirror. Not as green as before she thought and opened the door a crack. Rooster stood up so she could get out.

"You should probably move. It smells pretty bad," she warned.

Rooster obliged and sprawled out on Preston's bed. She walked to their bed and perched on the edge.

"So, how are we going to get out of here?" Jupiter asked.

"This is all your fault," Rooster smiled.

"My fault? You're the one who made me drink all of that tequila."

"Oh no sister, you did that of your own free will."

"Seriously though, how are we going to get out of here?"

"Let me go see what I see."

"That doesn't make sense."

He smiled and walked out the door leaving her alone in the room. She stood gingerly and pulled the borrowed jeans over her shaky legs, slid her feet into the white Keds, stepping on the backs so she didn't have to lean over and tie them. She then made her way very cautiously to the door. She pulled it open and walked to the landing.

"Jupiter," Rooster yelled, "Come on."

She looked out and saw a gigantic cattle truck pulled off onto the side of the highway.

"Seriously?"

"Come on, hurry up."

"Cattle?" Jupiter asked as she reached the bottom of the stairs.

"Beggars can't be choosers, darlin'." Rooster helped her walk to the truck and lifted her into the cab of the semi.

"What up bitches?" said a young scraggly blond, very white, red neck kid as he leaned his elbow on the enormous steering wheel while actually chewing on a piece of hay. Jupiter looked back over her shoulder at Rooster. He gave her butt a push and squeezed in next to her. The white kid dropped the truck into gear and pulled onto the highway.

"This is Jasper. Jasper, this is Jupiter."

"Nice. After the planet?"

"Yes."

"Parents hippies?"

"No."

"Why the name?"

"Why the questions?"

"Sorry, just tryin' to be friendly."

"Who lets you drive this?" Jupiter asked.

"Who let you drink so much you've been puking your guts out all morning?" Jupiter gave Rooster a dirty look.

"What?" Rooster whispered innocently.

"Seriously though, how old are you?" she continued.

"Probably older than you."

"Yeah but I'm not driving a thousand cows across the state."

"It's only a hundred and they're gonna die anyway so I guess they figure they got nothing to lose."

"How do they kill them if you don't first?"

"Three-hundred volt and two amp shot to the kisser," he said hitting himself in the head, "Then they hang 'em and slice the carotid artery and the jugular vein and they bleed out."

"Oh." Jupiter put her nose into the Styrofoam cup of ginger ale and inhaled deeply.

"Why?" the skinny white kid asked.

"Why what?" Jupiter answered.

"Why'd you want to know?"

"Just did."

"Jasper here is going out of his way to drop us off."

"Our lucky day,"

"Christ, Rooster, that's your name right? I hope she's a fantastic lay cuz she's a real pain in the ass."

"He wouldn't know," slipped from Jupiter's lips and she blushed.

"Well then what the fuck is he doing with you?"

"No idea, Jasper." She said.

"Any insights there Rooster?" Jasper pressed.

"Another dude in the room."

"Awwww not into the kinky shit?"

"How'd we get on this?" Rooster asked.

Jupiter folded her arms across her chest with cup in hand.

"Maybe she's such a bitch 'cause she needs to get laid?" Jasper offered.

"Naw, she's always like this."

"What do you mean always? You've known me for a week."

"And so far you're a pain in the ass with moments of sunshine and for the record... I don't just have sex with any random chick," Rooster said, playing with the knob of the glove compartment.

"Well, why not?" Jasper asked.

"Do you have anything to eat?" Jupiter inquired.

"Not worth the trouble," Rooster said staring a hole through her.

"Ritz crackers," Jasper said pulling them from under his hip.

"Were you sitting on them?"

"No."

Jupiter snatched them out of his hand.

"How old are you really?" Jupiter asked again, chewing the rims off of the crackers and handing the centers to Rooster. Then she poured the rest of the ginger ale into the cup, crushed the center of the can and dropped it onto the floor of the cab.

"Hey, pick that up," Jasper ordered.

"How'd you get this job?"

"Have you ever had a job?" Jasper asked.

"No." Jupiter said a little quieter.

"Thought so."

"What's that supposed to mean?"

"Not really qualified to do anything?"

"That's rude,"

"Did you graduate from college?"

"No."

"Why not?"

Jupiter didn't answer.

"Failed out? Quit?"

She stared deep into the Styrofoam cup and tried to hold back the wave of tears that was about to erupt.

"Huh?" Jasper pressed.

"Because my mom died and no, I've never done anything, not a fucking thing." She was full-blown crying now and Jasper and Rooster stared straight ahead not really knowing what to do. They rode in silence with Jupiter sniffling every now and again.

"I have to go to the bathroom," Jupiter said finally, wiping her nose on the side of her arm.

Jasper looked over at both of them and scratched his head. He pulled off at the next exit and drove into a Texaco station. Rooster jumped out so Jupiter could climb down. He watched her skinny legs tumble over each other in his sister's jeans. She struggled to pull the door open, her shoulders rising up against the force and then finally success. Inside the store, the fat lady behind the counter handed her a key on a long wooden stick. She walked back out and around to the side of the building.

101

47 men

"You should go," Rooster said to Jasper, still watching her.

"Why?"

"It's cool."

"You sure?"

"Yep," Rooster said.

"Well alrighty then." Jasper dropped the truck into to gear.

"Hey Jasper, how old are you?"

"Seventeen." Jasper grinned back.

"Thanks man, drive safe." Rooster patted the door of the cab and jumped down. He walked to the door of the Texaco and pulled it open with relative ease, which made him smile. He asked for the pay phone and the fat lady told him it was on the wall in front of his face. He picked up the receiver and waited for the dial tone. Made a call and as he did had a perfect view of Jupiter who walked out of the bathroom and searched hard for the truck as she pulled at her pant leg. She looked like a lost seven-year-old girl; something about her always seemed to get to him. She spotted Rooster just as he was hanging up the phone.

"He left us here?"

"He did.

"How are we going to get home?"

"I called Preston."

"Great."

"How do you feel?"

"Terrible," she said, looking like she might cry again.

Jupiter dropped the key on the counter, then went outside and sunk down onto the curb. Rooster bought her another ginger ale and some barbeque pork rinds and joined her.

"I can't believe he left us here."

Rooster handed her the open bag, which she held up for inspection and took a whiff of the barbeque fatty deliciousness. She pulled one out and bit into the irregular shaped crackle that popped as she chewed. She peered back in the bag as if it were a science experiment.

"Who invented these?"

"Black people from the South. At least the barbeque part. The Spaniards take credit for the initial discovery of the fried pork skin.

"Why do you know that?"

"Because I'm a huge fan of the air-puffed pig skin."

Rooster pulled one from the bag and clamped down on it with his incisors, "Ah delicious," and barbeque pork shards flew from his mouth into her face.

"Ewwww," she said wiping it off and then removing another one from the bag.

"It's a whole new world for you, cockfighting and pork rinds... now you can die happy."

"Awesome." She shaved off a bit with her two front teeth.

"Ahhhh, don't do that." Rooster moved his arm up by his ear.

Jupiter did it again.

"Ahhhh, you probably bite popsicles with your front teeth."

"Where's your camera?" Jupiter asked.

Rooster didn't answer for a moment.

"Forgot it."

"That's weird."

His eyes shot down to his feet and his face flushed. This was the only time since tenth grade that he had forgotten his camera. Something about her was so infectious; she yanked at his core, made him forget the most essential things. The expression on his face made Jupiter look away as if he were naked and she, a shy Amish girl. She hunkered over the pork rind bag and attempted to change the subject without words. She waited a minute and slowly reached her arm forward underneath his leg. She delicately slipped her hand into his. He barely moved but gently wrapped his fingers through hers. Her heart tumbled through her chest as he did this.

She wondered again how this strange boy was able to make her do so many unusual things. They stayed carefully holding on to one another.

"Your savior has arrived!" Preston shouted from the truck window.

They dropped hands and Rooster stood up as Preston pulled the truck around.

"Hey puker." Preston nodded in Jupiter's direction.

"Hey bloodsucker," Jupiter returned.

"This ought to be fun," Rooster said, opening the door for Jupiter.

"Hey Roo, your momma's been callin' me like a crazy person, she thinks you're dead or married. You oughta go call her."

"Alright," Rooster said and turned back toward the store, "Be right back"

Jupiter was already in the cab and wanted desperately to retreat but could not.

Preston grabbed her wrist.

"I don't want you fuckin' with my boy, you hear me?"

"Are you his father?" She said pulling her arm away.

"In a manner of speakin', yes. And girls like you are a dime a dozen. Leave him the fuck alone."

"Fuck you."

"What are you doing here anyway? Huh? What kinda crazy is a chick who follows a dude from a cockfight in Connecticut?"

"You're in no position to call me crazy."

"I can call you whatever the fuck I want. Just cuz you fooled them doesn't mean you fooled me. I saw you in that game; you had sex with five guys in one day. I saw it on you, you some kinda whore? What kind of fucked-up mission are you on?"

"I did not—" but Jupiter felt the rush of blood to her cheeks.

"Liar."

"I'm no—"

"Just stop yourself. You really are more my speed. Rooster's too good for you."

"Fuck you."

"You'd like that wouldn't you," Preston paused, "I heard you last night, tryin' to take him down but he turned your ass down, didn't he?"

"Shut up." Jupiter turned her back to him and folded her arms in front of her.

"Oh don't get me wrong, I'd fuck ya for sport."

Rooster hopped up on the bench seat next to Jupiter and she jumped three feet.

"Sorry, didn't mean to scare you. Christ, that woman can make a career out of worrying."

"Amen to that, let's get you home." Preston winked at Jupiter. She wanted to punch him as hard as she could but sat quietly back into the seat and stared straight out the windshield. When her attempts to thwart the forward progress of her brain in its plot to kill Preston were unsuccessful, she closed her eyes. Think about warm, she thought to herself, laying on the hot pavement next to our pool, my dad swimming laps and my mom on a chaise in her yellow straw hat and matching Pucci bathing suit, sipping iced tea and reading *Harper's Bazaar*. My skin toasty, chlorine crusted...

"There's Preston's house," Rooster said pointing and snapping her back to reality.

Jupiter followed his arm to a huge sterile French colonial with a perfectly manicured garden and matching topiaries stationed at either side of the front door. A stiff, stodgy, perfectly appointed mansion.

"Cozy," Jupiter sniped.

"Just like me," Preston said, elbowing her in the side.

"Sweet that you still live with your parents."

"Enough," Rooster said, fed up.

Preston veered to the right and turned left pulling up to the Boudreaux compound.

"Okay kids."

Rooster opened the door, hopped out and Jupiter ducked under his arm, stepped out on to the front lawn and kept walking.

"Thanks buddy, I owe you one." Rooster turned to follow Jupiter toward the house.

"Roo?"

Rooster turned back and leaned into the window.

"Yeah?"

"Watch yourself with this one. She's trouble."

"It's all good, buddy," Rooster reassured.

"What's she doin' here? Have you asked yourself that question my friend? It's fuckin' weird. I'm just sayin' I don't trust her."

Rooster reached across and punched him in the arm.

"Lighten up, it's cool."

"Boudreaux, I'm not fucking around."

"Gotta go." Rooster patted the roof and ran toward the house. Jupiter was swinging back and forth on the porch swing, the light cutting across her face. He looked back at Preston, who was still watching him, and waved. Preston's head shook slightly and he peeled out as Rooster walked toward Jupiter.

"Momma," he called out as he jogged up the steps.

"I don't think anyone's here." Jupiter surveyed him closely to see what Preston had shared.

"Momma?" He called out again opening the front door and waiting. He turned around in his two-day-old wrinkled jeans and blue shirt and smiled.

"We're finally alone." He plunked down next to Jupiter, picked up her hand and looked her square in the eye.

"What are you doing here?" he asked her plainly.

"What?"

"Why are you here?"

Jupiter felt her stomach drop, the intimacy scale and the fifty and now Preston. She didn't answer for a bit.

"I don't know," she finally offered.

"Come on," Rooster said, annoyed.

"I... well... I—" Jupiter stopped.

"Preston thinks I should stay away from you."

"Preston sucks the blood of poultry."

"I need you to be straight with me. What are you doing here?"

"You make..." Jupiter's voice croaked in her throat.

Rooster waited, pushing them back and forth with the toe of his thick brown boot. Jupiter looked at him, the mop of hair, the soulful blue eyes and she pressed her feet to the floor stopping their motion.

"You make me forget about myself," she said boldly, her voice raspy.

Jupiter leaned in and kissed him, lightly at first and as he returned her advance, she was overwhelmed by this simple delicious gesture. Their faces, arms, tongues, legs and hands intertwined. His hand gently cupped the side of her face and she opened her eyes. Rooster was watching her, recording her every movement. She put her hand up to the side of his face, he laughed and closed his eyes and brought his mouth instinctively back to hers. Her heart tumbled through her chest and with that came the burning fear and the toot toot toot of a car horn. Jupiter opened her eyes and looked out. Rooster pulled away and got up waving to his mother who had June Bug planted in the front seat of her car.

Jupiter leaned back in the swing and pulled her knees to her chest holding them tight against her heart, which felt as if it were cracking, exploding and breaking, simultaneously. With the death of Ruth Ann some part of Jupiter believed she would never be loved again. Somehow she was undeserving or she had already taken too much and would be punished for the rest of her life. Jupiter remained in her ball as Mrs. Boudreaux and Rooster walked a frail June Bug very slowly up the steps toward her. They were somber and no one acknowledged Jupiter's presence.

FOYER
Boudreaux home

R ooster and Mrs. Boudreaux finally came back out. Mrs. Boudreaux put her hand on Jupiter's shoulder.

"I am so sorry about all this sweetie,"

"What happened?" Rooster asked and plopped down on a wicker chair across from his mother, who sat very small and alone on the sofa.

"Well, Darryl tried to come visit your Auntie June. It was a *real* disaster. She is *real bad* this time, Roo. Doctor Poulson's had to come over a couple times just since you two been gone. He says she should be okay. He gave her some new medicine. I told Darryl and he thought that musta meant she was better. So he came and didn't tell me he was showin' up. Brought a huge bouquet of Calla lilies, walked in whistling. I was in the shower when he got here. When I got out all I could hear was this shrill scream and *GET AWAY FROM ME... GET OUT OF HERE*. I ran down to see what was going on and there was Darryl sitting on the floor in the front hall. There were flowers all over the marble and he was sobbin' like a baby. I said 'Darryl, why didn't you tell me you were comin'?' He said he was afraid I would say no. 'Well wouldn't that have been better than this?' I said to him. So then I went to her room to check on her. She was curled up in the corner, some weird noise coming out of her and she was bleeding. I had to get the doctor back over and he sedated her."

"I'm sorry, Momma," Rooster said.

"I need you to come look at a place with me."

"What do you mean?"

"Doctor's real worried. Says she needs to be somewhere safe. He recommended this place." Mrs. Boudreaux pulled a brochure from her pocket.

maguire

It had a sunny picture of a white plantation on the front. *Sunny Hill* was printed on the top in yellow script.

"Of course." Rooster looked over at Jupiter who was sporting a glassy stare. "We'll be back soon."

"Oh, sure, right, don't worry. I'm good here," Jupiter said, her mind still stuffed with the cotton balls of her hangover mingled with the deliciousness of Rooster's kiss.

Rooster walked into the house, his pockets jangling with the sound of keys and money. He grabbed a set car keys out of the sterling dish on the entry table. Jupiter watched Mrs. Boudreaux wring her hands, which were still adorned with the baubles of a married woman.

"I just gave her a sleeping pill, sweetie, so she'll sleep the rest of the day." Mrs. Boudreaux said.

"Okay," Jupiter nodded.

"Thank you, sweetie."

Rooster kissed the top of Jupiter's head, grabbed his mother's arm and suddenly they were in the car and out the driveway.

Jupiter's toes ran up and down the painted white boards of the porch. She pushed the old wooden frame swing with its tattered Toile cushion. Her eyes fixed on the ground as it rose and fell behind her toes. Her stomach gurgled aloud and she realized she was ravenous. She tiptoed through the foyer to the kitchen and opened the fridge. It was full but empty at the same time. She lifted the orange juice carton and glanced over her shoulder. She tipped the cardboard spout to her lips and poured the liquid down her throat. She peered into the cupboards, all food that required preparation. Junk food did not seem to be part of the Boudreaux DNA. Jupiter fished out a ten-year-old box of Kraft Macaroni and Cheese and put the water on to boil. She dropped down onto the yellow linoleum floor and waited until she heard the bubbles start to pop. Her mind settling into Rooster, the flesh, the mouth, the tenderness, the connection of their hearts. The bubbles popped, she stood and poured the elbow macaroni into the pot. The water and noodles made an oozing white froth that reminded her of the bile from earlier in the day. Jupiter searched for a strainer in the cupboards. She finally found one, strained the milky noodles and prepared the orange concoction. She returned to the butter-colored floor with her cornflower blue bowl of macaroni. She ate quietly and quickly. No smell or taste registered in her brain, just putting back in what had been purged earlier. She got to the bottom of the bowl and...

BAM!!! The entire house quaked.

Jupiter spun around trying to figure out where the sound came from.

She bounded to the front window in the dining room and looked outside. Heat from the late afternoon steamed up through the cracks in the sidewalk. Nothing. She craned her neck to see into the cavernous living room with its golden dapple of light. Nothing. Jupiter trudged to the front door and opened it, the late afternoon heat swatting her across the face. Nothing. She surveyed the sweeping front porch. Nothing. Jupiter was starting to think she had imagined it. She walked back inside.

A foot caught in the corner of her eye.

At the end of the dark foyer, a form swung softly in the space next to the chandelier. Jupiter tiptoed toward it, her eyes adjusting to the light.

A woman in a violet ball gown or a prom dress, she thought, hung from a thick white rope, dangling just high enough that Jupiter could only reach the ends of her frigid toes.

She galloped to the top of the staircase. She tried to pull the suspended body up.

"Help," Jupiter said quietly. And then louder. "Help, someone please help me."

Nothing.

She ran to the phone in the hallway and picked it up to call Rooster. Over her shoulder, June Bug's dead body swung from the banister in purple organza.

She thought of her mother. And then her father.

Rooster had no phone.

Brain pounded the inside of her skull. She placed the receiver carefully back into the cradle.

June Bug. Cold feet. Regal fabric. Bulging eyes. Heather-colored skin. Hunks of hair cut off. Mascara neatly applied.

And a pristine mouth of crimson lipstick, preserved.

Then nothing.

PLEASANT STREET
New Orleans

"WHAT SHOULD I DO?"

Jupiter stood listening to the drips of liquid coming from the body and she couldn't get the image of the bleeding out slaughtered cow from her head.

"Don't sit under a dead woman waiting for someone to come. Get up. Get help. But who?"

Jupiter's voice echoed against the hard surfaces and then Preston popped into her head. She didn't know his phone number but she knew where he lived. Every cell in her body rebelled against this idea but there was no other choice, she had to go.

Jupiter fished her car keys from the silver plate by the front door, twisted the massive knob and stepped across the threshold, finally turning to behold June Bug dangling like an earring from the banister of house.

She ran to the car, jumped in and bumped across the cobble driveway. Jupiter turned right then veered left trying to recall the direction that Preston's truck had taken them from the highway. She remembered a huge Magnolia tree on the corner and then she saw Preston's house up ahead. His truck was parked out front; she slowed down surprised at her relief and pulled in behind it. Her head fell against the steering wheel, how was she going to explain this, especially to him.

Jupiter got out and walked with much trepidation to the front door. She hit the knocker three times hard against the black door. She looked around impatiently as she heard footsteps coming closer.

The door opened to reveal the one and only Preston Pickett in light blue boxer shorts, no shirt and red-striped socks eating peanut butter out of a jar with his finger. She was at once both repulsed and grateful.

"What are YOU doing here?" Preston said, his voice dripping with disdain.

"It's June Bug," Jupiter said meekly.

"Yeah, what about her?"

"She's dead, she hung herself. No one's home and I don't know what to do." Her voice sounded high-pitched and strange.

"You were supposed to be watching her?" Preston asked, his arm blocking the doorway.

Jupiter could only nod her head.

Preston paused delighting in Jupiter's discomfort and removing his arm, waved her ceremoniously through the door.

"I have to get dressed, it's not like she's going anywhere."

Jupiter entered Preston's parent's home tentatively. Decidedly grand, somewhat sterile, many *objet d'art* and all of the shades drawn. Jupiter followed him across the checkerboard marble entry hall as he padded along in his stocking feet. They passed several nine-foot tall mahogany doors until finally he turned into the only open one, revealing his lair. He had his own living room with an eighty-inch television mounted on the wall blaring a movie in French.

"You speak French?" Jupiter asked surprised.

"My mother's French."

He kept moving, leading her into another room, black as night and everything "done" in burgundy hues. Once she was in the room he slammed the door behind her and locked it.

"What are you doing?" Jupiter turned around suddenly realizing she was trapped in his bedroom.

Preston with one swift hand grabbed her wrists and pulled her toward a black lacquered box on his nightstand. He flipped it open with the other

47 men

hand and pulled out a black zip tie, whipped it around her wrists and pulled tight as she struggled to break free.

"What are you doing?" Jupiter yelled.

He did not respond, just pushed her up against the wall and pinned her with one open hand between her breasts. She tried to kick him, pulling her knee up toward his crotch.

"Is this what you do? You freak." She screamed at him as he stepped down on both of her feet. He slapped her across the face with his free hand.

"Shut up."

Then he spun her around, arms tied behind her, and pushed her face up onto his bed. He mounted her, still in his boxers, immobilizing her legs and then ripped open her shirt. The buttons flew; he pulled at her bra, exposing her breasts.

"Nice tits." he said hitting each of them with an open hand. Then he unbuttoned her pants.

"NO," She yelled, wriggled and tried to kick herself free but he was too strong. He pinned her thighs tighter with his legs and ripped down her pants and underwear. She struggled against him and in response; he grabbed her by the throat, pressing her head into the mattress, making it difficult for her to breathe. Her denial seemed to arouse him. He shimmied out of his boxers to unveil a sizeable penis that he thrust toward Jupiter with force.

"This is rape," Jupiter said in a raspy whisper. He tightened his grip on her neck and the smell of peanut butter from his fingers wafted into her nostrils.

"Just how you like it, baby."

Jupiter spit in his face with all of the force she could muster.

Preston slapped her face hard. Her eyes welled.

"I'll scream." She said knowing it was futile.

"Good fuckin' luck princess, no one in this house will hear you."

Then he laughed in her almost purple face and prepared to mount. Jupiter tried to knee him in the balls and started to cry.

"I hate you." She whispered through her tears.

"I hate you too." Then he slapped her across the face again. She winced in pain and made another futile attempt to escape. He pushed harder against her groin but she realized as he continued to press for position that his penis was flaccid. Jupiter couldn't help herself, she started to laugh through the tears as his limp member slapped against her leg.

"Are you kidding me?" she said.

"Fuck you." He said pressing all of his weight on her shoulders and then cocking his arm back he punched Jupiter across the jaw. She felt the bones of his fingers collide with the edge of her face; the pain reverberated through her skull. Her eyes stared straight out in shock and her head shook like a bobble head bouncing on its axis. It felt like the hinge of her jaw had been eviscerated but the punch had thrown him off balance. She scrambled out from underneath him and used the opportunity to finally escape. He recovered and caught a handful of her hair and yanked her head back. Jupiter ripped her head forward as hard as she could and with her hands behind her, spun around backwards to open the door. Then she ran.

"You fucking bitch," he yelled dropping a handful of her hair and gathering himself to chase after her, "I'm gonna tell Rooster you tried to fuck me."

Jupiter pulled up her pants as best she could and ran half naked through the dark hallway toward the front door. His lumbering footsteps were gaining on her so she screamed at top of her lungs. Her jaw winced in howling pain with the motion.

"Preston, honey is that you?" a sweet voice with shuffling feet called out.

Jupiter listened to his footsteps slow and come to a stop. The scent of cooking onions flooded her nostrils, Willy flashed through her mind.

"Yeah, Mamman *c'est moi.*" Preston's voice calmed when he spoke to her.

"What's all the commotion?" she asked in a thick French accent.

"Nothing, everything's fine."

Jupiter grabbed the doorknob and turned it.

"Your son is a rapist," she screamed and slammed the front door behind her, her jaw throbbed. She ran to the car, jumped in and locked the doors. She threaded her body through her arms so her hands were in front of her. She removed the key from her pocket. Her hands still bound shook violently as she tried to put the key in the ignition. The engine started and she pulled on to the road without looking, a car honked, her body jumped and she started to cry again. She made her way to the main road and pulled over. Jupiter looked down at her ripped shirt and started to sob. She bent in half and held herself, hanging on to her last bit of dignity.

Slowly, she regained her composure and looked for something to cut the plastic tie. She remembered there was a Swiss army knife in the glove box. It was an ancient one with tools that her father had put in there just in case her mother needed it. She pulled the saw blade from the knife and placed it upright between her legs and attempted to cut through the plastic. Finally after many tries, the plastic gave way and Jupiter was free. She rolled down the window, took in huge gulps of thick air and closing her eyes tried to erase the events from her mind.

She finally looked into the rearview mirror to survey the damage to her face; she'd turned her head as he punched so she did not receive the total impact of the blow but her cheek was emblazoned with a crimson knuckle mark. She touched the spot gently with her fingertips and winced. She moved the mirror to review her whole face trying to determine if he had broken her jaw. She looked mostly like herself but there was an odd hollowness to her eyes so disturbing she had to look away. She attempted to tie her shirt closed but the fabric was bulky and uncooperative. For a split second she thought about going back to Rooster's house to get her things, but tears filled her eyes.

"He would never believe me." She said aloud.

She started to cry again, holding herself around the middle, the pain of her jaw and her heart fighting for position.

"I want my mom," she cried out through sobs.

BOUDREAUX HOME
Coliseum Street

The house was dark, formidably dark in fact. Rooster peered through the headlight mist searching for anything unusual. The Mercedes was gone. Rooster parked his truck where he always did and put his hand on this mother's knee.

"Momma, I think you should stay here. Let me make sure everything's a-okay."

He did not wait for an answer, hopped out of the truck cab and loped toward the front door. He turned the knob cautiously as if something in him anticipated the tidal wave waiting on the other side. He pushed it open.

"Hello, hello... anyone home?" he called out as he flipped the switches to illuminate the long hallway.

"Jupiter? You here? Junie?" The similarity of the j sounds struck him as each name came off of his tongue.

There was only silence.

His gait slowed as he continued down the hall in the low light.

Then he saw a dark form hanging in the line of his vision.

He stopped, turned and ran toward the front door. As he reached the threshold her grabbed his momma's arm and pulled her away.

"Rooster, dammit you scared me."

He maneuvered her toward the porch swing and positioned her facing away from the open door where, when he looked back he could now pick out June Bug's hanging body. He slid in next to his momma and picked up her very small shaking hand in both of his big warm paws.

"Momma..."

"She's dead."

"How'd you know?"

"Women's intuition."

"Well, it ain't pretty from what I can tell. I don't want you going in there to see that, you hear me."

"Yes, sir."

A huge tear welled in the corner of her eye.

"Who should I call?" Rooster said his voice filled with dread at the thought of poor Darryl.

"Can't you just cover her up and I'll come help you?" Mrs. Boudreaux said with an air of pragmatism only a mother can muster in the face of disaster.

"Momma, it's June Bug, you know she couldn't make anything easy." This sentiment made his mother laugh. Rooster looked at her in shock.

"Oh sugar, you knew this day was comin' and you are just so right. She couldn't make anything easy... my whole life."

Then she leaned over and held Rooster and whispered "God rest her soul" in his ear.

She sat back up straight as an arrow and rattled off a list of orders. The first was to bring her a pad and a pen before he got started. Then she told him to call Preston to get on over here and help him cuz she didn't want the last words about June Bug to be about how crazy she looked or how she'd offed herself, she wanted her soul to finally get some peace and a little dignity. Then she told him to go on and turn on some Neal Diamond cuz that was June Bug's favorite music, Lord knows why but real loud so she didn't have to hear anything from anything about what was going on in that house. She said she wasn't gonna come in until Rooster felt like she would never know anything bad had happened in there. Then and only then they would call the coroner and Darryl, cuz lord knows Darryl didn't need to see anything from anything either.

Rooster did wonder for a moment why it was okay for him to see it but did as he was told. He found a yellow lined pad in the library and called

Preston from the phone in the front hall. He was on his way. Rooster tried to figure a path to the stereo whereby he wouldn't have to pass the hanging body. Preston was good at this shit. He would get all military and delegate the appropriate functions, tenth grade military school to shape his ass up; all it did was make him more organized at being bad.

Rooster stood by the phone humming the "Star-Spangled Banner" waiting for Preston to arrive.

"Oh for Christ's sake, stop it with the hummin' would you? Or else I'm not gonna help you at all."

Preston pushed the door open, Rooster saw his little momma scribbling furiously over his shoulder. Preston walked straight to Rooster and wrapped his arms around him.

"I'm sorry brother."

"I know. I don't know how bad it is. Have you been eating peanut butter with your hands again?"

"Let me go first." Preston said bounding for the light switches on the wall. He flipped all the lights on and Rooster saw the purple form hanging in the distance. He turned his head away, faced the door and listened to Preston's feet hitting the marble, pacing in circles.

"Well, Roo, gotta admit, shit's pretty disgusting so..."

He heard him gag a little and then try to keep going.

"You need to get some trash bags and paper towels, and maybe a mop. Fuck I wish Letty could come do this. OOF. Go on now, go get me the stuff. Then we gotta to get her down, you're gonna have to help me with that."

Rooster told him the paper towels were in the kitchen and he was going to get the rest of the stuff from the garage. He walked past his momma on the porch and didn't say a word. He went to the garage and held the wall up with his hand.

"Fuck," he said it quietly, under his breath almost. He then gathered the mop, a dozen lawn-and-leaf bags and some disinfectant that his father used when the dogs were puppies and pissed in the house. He carried everything

47 men

in his arms, trotted dutifully up the steps and his mother looked at him. He stopped in his tracks.

"She'll come back." His mother said softly.

"God I hope not."

"Jupiter."

Until his mother said her name he had removed the thought of Jupiter from his brain. The detective work it would take to figure out what had happened was beyond him at this juncture.

He did not respond, resumed his task and marched through the doorway.

"Can I come down there?"

"No man, not yet." Preston choked on his words as he spoke them.

"You okay?"

"No dude, this is fucking disgusting, I told you."

"You're better than any brother a man could have."

Rooster put the disinfectant bottle down on the front table and glanced at the silver dish looking for the heart shaped key ring, which had sat comfortably on the table for the last week. Gone.

The hush puppies from dinner churned in his stomach, the sight of June Bug in his peripheral vision, the crazy people at the "home," his mother's laughter at June's death, his friend cleaning up God knows what at the other end of the hall, it bubbled up from his guts. He swallowed hard to put it all back where it belonged, picked up the bottle and walked down the hall toward his friend.

Preston was on the floor wiping up the last of her shit and piss from beneath the body.

"Holy Christ, what's that smell?"

"Purge fluid. Roo, I told you," Preston's eyes watered.

"How do you know what that is?"

"Grand-mère, Grand-père, two maiden aunts and an uncle. By-product of old parents." Preston answered without looking up from his diligent cleaning.

Rooster held his breath and looked up at her.

June Bug hung, in a purple dress, her face no longer looked like her own. It was bulging and now matched the dress; maybe that had been her plan. There was a hunk of hair missing and red lipstick shaped what had once been a beautiful mouth but was now grotesque. Rooster held open a trash bag for Preston to throw the rancid towels into and continued to breathe from his mouth, alternating between that and holding his breath. It reminded him of driving by a slaughterhouse with his father's hunting dog Marshall in the car with them. The dog freaked out, first started whimpering, then barking, finally the big old Lab lay down on the seat and covered his snout with his paws. Rooster felt like that dog. He looked up at her again.

"How are we going to get her down?" Rooster asked.

Preston finally stood up and followed Rooster as he mounted the stairs. Why the fuck did she have to do it here, he thought as he reached the top step. They followed the rope to its origin and found a feat of engineering which actually impressed both of them.

"Christ Roo, that's some handy rope work." Preston said standing behind him.

She had planned this for a long time he thought, just waiting for the right time. The rope was brand new, a glowing silky white and she'd rigged it in a manner requiring some thoughtful investigation.

"I was just thinking the same thing." Rooster said.

They walked to the edge of the banister and peered down at her barely swaying body.

"Think one of us has to go down below. Think it should be you, then I will lower her down. She's gonna be real heavy."

"We have to wash her." Rooster said wiping his nose like his father's dog.

"Do you have a wheelbarrow in the garage?"

"Yeah, but..."

"She's dead; just don't let your momma see. Then we can take her outside and hose her off in the back yard. Trust me it'll be easier. Then we'll get your momma to come pick out some clothes and we can lay her down on the marble. They can get her from there."

"Can't we put her on the couch or something?"

"Why would you want to ruin a perfectly good couch? Dude the shit keeps seeping out, you just can't stop it. Go on and get it, just don't let your momma see you."

Rooster followed orders, snuck out the back door and then back in, positioning the wheelbarrow under the purple mass. "I am I said" rang through the house in accompaniment to their next act.

"Okay, ready," Rooster called up the stairs to Preston.

"Wait..." Preston yelled running down the stairs holding an envelope.

"Shut up, I don't want Momma to hear you." Rooster said looking down the hallway to the front door.

"It's for Darryl, can we read it?" Preston whispered.

"Hell no, where did you find this?" Rooster snatched it out of Preston's hand and walked with him back up the stairs.

"Come on where was it? She obviously planned this shit out; let the woman have her day."

Preston showed him to the small desk in his little sister's room.

"It was there." He said pointing.

Two white pentagonal shaped pills sat untouched beside a half full glass of water. Rooster replaced the envelope with June Bug's scrawl on the front.

"What else?"

"The lights were all off and the bathtub's full of water. There's a rubber duck in it."

"What else?" he said firmly.

"I have a confession," Preston said looking down at his feet.

"Now?"

"When we were in eigth grade, June Bug taught me how to French kiss."

"Oh for God's sake, I didn't need to know that. What else?"

"Just the picture," he pointed to the bed.

Rooster stood up, it was the picture that he and Jupiter found of his mother and June Bug from the day at the Columns. It rested on top of the sheets staring out at both men.

"Those two must have been a real handful." Preston said shaking his head.

The phone rang; they froze looking at each other.

"Should we answer?" Preston asked.

"Hell no," Rooster replied.

Then the sound stopped.

"Come on, we gotta get going," Rooster bolted out of the room. Preston followed eyeballing the envelope.

"Shoulda just read it," Preston said under his breath.

"What do you need to cut the rope?"

"Nothin," Preston handily dissected her rope skills and quickly had her loose from the banister.

"Go on, she's heavy." The muscles in his forearms bulged under the weight.

Rooster galloped down the stairs and tried to line up the wheelbarrow with the body. She now looked like a piñata on the other end of Preston's rope and while the thought of this struck Rooster as funny, he did not laugh.

"Jesus Rooster, what the fuck are you doing? Stop moving around."

Rooster stopped and Preston let go of the rope. Her body hit the handles and bounced into the rusty carrier part. The weight caught Rooster off balance and she almost tipped out and fell on the floor. Rooster held tight steadying the handles.

"Shit, that was close," Rooster said looking up the stairs at Preston. "Do you think she heard that?"

"No." Preston said jumping down the last few steps and bee-lined it toward the back door. He hollered over his shoulder for Rooster to get a move on.

Rooster followed, his aunt's limbs crashing hard into the walls and doorjambs.

"Oops,"

"She's dead Roo, can't feel a thing."

Rooster drove the wheelbarrow to where Preston was standing with the already running hose.

"Okay, get her clothes off."

"Why me?"

"You're her relative and I already cleaned up all the shit."

Rooster acquiesced and bent her in half and unzipped the back of the dress.

"Fuck, she has a bra on."

"Maybe you can leave it if it's not dirty."

Rooster pushed her back up. There was runny blood all over the front of the dress.

"No such luck."

"Well, get it off then."

Rooster stood motionless.

"I can't."

"Sack up."

"No come on, I'll do the rest. I just can't touch my aunt's boobs."

"But you're cool with the cootch. I don't get you sometimes, Boudreaux."

Preston dropped the hose, walked over to the body, unhooked the bra, pulled the top half of the dress off and removed it, never touching her breasts, it was masterful. He then stepped back and held his hands in the air and said

"Voila, all yours, brother."

Rooster gingerly pulled down the edges of the dress.

"Just do it, she's dead you don't need to be careful."

Rooster yanked the fabric down and used a clean piece of the dress to pull it all the way off.

"WHAT?" Preston yelled out.

Rooster looked into the rusty wheelbarrow to see a huge tattoo of an arrow pointing at June Bug's bald vagina. Rooster's eyes looked like they were going to pop out of his head. Preston started to chuckle. Rooster looked over like he was going to kill him, but the absurdity of holding a purple ball gown over a dead naked tattooed body shoved in a wheelbarrow took precedence over decorum and he started to laugh too. Pretty soon they were like two hyenas with the giggles so bad that Preston was curled up into a ball crying and Rooster had dropped the dress and was kneeling in the grass about to pee his pants. But Rooster's laughter caught up in him and suddenly he dissolved into tears. Preston didn't notice for a bit and then saw his best friend's anguish.

"Awwww Roo."

"Sorry man." Rooster said through tears. "It was the fucking duck."

"What?"

"The duck in the tub, she always left it for me."

"What do you mean?"

"It was her code that something crazy and great was coming my way. One time she snuck me out of bed at three in the morning and we drove to Atlanta for a Falcons vs. Saints game... Fuck."

Then he couldn't speak, smashed his forehead into his knees and cried. Preston watched uncomfortable with this raw display of emotion. He stood up, paced around in the dark for a bit. Finally he couldn't take it anymore.

"Alright brother, we gotta keep moving here. Go on and get some underwear outta your momma's drawer. She can't see that." Preston's head nodding in the direction of June Bug's crotch. "I'll hose her down while you're gone."

Rooster picked up his heavy head from his knees and wiped his nose across his sleeve. He stood slowly not looking at June Bug's body.

125

47 men

"Okay."

Rooster walked toward the back door, his head feeling like a huge watermelon balanced on his neck.

Preston retrieved the hose. The hose had a yellow gun nozzle. He lifted it up with two hands, like a real gun, pointed square at June Bug's vagina and pulled the trigger.

Rosie Boudreaux sat stoically on the porch listening to her son, the coroner, Preston and the attendant. She heard the sound of the gurney being wheeled across the marble floor of the foyer. She heard the zip of the body bag, the hushed words, whispers of speculation. Whispers that she had so long been the architect of, were no longer necessary. She took this information into her body through her breath. Finally, the wheels crackled and squeaked back across the foyer floor, banging into the threshold and bumping clumsily across and Preston's footsteps hitting hard behind the gurney, his voice full of instruction to the attendant to be careful.

Of what? she thought, June Bug is already dead.

Rooster quietly slipped into the wicker chair beside her and collected her hand in his. He instructed her to stay put. He and Preston would go to the morgue and meet Darryl. Rosie nodded, patted his hand and watched as they shoveled the body bag into the corner's vehicle. The car doors slammed, Preston's engine revved and she stood as they all drove away.

She walked to the front door and pushed it all the way open looking down the long hallway. There were dark green trash bags stacked by the stairs; she wished they weren't there. She traveled slowly, taking it all in. At the foot of the stairs, the three trash bags sat neatly lined up with a white rope perfectly coiled next to them, Preston, she thought. She studied the rope; red marred its pristine whiteness, lipstick perhaps, too red for blood. The trash bags were full to the brim and a foul odor, masked slightly by Lysol, permeated the air. She picked up the bags and walked outside, leaving them by the back door. She returned to the stairwell to study it, where had she hung from? She surveyed the banister for signs something had gone awry. She scrutinized the rope again and wondered briefly what the scene must have looked like, then she went to the bar. She retrieved a low-ball Baccarat glass, a wedding gift from her favorite Aunt Bess. She filled it with square cubes from the icemaker and poured Crown Royal almost to the brim. She popped a can of Coca-Cola and poured a floater across the top. She opened a small wooden drawer filled with corkscrews and bottle openers, reached to the back where you couldn't see and retrieved a pack of Marlborough Reds. She opened a cabinet, got an ashtray and picked up the crystal match holder. Her hands full, she walked back to the staircase and placed all of the items on the third step. She went to the dining room and dragged an upholstered chair by its back across the floor, placed it within reach of the third step and adjacent to the white rope with the red lipstick. She could not bring herself to touch it, so it remained, staring at her. She sat down squarely on the chair, looked up, lifted her glass with conviction toward the ceiling and then took a huge swallow, letting the liquid combination of sugar and alcohol burn down the tunnel of her esophagus. She removed a cigarette from the box and lit it. She hadn't smoked for twenty-five years and it scorched her throat. The smoke billowed above her head; she followed an s-shaped plume as it reached for the ceiling. She heard her own voice scolding her husband about smoking his pipe in the house. She smiled thinking about him smoking in the garage with her boy lying on the floor at his feet drawing away on a huge white tablet. She settled into the place of missing her husband and wondered if eventually she would miss June. She closed her eyes and opined as to what might have been the final straw for her sister. Finishing the cigarette and mashing the butt into the ashtray on the step, she got to the fact that it didn't matter anymore. She took another huge gulp from the glass on the step. Then stood and leaving everything just as it was, she mounted the stairs to her bedroom to enjoy her first good night's sleep in forty years.

FIVE (5) DAYS

(5) Days
Post mortem – body begins to bloat and swell
grotesquely. Fluids leak from mouth, nose,
eyes, ears, rectum and urinary opening.

(5) Days
22 hours and 54 minutes – duration of Apollo
13's mission to the moon and back.

(5) Days
Woman survives five days in an avalanche in Tahoe City,
Ca. before being finally sniffed out by rescue dogs.

(5) Days
Jupiter Campbell's clock is ticking… only
five days left: seems to have lost her killer
instinct, should she give up the hunt?

I-10
North Biloxi, Mississippi

The incessant grinding sound of a leaf blower buzzing noisily past the side of the car woke Jupiter. Coiled in the driver's seat, arms folded across her body and hands clasped in her lap, like a child in church, she regarded the clock. It was seven in the morning. The flood of information avalanching into her mind was overwhelming. The man wielding the blower stared at her through the windshield as she moved to sitting. She tucked her shirt in around her. His gaze irked her as she scrambled around to find the keys. She started the car and finally he looked away.

Ugh, she thought pulling onto the road and running her tongue over her teeth. Then she was stunningly reminded of her plight as she tried to open her mouth. The stabbing pain incinerating into the hinge of her cheek caused her to see stars. She managed to find the highway and merge into the rush-hour traffic, no idea as to her destination, just desperate to get out.

One hour and twenty-three minutes in the car and the throbbing of her jaw had reached a decibel her brain could no longer tolerate. She spoke "find pharmacy" into her phone. She chose Cedar Lake Pharmacy because of the name and proximity. It sounded soothing, cool lake water; she imagined her chin resting in the deep blue. Jupiter examined herself in the rear-view mirror again. The color was changing, the knuckle mark beginning to look like a raspberry colored gash against her white cheek and a deep purple hue was developing at her jaw line and behind her ear. It wasn't very swollen but the pain was excruciating. She pulled off of the highway onto Cedar Lake Road and then into a massive parking lot. Not quite the naturalistic setting she'd envisioned. She parked and slowly scavenged the back seat for something to put over her ripped shirt. There was nothing. She held the two pieces of fabric closed with her fingers and moving very slowly, ventured toward the trunk. She thought about the beach towel she had used the first time she met Rooster and quickly pushed the button to open the trunk. It smelled like old car and motor oil. There were some jumper cables, a first-aid kit, a pair of unworn running shoes and in the back, underneath some sort of earthquake kit, she spotted the corner of a pale blue wool sweater. Jupiter ripped it out from underneath and the swift movement caused her to shriek out in pain. Maybe she should go to the hospital she thought as she settled back into the driver's seat, gingerly removing what remained of her shirt. She pulled the itchy sweater over her head stretching the neck as wide as it would go. Once on, she hurried inside the pharmacy with eau de her mother wafting from the wooly knit. The pharmacy had a faint anti-septic scent combined with the pleasurable odor of counter candy. Jupiter made her way to the back of the store where she saw an elderly woman at the cash register and a chubby bald man with a pink face and glasses on the end of his nose. He was trying to read the label on a tiny pill bottle and addressing an older, very tan, woman at the counter.

"Marilee, you can't take old medicine. This expired five years ago."

"Well, I just don't see the harm in it, Paul. I mean, seems such a waste to throw them all away.

"Marilee, we have been through this a million times. Let's look up the paperwork and we'll just see if we can get that refilled for you. Go on and do the rest of your shopping." Then he looked to the old woman.

"Can you do that?"

But the old woman was staring at Jupiter. Jupiter looked down at her-self wondering if she had missed something vital, like blood spatter or a stab wound, based upon the intensity of the woman's stare.

"We got another customer here, Paul. You gonna help her?"

The pharmacist looked up from his glasses and also regarded Jupiter. He stood; he was a huge man with sweet eyes.

"How can I help, miss?"

Jupiter took one step toward him and opened her mouth to speak but nothing came out. The old lady stepped away and he reached out to touch Jupiter's elbow.

"You alright?"

Jupiter blinked hard and then stammered, "I was hit in the jaw and I'm not sure if it's broken but it hurts so much."

"Don't you think you should go to the hospital, sweetie?"

"No, please, I can't, I—" and then there was too much to explain and she started to cry.

"Shhhhh, now, don't cry. Let me see what we can do here. Come sit down."

There was a light blue plastic chair to the left of the counter. Jupiter sat hard. He gently put his cool hands that smelled of Betadine around her face, and touched the area lightly where the raspberry color had formed. Then her jawbone, he pressed in a bit at the joint and Jupiter winced.

"Can you open your mouth?" he asked quietly.

Jupiter slowly opened. He reached into a drawer behind the desk and pulled out a wooden tongue depressor. It reminded her of gagging at the pediatrician when she was five.

"Good," he said, "now let's see if you can hold this between your teeth." He put the stick in her mouth and told her to bite down, which she did without trouble.

"Well, I think what we have here is just a bad bruise. So some time and a lot of Advil should do the trick." He pulled a bottle off the shelf. "Take three at a time and make sure you eat something."

"Thank you." Jupiter said through wet glassy vision.

"And y'all stay far away from that man, you hear?"

"Yes, sir. Thank you again."

Jupiter pulled a twenty from her wallet and handed it to him.

"I don't know how to work this thing. Hey Mary, could you come back out here and ring her up?"

The old lady shuffled back out and did as she was told. Jupiter waved to him with her red-and-white striped bag in hand.

"Be careful out there." He called from his pharmacist booth.

Jupiter nodded and retreated to the familiarity of her car. She buckled her seatbelt and headed off in pursuit of food. KFC mashed potatoes and gravy, a Coke and four Advils later, she hit the highway again with the glaring realization she had no idea where she was driving. There was a green freeway sign up ahead with "Atlanta Ga. 385 miles" printed in white type. She thought of Atlanta... the last time Jupiter had been there she was a raucous eight-year-old. Her family had arrived at the Ritz Carlton in Buckhead; her mother went straight to the suite and her father marched directly to the bar. Jupiter had followed him but hadn't been allowed to belly up because she was *under age,* according to the bartendress, who whispered even though there wasn't a soul in the bar. Russell drank a Maker's Mark neat, alone, and Jupiter retreated to the lobby. She chose a salmon moiré wing-backed chair facing the bar and her father. Her feet dangled above the floor. She chewed Bubble Yum and waited patiently for her mother to exit from one of the elevators. Ruth Ann finally stepped out from the opening doors. Two men in business suits admired her mother in her black dress and pearls. She'd been crying, eyes puffy; make-up attempting to cover up the baby that fell out of her. She glided right past Jupiter who pulled up her feet and tucked herself behind the wing of the high-backed chair so she could watch her parents. Her mother found her father swimming in his bath of whiskey. Russell threaded his arm through Ruth Ann's waist and she rested her head on his shoulder.

There are some things a kid should never see. The remnants of a human floating around in the toilet bowl should always be flushed. A child does not have the wherewithal to understand. According to her eight-year-old brain, her mother was dying. The toilet water was crimson like *no parking curb paint,* shiny and wet. They had explained to her a hundred times that the fetus wasn't really a person yet but, whatever, she thought her mother was peeing out her guts.

133

47 men

Noreen Kellogg was the reason that her father brought her mother to Atlanta after the baby died. Noreen lived in Alpharetta, Georgia with her wealthy husband Jimbo. Russell thought Noreen was "a wing nut" but the trip to Atlanta was to boost her mother's spirits. Noreen had thinning blonde hair, gigantic low hanging boobs, color-coordinated outfits and her cocktail of choice was the Singapore Sling. She'd sent Jupiter her first bra at age nine, seven years premature. When Jupiter was sixteen a carton of condoms arrived with *Just in case* scrolled in perfect script on the outside of the box. Ruth Ann was appalled. For the occasion of meeting Noreen, Jupiter dressed up in a lavender ice-skating dress that she'd smuggled in her suitcase.

They'd waited for Noreen, her mother nervous and excited and so out of it she hadn't noticed Jupiter's unique fashion statement. Noreen finally arrived at the hotel in a turquoise-and- lime-green outfit, with shoes and purse to match. She held a Cabbage Patch doll in her arms also in a matching outfit. Noreen kissed Jupiter on the head and handed over the doll. The women retreated to the bedroom and closed the door on her. Noreen had no children.

Jupiter planted herself outside the white double doors on the scratchy green carpet and listened. She heard her mother laugh. Clear, loud, sunny, and hopeful. There was a joy in her laughter that her life with them did not possess. Jupiter fell asleep on the scratchy green carpet in her lavender polyester skating ensemble. Her father woke her up and whispered to come on; they needed their "time" together. Russell took Jupiter to Piedmont Park and they fed ducks and geese, ate hotdogs and a strawberry shortcake bar. She asked for cotton candy but he said no. Instead he invited her to sit on a park bench in front of a pond where he very insightfully described to Jupiter the biology of the goose species and the intricate psychology of that order and their place in the chain of the animal kingdom. Somehow Jupiter felt he was trying to explain the death of the baby as being a part of natural selection without using the words to do so. Though she did not understand it at the time it was the moment that changed their relationship forever. Russell had decided on that day that his weird little daughter deserved to be treated like a human being. They were of the same genus, though not the same species. Jupiter and Russell returned to the hotel holding hands. Noreen had departed. Her mother was aglow, smiled the rest of the night and even for a few days when they'd returned to Connecticut.

Noreen had been gutted by the news of Ruth Ann's death. When Jupiter called to give her the details the line simply went dead. Jupiter had dreaded the call but there was no one else who could have made it. She'd thought there would be tears, hysteria but no. Noreen's husband had called back ten minutes later to apologize for his wife's behavior and to say he was so sorry for her loss. If there was anything they could do and all that. Jupiter had politely responded and said she would call back with details for the funeral. That was almost two years ago, Jupiter hadn't heard a peep since. She wanted to see Noreen, talk to her, maybe she knew something. Atlanta was five hours and twenty-five minutes away according to her phone. She could be there by sunset if she drove fast. Simon and Garfunkel time seven, Jupiter suffered through the Carpenters times two, four more Advil and finally another green sign told her she was *Now Entering Atlanta*, population 5,312,283. She looked for a gas station having no clue where Noreen lived and only an eight-year-old's memory of the city, which proved to be of no use. She pulled into the midtown BP and went inside to ask for a phone book.

SAINT LOUIS CEMETERY #1
Basin Street, New Orleans

ooster stood solemnly at the front of the church in his dark suit with a weird tuberose boutonniere that June Bug requested the men wear. He waited for the line to die down before he went to pay his last respects. Darryl, red nosed and sad eyed, sat in a heap in the front pew with Rosie next to him holding tight to his hand. Rooster took a deep breath and got in line. The coffin was open; June Bug actually looked pretty good he thought. Her hair curled in auburn rings and her face minus the purple hue he'd last seen. His eyes shot to her crotch and he blushed at the thought of the arrow, now concealed by the white gown. He stood over her body and thought about her feet. He'd taken thousands of pictures of her feet, which were now oddly trapped in white high heels. Rooster wanted to remove them and get one last look at her craggy baby toes and the big toe on the left that veered out like it wanted to escape off the island of her foot. She'd tried to cover them lately, told him he had enough pictures already; he wondered if that meant anything.

"Rest in peace," He said quietly and patted the top of her hands. They felt like rubber and reminded him of Jupiter and her gray crayon reference.

He returned to his seat next to his mother. A minister spoke and he stood up and sat down at all the appropriate times without thought or feeling, his mind elsewhere. His mother nudged him and he looked at her, her head motioned toward the podium. Oh… right, the poem, he thought. Yeats, her specification, one stanza, and Rooster was to read it. No one else would be allowed to speak. He took the folded piece of paper from his jacket pocket and went to the podium.

"I'm June Bug's nephew, Darwin Boudreaux. This is what she wanted read, it's by Yeats.

> *The South is pouring down roses of crimson fire:*
> *O vanity of Sleep, Hope, Dream, endless Desire,*
> *The Horses of Disaster plunge in the heavy clay:*
>
> *Beloved, let your eyes half close, and your heart beat*
> *Over my heart, and your hair fall over my breast,*
> *Drowning love's lonely hour in deep twilight of rest,*
> *And hiding their tossing manes and their tumultuous feet.*

That was it, all she'd wanted. He folded the paper up and returned it to his pocket. He squeezed back into the pew and his mother patted his hands exactly as he had patted June Bug's. He wondered if that was where he learned it.

Rooster stood,

Followed,

Placed a white rose,

Put his arm around his mother,

Hugged Darryl,

Shook hands with Preston

And finally crypt closed, back to standing.

It was dusk. He was alone in the cemetery and leaning against Homer Plessy's tomb. The smell of the tuberose, so sweet it was almost acrid, stung his nostrils and made his stomach churn. He unpinned it from his lapel and placed it purposefully on the step. He wondered if she'd meant for the scent to be disturbing. He felt like she did. He told everyone to go on ahead without him that he needed a few minutes alone.

Rooster settled down onto Homer's step, pulled out a cigarette and lit it. Felt a little like he shouldn't but did it anyway. He reached into the same pocket that had the poem and removed a flask, sterling silver, dented, with his father's monogram. He twisted off the top with one hand, looked up into the sky and held the flask high above his head.

"Cheers big ears." He said aloud and took a pull of whiskey.

He mashed the cigarette out into the step of the tomb and returned the flask to his pocket. He got up, looked around at the cemetery in twilight. His eyes settled on the decaying boutonniere and the cigarette butt and he wished he had his camera.

Rooster Boudreaux walked away feeling an unnerving sense of relief.

FOUR (4) DAYS

(4) Days
Duration of the Woodstock Festival August 15–18, 1969.

(4) Days
The time it takes for cocaine to be
undetectable in a urine test.

(4) Days
The Bay of Pigs Invasion – Playa Girón, Cuba.

(4) Days
A quarter-inch piece of banana peel will eliminate
visible signs of pimples in just four days.

(4) Days
Yo, Jupe, git on it - four days left sista… tick tock.

ALPHARETTA

Black dress from gift shop.

Hair twisted and held in place with paintbrush courtesy of Rooster Boudreaux.

Darling Boudreaux's white Keds.

Sunglasses.

Rainy day.

Black coffee.

Twizzlers.

Umbrella.

Alpharetta, Georgia was one hour and twenty-eight minutes from Buckhead. Jupiter had called the Pioneer Taxi Company to meet her at Cherbury Lane. The one night of sleep, new dress, make-up to cover the bruising, cream of tomato soup and a game plan had done wonders for Jupiter's demeanor. She would deliver the car to Noreen, ask her if she knew anything about her mother's wishes and then Jupiter would go to Manhattan, finish her quest and return to her father to deliver the shock of his lifetime. Rooster's smile cracked its way through her plan but she shut it out, had to move on, Rooster would never believe her; this was her only solution.

Jupiter blared Ruth Ann's music through the ancient speakers in an effort to distract herself. She began to think about what she would say to Noreen... the words ran through her head... *Noreen... You were her best friend in the world... she would have wanted you... No... she adored you... no, that's weird... God, for a relatively intelligent person I sound like a retard. Okay. Noreen... you made my mother so happy, happier than anyone else in the world. I want you to have her car to remember her. That's weird too. And how do you ask someone, oh hey, by the way, did you and my mom ever chat about her burial wishes? No, I suppose not.*

A blush rose to Jupiter's cheeks as she thought the words. She couldn't go up and ring the doorbell and just... A note, she thought, that way she can process it. That's it... a note.

The car crept down the lane and Jupiter pressed hard on the brake pedal coming to a complete stop in front of a colossal colonial home with no gate. Excellent. Circular driveway, brick with huge pillars and opulent landscape. She put the car in reverse and parked a few houses away, she had to write the note before the taxi arrived.

Dear Noreen,

You were an enigma to me, like a lovely dream. You were my mother's freedom. When she was stuck with us in Connecticut, her car was her freedom. Somehow it just makes sense to me that her two freedoms should be together. I wish I knew you better, but please accept this gift in honor of the memory of my mother who loved you so very much.

Fondly,

Jupiter Campbell

It wasn't perfect but it was the best she could do within the time constraint. She tried a couple of different lines about her mother's wishes but it seemed too creepy.

The Pioneer taxi pulled up and Jupiter waved and motioned one minute to the driver. She folded the piece of paper in half and turned the ignition key. The engine roared. She pulled into the drive of Noreen's *Gone with the Wind*-esque manse. Jupiter opened the door of her mother's car, pilfered one of her tapes, retrieved her purse, the light blue sweater and snuck up the steep brick steps to the lacquered ebony front door. Her finger pressed the bell, a loud chiming long-winded series of tones rang through the thick Georgia air and then she ran.

She jumped in the back seat of the cab and hid.

"Can you just wait here for a minute?" she asked the driver.

"Alright," he returned in almost a whisper.

Jupiter's view was perfect. A black housekeeper packed into her gray uniform complete with a white scalloped apron answered the door and walked out on the porch. She stood at the top of the steps and walked down slowly, puzzled by the empty car. She bent over to look in, her large gray buttocks square at them, then she turned with her hands on her hips, surveying the grounds to search for clues. She spun on her white nurse shoe heel and returned to the house yelling, "Mrs. Noreen! You best come out here!"

Noreen appeared in the doorway wearing a lavender ensemble with a dishtowel drying her hands. The car took her breath away and she stepped back slightly, then she looked out toward the street. She cautiously walked down the steps and looked in the car window. She released the door latch and sat sidesaddle in the front seat. She picked up the letter and read. Then Noreen started to cry, hard, and the housekeeper ambled down the steps toward her. Noreen handed her the letter. The housekeeper read it and she cried too. Then the housekeeper hugged Noreen. They said a few words looking out at the street and slowly walked back in the house, the housekeeper's arm around Noreen.

"What?"

"Sorry miss?"

"Nothing," she paused. "I thought it would make her happy."

"What?" he said looking into her eyes from the rear-view mirror.

"Can you take me to the airport?"

"Of course," he said and drove away from the house.

"I thought she would..." and then she stopped, touched the side of her cheek and closed her eyes.

It was quiet save for the windshield wiper blades thumping back and forth.

ARTIST LOFT
Dauphine Street, New Orleans

Rooster shuffled through his studio. His show was hung, party was in two hours. Darryl's sobs seemed cemented in his brain; he didn't want to go, didn't want to have to talk to anyone else. He'd tried to cancel but the gallery said no.

He poured a shot of Jack Daniels into a dirty glass and sat on the edge of the couch surveying his current landscape. Shit was everywhere, pizza boxes, beer bottles, cigarette butts. Then he saw the corner of a pad under the edge of the coffee table. He kicked it out with the toe of his boot and picked it up.

Rooster flipped through the pages, an ink drawing of June Bug's foot, a pencil drawing of a dog's ear, a line drawing of the brim of a fedora, a charcoal drawing of a bull's horn and eye just prior to gouging a matador. He turned the page and there she was, the sleeping Jupiter. Lying in Delilah's bed, her body curled in a "c" and her head snuggled into the edge of the pillow. Her lips slightly parted, eyes closed, hand up close to her chin, hair unfinished, but the lines beginning to curve their way across the pillow.

He lifted the glass and downed the contents. Stood up, picked up the phone and called Preston.

"Can you meet me before, I need a drink."

"Yep, I'll come get ya."

"Be waiting outside."

"It's gonna take me a minute or so to get there."

"I need to get out of here."

"Suit yourself."

Rooster looked once more at the drawing. He held the tablet and carefully tore the sheet from the pad. He walked to the handle bottle on the table and poured another shot into the glass. He threw the Jack down his throat, picked up the piece of paper and held it up in front of him. Rooster ripped the drawing in two, dropped the pieces on the table and walked out.

He didn't lock the door or take his keys or camera.

He stood outside the old brick building jamming his hands down to the bottom of his jean pockets, trying to get her image out of his head. He lit a cigarette, paced, kicked some rocks and started to hum the "Star-Spangled Banner" again.

"Fuck." He said to no one, "Stop." He said to himself.

He lit another cigarette, kicked some more rocks and started humming again. "Fuck... hurry up."

Preston's truck finally rounded the corner. Rooster flicked the lit butt into the night air and jumped in.

41,000 FEET

J upiter, looking quite forlorn, walked up to the first counter with no line. Delta international, first class. A lovely looking petite French girl stood behind the desk in a navy suit jacket and red scarf, smiling at Jupiter.

"May I 'elp you?"

"Uh, oui. Do you have any flights going to JFK?"

"When would you like to go?"

"Now if possible."

Jupiter pulled out the platinum Amex and attempted to conceal the side of her face with the now eggplant-colored bruise. The agent's eyes registered the card, not Jupiter's face.

"Let me see what I can do for you." She said her fingers clicking away at the keys. "There is one seat left on the one-forty-seven, which goes on to Paris. Do you have baggage?"

"No."

"Okay, then, I think I can get you through."

She swiped the credit card, asked to see Jupiter's identification and told her associate she'd be right back.

It was ten to one. The French girl maneuvered Jupiter through Hartsfield Airport, navigating like a salmon spawning. Expertly whisked through security, Jupiter was officially the last person to board the aircraft.

First class was a marvelous institution. *L'Espace.* She had her own personal chamber and a gentile steward who presented a flight kit with light blue socks imprinted with dark blue treads, ear plugs, a navy eye-mask, toothbrush and paste, cologne and eau-de-toilette, all in a smart navy carrying case. Next, another uniformed attendant arrived with a glass of champagne, a bit of foie-gras on a circular piece of toast, and le menu. She bit heartily into the delicate slice of fat, somewhat surprised by her ravenous hunger.

Jupiter's seat neighbor, 3B, sprayed a lavender mist all over her face and turned to Jupiter.

"It helps the skin. Hope you don't mind?"

3B was a sophisticated middle-aged woman, clad in a two-piece suit of pale gray cashmere, complete with a matching blanket. She was obviously a professional in the art of travel; various tonics and elixirs were displayed in front of her, as well as containers of macrobiotic foods designed to mitigate the effects of jet lag.

"I do this trip often," she explained.

"Where are you from?" Jupiter asked.

"Manhattan, originally. Now I live in Los Angeles."

"What are you going to be doing in Paris?" Jupiter asked.

"I'm a writer. French *Vogue*."

"Really? That's interesting. What do you write about?"

"Nothing important." She downed a blood-orange colored concoction and winced at the taste. "Awful, but it works miracles. What's your business in France?"

"Well, actually, I'm just going to Manhattan. But how would I go about answering that question? Honestly, I need to find a few men to have sex with so I can get to fifty. Why fifty? It was an arbitrary figure, which at the time seemed both shocking and plausible. But now I'm just not so sure about any of it. So yeah, I guess that's what my business is."

"Fascinating," 3B replied, "Do any stand out?"

"The first few, ten or so, the middle chunk... not so much and then the one that was supposed to be forty-seven."

"What happened?"

"I don't know. He... he... really got me off track."

"What do you mean?"

"Fifty didn't seem to matter anymore; I just wanted to be with him."

"Well, why aren't you then?"

"It's complicated."

"Isn't it always? In my experience, if you find one you just want to be with, you should stay right where you are."

Jupiter felt like she might cry so she just nodded her head in agreement.

"I have an extra Gingko if you'd like one," 3B offered, changing the subject.

"What's that?"

"Increases stamina and boosts energy levels, darling. Sounds like you might need it. You'll go go go. I highly recommend it."

"Okay, thank you."

3B delved into one of her secret compartments and unveiled a box of pills labeled with the days of the week in Swarovski crystals. She picked out a grayish-green tablet and delivered it to Jupiter's palm.

"Wait until after you eat, then take it. I'm Lesley, by the way."

"Jupiter. Thank you again."

"Of course," she said as she opened a curious box, which housed a satin eyeshade the color of a sterling rose.

"Good luck to you." Lesley put the mask over her eyes and leaned back into her plush cocoon.

Jupiter clutched the pill in her sweaty hand. She adjusted her headphones and found the most action-packed film in the queue. She wolfed down the simulated French cuisine, Beef Bourguignon and whipped potatoes and then swallowed the pill with warm airline champagne. Jupiter delicately set her glass down on her airline tray, suddenly feeling monumentally depressed. She closed her eyes… why was she doing this?

I walk into his office at what used to be his cocktail hour. He languishes in relative darkness. I flip on the lights, go to the bar and make him a Hendricks and tonic because that was his favorite summer drink; he was always happier in the summer. I deliver it to the small wood table next to him where his glasses rest, as if he might put them on at any moment and start to read the paper. I drag over a chair and sit with my bare knees touching his corduroy ones. I hold his face in my hands and speak very softly looking directly into his eyes.

"She's dead, Daddy."

Delta flight 1153 slammed to the ground with a vicious impact, jarring Jupiter from an angst-ridden sleep. She surveyed her surroundings and Lesley, now with her mask resting on top of her head, waved happily.

"Did you take the pill?"

"Yes." Jupiter said trying to smile.

"Some say it's also an aphrodisiac. Enjoy the city."

"Thank you."

"Perhaps it's a sign, you know."

"What is?"

"Forty-six might have been the limit. You're quite lucky nothing terrible has happened to you."

"Like what?"

"Disease, pregnancy, rape."

Preston's face flashed before Jupiter's eyes. She shuddered and flushed crimson.

"So that's where the bruise came from? Something bad did happen."

"Almost."

"Why don't you go back to forty-seven?"

"I can't." Jupiter teared up. Lesley patted her hand.

"The universe will give you your answer; you just have to be listening."

Jupiter gathered her belongings and stood up.

"You're a beautiful girl, don't waste it. It's gone before you know it, darling. And get some Arnica for that bruise."

Jupiter nodded and tried to say goodbye but the words stuck in her throat. Lesley waved a little wave and Jupiter walked off the plane feeling like she might vomit.

47 men

ARTIST LOFT
Dauphine Street

The door burst open; Rooster stumbled, tripping across the threshold. He fell to the floor and stayed there, leaving the door wide open. Faint Zydeco music and the low hum of voices filled the corridor. A meow echoed against the walls of the hallway. It grew louder and closer and finally a large orange Tabby cat peered in the door with the air of superiority only a cat can muster. He meowed loudly. Rooster's eyes opened.

"Randolph."

The cat meowed again.

"Where ya been?"

The cat looked at him as if to say: "Do you think I can actually talk to you, moron?"

"Right, you can't talk. Fuck." Rooster rolled over and lifted himself up so he could speak to the cat.

"Every single one sold. A lot were of her and how's that? I take all these pictures and they all sell and now she's gone. Disappeared into thin air. What do you do with that?" he slurred the last sentence.

Randolph meowed again and walked over to Rooster purring like a motorboat.

"At least you like me."

Rooster tried to scratch his head but his hand completely missed the cat and hit the floor.

"Fuck." He picked up his hand looked at it and looked at the cat again.

"Why did she leave?" he asked in earnest.

Randolph rubbed up against him with his ass in Rooster's face.

"Why?" He asked again and rested his head on his arm and closed his eyes. Randolph licked the edge of Rooster's ear with his sandpaper tongue and moved to his face, which seemed to have some delicious food remnant on it. Rooster didn't move.

The sound of music was suddenly louder and a woman's voice called out "Randolph, Randolph, where are you?" Her footsteps came closer and finally she was in Rooster's doorway.

"Rooster? You okay?" asked a stunning African American woman with a turban on her head.

He roused momentarily, "Huh? What arr—" and that was all.

She laughed. Then picked up the cat in one arm, pulled the blankets off the mattress and draped them gently over Rooster's passed-out body. She snapped off the lights that had been on all night, shut the door and left with Randolph in her arms lodging a massive protest.

JOHN F. KENNEDY INTERNATIONAL AIRPORT

J upiter bee-lined from the aircraft toward the nearest bathroom. She hunched over the toilet bowl and spit, but nothing came. She stuck her finger down the back of her throat but only made herself gag. Finally she gave up and wiped her watery eyes and saliva on her sleeve. She looked at her face in the florescent light as the warm water ran over her hands. Was Lesley right? Should she get back on a plane and go find Rooster? The humiliation of the explanation played in her mind, which shook the idea straight from her brain. *He won't believe me.* Back to the plan, she thought, and waded through the myriad of nationalities and queued up amongst the hordes in the taxi line.

"The Carlyle, seventy-sixth and Madison," Jupiter said, as she settled into the back seat of the taxi.

Jupiter adored the Manhattan apartment, as did her father. It was located on the twenty- sixth floor with views to Central Park and down Madison Avenue. There were magnificent sunsets, spying on the apartments across the way and the majestic roof gardens. It was all pretty magical. Jupiter had spent hours of her childhood sitting on the floor Indian style looking down at the city bustling below. Russell favored the view facing Central Park and would position himself accordingly so that when he glanced up from his papers he would be greeted by the verdant treetops and cornflower-blue sky. Jupiter would scrunch into the exact corner where the two banks of windows met in order to maximize her vistas. When she was about eleven her father had asked what she thought about with her nose pressed to the glass. Jupiter started to laugh.

"Daddy, you don't care."

"I do," he said.

"No you don't."

"Yes, please tell me."

"I was thinking... as I looked down on all of these groups of people, of families with their children, why you and mom didn't have another child?"

Russell breathed in heavily and let the air back out like a tire with a slow leak.

"We tried... remember Atlanta, when we went?"

"Yes." The red toilet returned in a painful flash.

"After that the doctors told us your mother's body couldn't sustain another pregnancy that she would probably die."

Jupiter recorded her father's very sad eyes.

"Thank you, Daddy."

"For what?" he said, confused by her response.

"For telling me the truth."

"Such a grown up you are, my Jupiter June." He smiled and then looked out to the park, his eyes resting in the green before they traveled back to the black and white of the page in front of him.

Jupiter's focus returned to the street, to the people, to the families, with different eyes. Envy had been replaced by gratitude that her mother did not die and would be with her for the rest of her life.

"Here we are," the crusty old cabby growled, his voice surprising her.

"Oh, sorry." She reached for her wallet.

"Welcome to the Carlyle," a bellman said, swinging the car door open.

Jupiter paid and stepped out of the cab.

"Yo, Jup, I didn't even recognize you, turning into a real lady," a uniformed bellman said grabbing her small bag.

"Oh my God, George, I can't believe you're here right now."

"Yeah, you lucked out," George said with a wink.

47 men

Jupiter smiled thinking the tides of good fortune might be finally turning her way. George was her most favorite bellman; he had worked at the Carlyle since Jupiter was a little girl. Somewhere at home, there was a photograph of George crouched down next to Jupiter waving from her stroller.

George held up his hand to give her a high five, a ritual that began in her youth but now at twenty-four seemed a little goofy, though the gesture was sweet. She hit his hand and pushed through the revolving door, walked across the lake like black marble floor to the reception desk.

"Is Frank here?" Jupiter asked.

"May I ask your name?" a feminine brunette asked in an accent-less voice, a necessity for the discriminating clientele.

"Jupiter Campbell."

"Ah yes, Miss Campbell, I'll just be a moment." She disappeared into the back and Jupiter's attention turned to the elevators. As a little girl, the elevators were her most desired destination. Each had a velvet corner seat just the right height for her and most importantly an elevator operator to chat with. If one of her favorite operators was on duty she would spend hours riding up and down, greeting the hotel patrons from her corner perch. She would garner their vital statistics, where they were from, whether they had children and if they had been to Bemelman's Bar to see the paintings on the walls.

"You know the Madeline books?" she would explain, "Did you know that in exchange for painting the murals the artist was able to stay at the hotel for a year and a half for free? My father says he traded painting for his bar tab."

The receptionist returned to the desk. "I'm sorry, he's not here but he's instructed me to give you the keys to the apartment."

"Thank you."

"He also asked that I express his condolences."

"Oh, um... thank you." Jupiter said, taking the key and ending the conversation.

"Do you have any baggage?"

"Um," Jupiter said again, turning and looking down at her peculiar outfit of Darling Boudreaux's Keds, her black dress with the light blue sweater awkwardly worn over it and her mother's crocodile Birkin bag.

"No, I..." She felt ridiculous and very uncomfortable in her own skin. She clutched tight to her bag and didn't finish her sentence. She stepped into the elevator and eyed the velvet seat, now a putty color, but inviting nonetheless. She nodded to the elevator operator.

"Twenty-six, please." She said softly.

They rode in silence. Jupiter stared down at her feet and instead of the vomit feeling; she was now experiencing a brutal ache, a gut wrenching tearing at her heart. Rooster's blue eyes, the softness of his kiss on the porch swing, the purple of June Bug's feet.

"Here we are, Miss."

Jupiter muttered thanks and made her way to the door of the apartment; it creaked as it opened. She reached in and flipped all the light switches on the inside of the door. The dark parquet floor shone as the hallway light hit the surface. Her feet stuck, the smell of her mother wafted into her nostrils and felt like a slap across the face. She felt like a deer trapped in headlights not knowing which way to move. The ding of the elevator behind her forced her forward and she shut the door quickly behind her. The concept of her Manhattan excursion was far from the reality that was now presenting itself. She moved through the foyer and to the living room to her beloved view. Jupiter abandoned the bag and lunged for the curtains. She yanked at the strings and slowly the living room was bathed in city lights and her view was unveiled. She dropped to the carpet and watched the grids below through the glass. Her eyes were drawn to the yellow taxis bopping along in sunny bursts against the black asphalt and moved to the park and the silhouetted outline of the treetops.

She went to the coat closet and tentatively opened the door. Her mother's smell became even more pronounced. Jupiter pressed her face into her favorite coat of her mother's Mahogany-crushed beaver, she rubbed the fur and the scent of her mom all over her face. Then she wrapped her arms around coat and hugged it.

"Oh Mommy, I miss you so much."

She pulled her face out of the fur and tried to regain her composure.

"Come on, you can do this."

THREE (3) DAYS

(3) Days
The time it takes for bubble gum to pass
through the digestive track.

(3) Days
Jesus was executed by Roman crucifixion and entombed;
he was raised from the dead on the third day.

(3) Days
"Three-Day Rule" refers to dating etiquette that suggests
waiting three days to call a prospective love interest.

(3) Days
Amount of time required for oil-based paint to properly dry.

(3) Days
Number of days it takes Tony Robbins to
"Unleash the Power Within" ™.

(3) Days
Um Jupiter, One – two – three… chop chop…

ARTIST LOFT
Dauphine Street

"ROOSTER BOUDREAUX, get your ass out of bed. It's fucking enough already."

Preston pulled the blackout curtains back to let light in. Rooster's studio was in an old warehouse building with two-story windows and incredible light. The sudden exposure to daylight revealed a sorry state of affairs; pizza boxes, Chinese food containers, three empty handle bottles of Jack Daniels, a few smashed Coke cans, twenty or so beer bottles, two ashtrays full of cigarette butts and five empty crushed-up cigarette boxes. A coffee cup with mold nesting on the surface sat on a table near Rooster's head. There was a mattress on the floor that formerly resembled a bed, but now only the shiny pale blue tufted quilting remained.

"Close the fucking curtains," Rooster yelled with his arm covering his eyes. He was fully clothed, boots and all and now rolled over face down arms covering his head.

"No, motherfucker, enough with this shit." Preston kicked a pizza box. "When was the last time you bathed?"

Preston peered into the bathroom adorned with vomit spray and piles of dirty towels on the floor.

"Christ Roo, it's fucking disgusting in here." Preston flushed the toilet and turned hot water on in the sink. He started dialing his phone.

"Letty, I need you. Tell Momma it's for Rooster. Can you come down to the—"

"No, come on Preston; just leave me the fuck alone."

"Let me call you right back," Preston whispered into the phone.

"It's enough man. You need to take a fucking shower and eat a decent meal. Your momma is dyin' with worry. Rooster, she's not half as bad as you are. You had to see this comin'. June Bug was sick for a real long time."

"It's not fucking JUNE Bug."

Preston stared, not understanding.

"It's her."

"The demon seed?"

"Fuck you."

"Hell, she mighta been the one who did June Bug in."

"Fuck you."

"She was fuckin' rotten. I say good riddance to bad rubbish, or however the fuck you say it."

"You didn't even know her."

"Neither did you."

"Fuck you."

"She was one wicked bitch."

"Because she called you out?" Rooster was now upright, his hair matted to his head, white shirt with pizza stains down the front of it.

"You don't know the half of it, my friend."

"What the fuck does that mean? I love her. I think she loved me."

"I wouldn't be so sure."

"What the fuck Preston? If you think this is helping me, it's not."

"She's fucked up. Seriously fucked up."

"What makes you such an expert all the sudden?"

"I'm just sayin' it's a good thing she left. Come on man there's a thousand honeys out there just waitin' for y'all."

"Are you fucking listening to me?"

"Well you better fuckin' get over it."

"Why?"

"Because."

"That's not an answer."

"It's all you need to know."

"What does that mean?"

"Information is on a need-to-know basis and you don't need to know. Take my word on this one, Roo. She was fucking trouble."

"No, she wasn't."

"Oh, yes, yes she was."

"Preston, tell me what you're not tellin' me. My head fucking hurts. I'm not in the mood for your bullshit."

Rooster grabbed a pack of the cigarettes off the floor, pulled one out and put it to his lips. He rummaged around next to the mattress to find the lighter and sucked hard into the flame. Preston paced through the mounds of trash and dirty clothes.

"Can't."

Preston found a garbage bag under the sink in the kitchen and began picking up trash to avoid eye contact. Rooster sucked on his smoke and watched Preston's mounting discomfort.

"Dude, what the fuck is in your craw?"

Preston didn't answer, just kept at his task.

"If she's so fucking evil, don't you have an obligation to tell me?"

"She came over to my house and we fucked. Satisfied?"

Rooster stood up. "You did what?"

"I had sex with your sweet angel, who offered herself up like a dirty whore." Rooster walked slowly over to Preston.

"Look at me." Rooster dropped his cigarette. Preston glanced up.

"You slept with her?"

"Fucking whore, yes I did."

Rooster cold-cocked Preston, who was so stunned by this action that he collapsed on to the wood floor.

"Roo, come on," he said, with blood dripping out of his nose.

maguire

"Fuck you, you... she hated you..." Rooster searched the floor, picked up a jacket and found his car keys. "I don't fucking believe you."

"Truth hurts, my friend."

"I'm gonna find her."

Rooster stormed out, slamming the door. Preston got up smashed out the cigarette with his foot and fell backward on the mattress. He wiped his bloody nose on Rooster's sheet.

The sound of tires screeching made Preston smile a little.

"Go get her, Roo."

TWO (2) DAYS

(2) Days
Number of days three-hundred Spartan men were able to hold off thousands of Persians in the Battle of Thermopylae.

(2) Days
Time it takes for rigor mortis to set in on a human body.

(2) Days
Manson Family killing spree August 9th and 10th, 1969.

(2) Days
Time allotted to defrost duck for Julia
Child's Duck a L'Orange.

(2) Days
Gonorrhea, a bacterial infection of the genital tract, symptoms appear two to ten days after exposure. Symptoms include: thick, cloudy or bloody discharge from the penis or vagina; pain or burning sensation when urinating.

(2) Days
Jupiter Campbell, down to the wire, her quest in jeopardy of being a complete failure.

BARNEY'S NEW YORK
Madison Avenue

The daylight brought the unwelcome realization that Jupiter was down to just days. Her mission loomed large in her mind. She had eaten a breakfast of soft-boiled eggs, toast points and a pot of hot chocolate. Her mind was splitting time between a ten-year-old girl and a twenty-four-year- old woman. The imbalance was pulling her in directions of eerie bliss and mind-numbing sorrow. She needed to get out; the fresh air would do her good, her father's words. She wandered around the apartment terrified of opening another closet to the ensuing avalanche of memories. She had nothing to wear except for what she'd had on yesterday. She removed the heavy white robe, pulled the black dress over her head then the blue sweater and slipped Darling's shoes back on. She looked at herself in the bathroom mirror. The bruise was now yellow at the edges and a putrid greenish hue as it moved onto cyan, although behind her ear it was still solid violet. She pulled the beige make-up from her purse and dabbed it, quickly smoothing it over the cheekbone.

"It will have to do." She said to herself in the mirror. She used the Tiffany monogrammed sterling hairbrush from the tray to smooth her hair. Though she loathed shopping, she had to suck it up and ferret out the appropriate attire because she was certainly not going to brave another closet. She could feel the chill outside just from the color of the light and the stiff shadows, falling hard against the buildings. This unfortunate fact required a return to said closet.

She held her breath and quickly picked a sensible navy blue cashmere overcoat and slipped it on, then transferred the credit card from the inside zip pocket of her purse to her coat pocket. She grabbed the keys and went from room to room turning on every light in the apartment so it would be bright when she returned. She pressed the elevator button and the doors opened to the same awkward man as yesterday. "Hello again, Miss."

"Hi," she said, eyes shooting down toward her feet. The elevator experience stirred up too many memories, and then her shoes and Rooster, fuck.

The cold air hit her cheeks as she spun through the revolving door onto 76th street and she fell into her Manhattan stride. Her gait felt good, familiar, and she remembered walking with her mother as a little girl, down Madison Avenue, trying her best to keep up with Ruth Ann's long city strides. Once a month, they would go to meet Daddy *"in the city."* Her mother always wore a suit, a jewel tone, high heels and stockings. Jupiter was forced to wear white tights, an itchy blue wool coat with a velvet collar and hard black Mary Jane's with buttons on the side. The shiny patent leather slid across the pavement and occasionally the toe would catch in a crack of the sidewalk, causing Jupiter to stumble. Ruth Ann would look down like she'd completely forgotten Jupiter was attached to her hand. Ruth Ann, always a bit preoccupied in Manhattan, would realize she'd been dragging Jupiter for blocks along Fifth Avenue. Then she'd stop, stooping down to Jupiter's level, "Sorry darling we're just late to meet Daddy." As Ruth Ann's modus operandi was tardiness, Jupiter spent much of her childhood in this hurried state. Jupiter waited for it, trying to gauge when it might come. It was a particular combination of things, her mother's perfectly perfumed skin and the smell of hair spray. The fact that she bent down in those high heels just to look Jupiter in the eye, then the kiss her on the forehead and the words, which included Jupiter and little princess in the same sentence.

It was colder than she'd thought; no gloves, hat or scarf. Jupiter hailed a cab and jumped into the back and barked out her destination to the cabby with true city kid flair.

A bad Broadway anthem blared from the taxi's seat back and Jupiter watched out the window as the music provided an odd accompaniment to her trip down Park Avenue. She watched the women in their varied ensembles, each portraying a distinctive persona. Growing up, she'd wanted to be one of those women in a business suit with high heels and a briefcase, but now what did she want to be?

Rooster appeared again in her mind, talking to her from behind the camera lens, "What did you want to be when you grew up?"

"A veterinarian who wore business suits and carried a briefcase."

Rooster laughed at her, "Really?"

"I was a weird kid."

"What do you want to be now?"

Jupiter stared into the lens. The shutter closed once and then twice and then a third time. Her eyes didn't blink.

"I don't know," she said finally, a hollowness in her voice.

Rooster put the camera in his lap and looked at her.

"It's okay, you don't have to know," he said warmly.

"I'm scared though," Jupiter looked away, edging up to nine on the intimacy scale.

"Of what?"

"What if I never know?" Jupiter whispered.

"Ma'am," the cabbie shouted, "We're here."

The doorman flung open the door and Jupiter handed a ten-dollar bill to the driver. She stepped onto Madison Avenue, becoming part of the herd swinging through the revolving doors of the Barney's store. She was pressed against bodies in coats with shopping bags, herding like cattle through the jewelry department, past handbags and then finally dissipating at the elevators.

Personal shopper, seventh floor, ding, doors opened and Jupiter sniffed out the offices of the personal shoppers like a rescue dog. Personal shopper Marcel was wielding two phones and going through a rack of clothes when Jupiter tapped gently on his door.

"What?" he barked.

"Can you help me?" She mouthed to him.

He held up a finger, ended his call and stepped forward.

"Only because of the coat, Cashmere Chanel 1963. Marcel," he said offering Jupiter his hand to shake.

Marcel wore a tightly tailored Hugo Boss suit, a dazzling lime Etro shirt with a coordinating silk scarf loped over his left shoulder, acid lemon cashmere socks peaked out from his velvet Gucci slip-ons and to complete the look, painstakingly coiffed jet-black hair. He looked like a canapé on a tray waiting to be eaten.

"Jupiter," she said and held out her hand, mortally embarrassed by what lay underneath her chic Chanel exterior.

"Alright dah-ling, what do we need?"

"I'm not really sure."

"Something decadent, perhaps? Or something sexy/slutty?"

"Let's try decadent."

"Okay... SO where are we donning this ensemble?"

"Out."

"Out where? Marcel needs some parameters."

"Not sure yet. I need to find... someone... who..."

"Are we looking to meet someone?"

"Yes, sort of—"

Marcel put his hands on his hips. "You're looking to get laid?"

"Um... well... yes," Jupiter said relieved.

"Off to three then." He raised his index finger in the air and traced a small circle. "Follow, follow, follow."

Marcel slalomed down the escalators to the third floor. There was a secret room adjacent to the common dressing rooms with racks and racks of clothing. They were separated into sections. Marcel sifted through the stock tagged for a prominent young socialite. He pulled a Balenciaga micro mini, tiered ruffle dress in silk with a hot pink floral pattern.

"You cannot tell a soul that you have been in this room or that it even exists. This is perfection for you, and the shoes make the ensemble," he said, revealing from the box, a shoe of strappy fabulousness.

47 men

Jupiter nodded.

"Dah-ling, trust Marcel."

Marcel ripped clothing from the other racks in a whirling frenzy. Jupiter watched the master with rapt attention as he held items in the air, deciding if they were worthy of being tried on. When he was satisfied, they returned to his "room," both carrying armloads of garments.

They entered to the telephone ringing off the hook; Marcel dropped his armload on to a small velvety sofa and grabbed the receiver. "Ciao... Marcel at your service."

He listened intently for a moment.

"Oh that's a disaster, she's actually in JAIL?" Marcel rolled his eyes at Jupiter. "No, I don't... wait... HOLD please." Marcel put his hand over the mouthpiece. "What are you doing this evening?"

"Why?" she asked.

"Never ask Marcel why, just say yes."

"Okay, yes."

Marcel removed his hand and began to speak, "My friend, it is your lucky day, I just happen to have THE most delightful young thing in my room right now and I just might be able to persuade her to accompany you *ce soir*, Theodore." Marcel smiled at Jupiter, who smiled back.

"Stunning." He winked, nodding all the while as if the gentleman on the other end of the phone could actually see him.

"She's in from out of town. Dah-ling where are you staying?"

"The Carlyle," Jupiter said trying to deduce the other side of the conversation.

"She's at the Carlyle, arrive at eight, she will meet you in the lobby, wearing a divine Balenciaga. Of course, Theodore, you are most welcome. Just behave... no arrests. She's a good girl."

Jupiter blushed and turned away. Marcel hung up the phone.

"Well my dear, you have just procured the hottest invitation to the most spectacular event with the most eligible, albeit a bit notorious, bachelor in ALL of Manhattan."

"Wow, thank you. Where am I going?"

"You will be attending the Whitney Museum American Arts Gala, so let's get you out of here. Do you have hair and make-up?"

"Umm... No..."

Marcel looked at his watch and sighed heavily.

"I guess the hotel is the best we can do at this late hour." He picked up the phone and dialed from memory.

"The salon." He rolled his eyes at Jupiter.

"Hello Mona, Marcel here. Yes, I am sending a guest. I know it's late, but Teddy P. is taking her to the Gala tonight. Thank you Dah-ling, she'll be there in fifteen."

Marcel hung up the phone.

"Alright here are your instructions... Number one: Don't drink too much, you will need to keep your wits about you; Number two: He likes to fight when he gets drunk; and Number three: He has dated EVERY woman in this city so a thick skin will be required."

Marcel arched his eyebrows, looking for her acknowledgement. Jupiter nodded and put out her hand to shake his.

"You are the best!"

Marcel leaned forward and gave her air kisses on each cheek. An assistant arrived holding a small clip board with her bill. Jupiter handed her the platinum card and followed her out of Marcel's room.

"Oh and you can't make him wait or he'll just leave and call me to find someone else." Marcel called out after her.

"Got it." Jupiter said with her Chanel-clad exterior and many packages in tow.

MAGNOLIA SUPERETTE
Simon Bolivar Ave, New Orleans

Rooster Boudreaux stopped at the Magnolia Mart for a couple packs of Parliaments before he began his journey north. He strode in, asked for the cigarettes and took a quick look around to see what else he might need.

"And coffee, black."

"Serve yourself." The man behind the counter pointed.

Rooster poured stale coffee into a Styrofoam cup and put a lid on it. His hands shook. He thought about food but his stomach curdled with the anticipation of it. Then he looked over and the red bag of barbeque pork rinds caught his eye. He wanted to cry and punch the wall simultaneously. Rooster paid for the coffee and cigarettes and returned to the truck. He stared at the steering wheel in the dark. He peeled the red line off of the cellophane cover, crumpled it into a ball and threw it on the floor of the passenger side. He opened the top of the cardboard pack and pulled out the silver foil. He crumpled that as well, removing the smooth white cylinder. He put the cigarette between his lips and opened the silver butane lighter, his father's. He rubbed his thumb against the course metal, a spark flew. The flame ignited. He held the flame to the end of the cylinder. He sucked in hard. White smoked blew from his mouth and out of his nostrils. He put the cigarette back into his mouth, drew hard again. He threw the pack on the seat next to him. His head fell forward against the top of the steering wheel.

On the seat next to the pack of cigarettes was an announcement card.

Rooster Boudreaux, *The New Orleans Photo Alliance*, printed in 16pt Copper Plate 32BC at the bottom.

Above it—
A photograph
Of a girl

In silhouette
Against a bright
Blue sky...
A black swing
Attached with chains

And the girl flying through the air...

"Ahhhhh!" he shouted into the night.

WHITNEY MUSEUM
OF AMERICAN ART
945 Madison Avenue

A t 7:57 p.m. a freshly groomed Jupiter Campbell stood in the lobby with the glistening black floor as a backdrop to her dainty Balenciaga with her butter cream hair spilling down her back. Eight o'clock passed onto eight-fifteen and finally as her feet began to bark their discomfort, Teddy waltzed into the lobby in his tux, wearing black patent leather dancing shoes with bows. Jupiter wanted desperately to roll her eyes, but she refrained. His head was attached to a cell phone that he spoke into as if he were barking orders into his own brain.

"Hey." He covered the phone. "Teddy." He reached out a limp hand to her.

"Jupiter," she whispered.

"What?" He said, still covering the phone.

"Jup-i-ter," she stated loudly, enunciating each of the syllables carefully into his phone. He nodded, stepped back and gave her the one-minute signal with his hand and turned away.

"Babe, it's just a date for the party, nothing else. We'll get you out of there by noon tomorrow, the guys are on it. Me too. Gotta run."

Jupiter rolled her eyes at his back, which he caught as he turned around to her.

"Hi Jup-i-ter," he mimicked her pronunciation, "Sorry about that."

"Girlfriend?"

"She got arrested last night for cocaine possession and she had so much on her person they booked her. My lawyer's on it but apparently when you are arrested with a brick of cocaine in your Prada bag, there's a whole intent-to-sell issue they have to get past. So, what do you say we jet?"

Teddy held out his arm to her, she latched on and they floated up the steps and out the door. George the doorman tipped his hat to Jupiter as she was whisked into the back of a black Mercedes sedan. The door slammed behind her head.

"Teddy," he said, offering his hand to her again.

"I know," she said smiling.

"As billed, quite stunning."

"Glad you approve."

Teddy ran his fingers through his thick brown hair and his phone lit up again.

"Oh Christ. Sorry I have to take this. It's my attorney." He answered it and Jupiter cataloged his every move. His thin, perfectly tanned fingers, the hint of razor stubble, the strong patrician nose, the eyebrow that furrowed when he heard something he didn't like.

"Do whatever you can to get her out of there. Thanks Max." He hung up and turned his brown eyes to her.

"Where were we?" He half laughed and then looked straight into her eyes, "So what's your deal?"

"What do you mean?"

"Come on, stunner like you doesn't happen upon my door-step every day."

"It truly was random; some might say fate. Or Marcel."

"Ah, my man Marcel." He picked his phone back up and dialed. "Marrrrcel, you have truly outdone yourself."

Jupiter could hear Marcel's voice, first excited and then slowing with caution and instruction.

"I will take good care of her, Marcel. Thank you again my friend, you are a lifesaver."

"Excuse me, sir," the driver asked, "where would you like me to drop you?"

"Just up on the right, James."

"What time would you like me back, sir?"

"Let's say midnight. I'll text if it's sooner."

The car shimmied up to the curb; James was out in a flash and the door flew open for Jupiter's exit. The paparazzi cranked off a bunch of photos before they could figure out they didn't know who she was. Then Teddy stepped out and the bulbs popped away. He held her elbow from behind and gently guided Jupiter toward the line of photographers. They posed for pictures, a reporter asked whom she was wearing and they were suddenly in the center of a party. Teddy handed her a glass of champagne. He chatted effortlessly with everyone, introduced her around and was a positively delightful host. Teddy was everyone's love; men, women, and Jupiter was certain that puppies and babies were also in the repertoire of those who fell for his charms. She did get, as warned, many dirty stares and even a shove or two to move her out of the way.

He leaned in and whispered in her ear, "You are very good at this."

Jupiter curtsied slightly. "And you, kind sir, are the mayor."

He laughed and fished a fresh glass of champagne off of a tray replacing her half consumed glass. "Need to keep you happy according to my man, Marcel."

Jupiter nodded.

With that, the dining room was unveiled, a fuchsia and lilac Garden of Eden. Cascading tendrils of green, festooned with chunky garden roses, a mélange of senses being engaged, enticed and explored. Teddy grabbed Jupiter's hand and pulled her toward a canvas wall where guests were meant to draw to their heart's desire. Teddy began to draw a gigantic heart and Jupiter's mind leaped to Rooster...

They had slept in Delilah's small pink bedroom off of the kitchen; it had become their room. One morning, Jupiter felt a stirring and opened her eyes to find Rooster on the floor with a pad jimmied in his lap and a piece of charcoal in his hand.

"Don't move," Rooster whispered.

"What are you doing?"

"I'm drawing you sleeping."

"Why?"

"So I don't forget."

"Forget what?"

"Don't move."

Jupiter held still but continued, "Forget what?"

"Peaceful."

"What's peaceful?"

"You."

"Me?"

"When you sleep."

"Really?"

"Yes and the juxtaposition between that and when you're awake, is remarkable."

Jupiter sat up.

"What's that supposed to mean?"

"Don't MOVE!" he barked.

She lay back down to where her head had indented the pillow and remained still. She must have fallen back to sleep because he pushed her lightly to nudge her awake.

"What?"

"Want to see it?"

"Yeah."

175

47 men

Rooster climbed up on the bed and lay down next to her. He held the drawing on the pad above them. Jupiter sucked in her breath. Her favorite painting was "Breakfast in Bed" by Mary Cassatt. Her father had taken Jupiter and her mother on a field trip of sorts to Pasadena in the spring of her fourth-grade year to experience the Huntington Botanical Gardens and while it was supposed to have been a trip to the sunshine, it rained ferociously. This did not thwart Russell's agenda and they began their tour inside the museum. Jupiter wandered off on her own, found the painting and simply sat down on the floor in front of it, mesmerized.

"Jupiter," her mother called out exasperated.

"Mommy," she said, not moving a muscle, "Someone who doesn't even know you painted a picture of you."

Ruth Ann joined her daughter on the museum floor, wrapped her arm around Jupiter and kissed the top of her head.

Rooster had drawn that same woman nuzzled in her cozy pillows, eyes gently closed, only without the baby girl in her arms.

"See, peaceful."

"Have you ever seen..." and Jupiter rolled over and kissed him, her words inadequate.

"Come on," Teddy said snapping her back, "what are you going to draw?"

"Oh, God," Jupiter said trying to remove Rooster's face from her brain, "I don't know. I can't draw very well."

"Just do something, it's for charity."

Jupiter opened her tiny purse, removed her lipstick, applied a thick coat and kissed the canvas perfectly hot pink three times then signed her name underneath. Teddy watched the procedure carefully. When she finished, Jupiter kissed him, leaving a bright pink lip print on his cheek.

"Inventive," he said, leaving the kiss on his cheek.

Jupiter and Teddy dined under pink chandeliers in the Garden of Eden. A salad adorned with fuchsia edible flowers was placed at each setting. Jupiter was seated between Teddy and an elderly man with a hearing aid named Stan who yelled when he spoke. Stan owned a large chain of "big box" stores.

"I can see your nipple through your dress," he yelled. The entire table turned and stared, most notably his wife.

"That's awesome, sir," she yelled back. "You remind me so much of my grandfather," and then she patted his hand.

Teddy leaned in and whispered, "You have beautiful ankles."

"Are you kidding?"

"No."

"When did you see my ankles?"

"Habit, first thing I look at."

"Why?"

"Thoroughbred vs. a Clydesdale."

"How do you figure?"

"You start at the ankles and determine if it's worth moving up."

"That's terrible."

"Nope, effective."

"How effective?"

"I'd say about ninety percent accurate. Try it." Teddy looked around,

"Yellow dress twelve o'clock."

"She has a pretty face."

"Yes but look at the ankles... she's what... mid-twenties, I give it two years before she's got solid cankles."

"What about her brain?"

"Intelligence is overrated."

"So you like 'em skinny and stupid?"

"No, it just makes everything more complicated."

"And that's bad?"

"Not necessarily. Just depends on what you're in the mood for."

"Have you ever had a monogamous relationship?" Jupiter asked.

47 men

"Of course. Have you?"

"Yeah."

"The longest?" he asked.

"A year."

"Smart?"

"No, a football player."

"See."

"Eat your flowers and be quiet." She said smiling as the salad was removed and a banquet plate was set in front of her.

Jupiter ate a hard roll with butter and let the salmon in congealed sauce sit untouched.

"Not a fan?" Teddy said nodding in the direction of the plate.

Jupiter batted her eyelashes and mouthed no. Teddy picked up his Blackberry and sent a text.

"What did you do?"

"It's a surprise."

Teddy rose from the table ten minutes later.

"Meet me by Basquiat's Hollywood Africans in the Permanent Collection – fifth floor, ten minutes."

She waited and then excused herself, slipped into the stairwell and found her way to the fifth floor. She turned the corner and a security guard greeted her.

"This way please,"

"Thank you," she said and followed him gingerly into a small gallery where Teddy was seated at a table with champagne and pizza.

"No way," Jupiter said beaming at him.

"Best pizza in the city" he said as he stood to pull out her chair.

"Amazing," Jupiter sat down and devoured the first slice.

"Ahhh, I love a girl who eats. So rare."

"It is?"

"Yep. If they do eat, they generally evacuate later."

"That's gross."

"Yes, it is."

Jupiter held up her glass, "Thank you."

"No, thank you," Teddy returned.

"So... have you ever been in love?"

"Once."

"What happened?"

"She broke my heart," he said.

"How old were you?"

"Twenty-five."

"How?"

"I proposed, she bailed."

"Where is she now?"

"No idea."

"Aren't you curious?"

"No."

"Can I have another piece?"

"Of course," Teddy reached into the box and put another piece on the paper plate, "how about you?"

"No." she said too quickly.

"I think you're lying to me."

"No," she said again and then blushed.

"Your blush betrays you," he smiled and sipped his champagne, "Ready to dance?"

"Sure," Jupiter said, relieved he had not pressed further.

They got up, Teddy slipped the security guard a bill and they returned to the abundant garden. The crowd had moved to the sleek lower gallery for the studio party. Dancing, flowing champagne, sweaty bodies, Teddy slipped her right into the center of it. He was a fabulous dancer and Jupiter was enjoying herself for the first time in what seemed to be a long time. They were sweaty and thirsty so Teddy grabbed a huge bottle of Pellegrino off the bar and guided Jupiter to a dark corner of the room where they fell into a heap. He pulled her sweaty self into him and kissed her. A bit aggressive and slobbery but at this juncture she was not in a position to quibble. She returned the kiss, toying with him and then retreating – Jupiter fell into her groove. She opened the bottle of water, took a huge swig and put her mouth to his, slowing letting the water run into his mouth. She ran her fingers through his thick curly hair and then dappled them across his lips. She kissed him as her hand continued the exploration down his chest. Her fingers skimming along the top of his zipper, probing slightly to find the outline of his penis, which was dutifully erect. She slipped off her shoes and slid her leg over his, straddling him. She was on top of him and gently reached under the flounce of her skirt to unzip his fly, her fingers exploring inside to guide his penis to freedom. She held him in her hand, teasing the tip with her index finger and thumb. He sucked in his breath and she guided him under her dress, Rooster's whispering voice crept into her head: "Not here, not like this." She shook her head wildly from side to side trying to shake this memory.

"You okay?" Teddy asked.

Jupiter nodded. He grinned at her just as someone grabbed a huge handful of Jupiter's hair and yanked her back hard.

"What the fuck, Teddy?" a woman screamed into her ear.

Jupiter's head was then shoved forward and fell with a thud onto Teddy's chest.

"What the fuck is this, you douche bag? I was in fucking *pri-zon* and you're fucking some little debutante in the middle of a fucking event," the woman screeched at him.

At this juncture, Jupiter managed to roll off of Teddy, who had somehow stuffed what was once stiff back into his tuxedo pants and was up attempting to console someone named "Serena." Serena, a raven-haired fox, some years Jupiter's senior, was quite well-appointed: the Bulgari jewels, the Valentino gown, and the mink, definitely unnecessary in the current climate conditions. Serena hurled the fur at Teddy's feet, slapped him across the face and began to weep hysterically, which then transformed into uncontrollable cackling. Her fury was mounting and it was now suddenly and forcefully directed at Jupiter.

"Who are you? You fucking little debutante?"

Jupiter sat up. "Not a fucking little debutante. You must be the drug addict."

Teddy, now behind Serena, cracked a smile and then shook his head for Jupiter's benefit and mouthed, "Sorry."

"No worries, Ted," Jupiter said. "A for effort, F for girlfriend selection; and by the way... questionable ankles." She turned toward the girlfriend. "Serena, a pleasure,"

With her shoes in hand, Jupiter shoulder checked Serena as she darted by, sending Serena careening off balance into the banquette. Teddy watched Jupiter fly through the crowd and out the door. She reached the street in her bare feet. Sheets of rain impaled the sidewalk.

"Shit," she said, peering out through the torrential downpour.

Teddy's driver, James, stepped to the door with an umbrella.

"Can I give you a ride?" he asked.

"What about him?" Jupiter asked.

"He just texted me to take you home."

Jupiter cracked up. "He's a funny one that Ted."

James held the umbrella over Jupiter and escorted her to the car. She sat small and alone in the back seat.

"He also wanted me to get your information."

"Unlikely."

"Excuse me?" James said.

"No."

"Why is that, may I ask?"

"Self-preservation." Jupiter answered.

"You are wise beyond your years."

"I guess." She said.

"He also asked that I offer my services to you during your stay should you need them," James said, and then he handed her his card.

James pulled up and stopped in front of the dark entry.

"What time is it?" Jupiter asked.

"Three fifteen. Time flies." He said.

"Ha, please thank Ted for a mostly enjoyable evening." She said.

"He doesn't like to be called Ted. His father is Ted."

"I know, he told me." Jupiter smiled wryly. "Thank you for the card."

Jupiter got out of the car in her bare feet and ran to the revolving door and turned to speak to James.

"Thanks for the pizza, it was awesome."

"My pleasure, best in the city."

"Goodnight, James."

"Goodnight Miss."

Jupiter rode up the elevator silently with an elevator operator who had clearly been asleep seconds before her arrival.

"Goodnight," she said quietly.

Jupiter unlocked the door to the apartment and closed it behind her. She walked to the window, tilted her head against the glass and thought about Rooster's drawing.

"Maybe tomorrow will be better," she said as she unzipped her dress and let it fall to the floor.

Jupiter left on all of the lights, went to the closet, removed her mother's crushed beaver coat and walked to her room. She wrapped herself in the coat and climbed under the stiff linen sheets that she'd hated as a child. She curled into a tight ball, trying to keep her mind empty in the still darkness.

Rooster's fingers lacing through hers flashed through her mind.

"Fuck." she whispered into the darkness.

UNIVERSITY OF VIRGINIA
Charlottesville

Rooster exited highway 29 at the Fontaine Avenue off ramp and tooled his way around the small streets of Charlottesville in his white beast of a truck. He tried to follow the map to the address on the birth announcement but was straight up lost.

Lydia and Billy Wyler are pleased to announce
the birth of their son,
Darwin Jasper Higgins Wyler

"Why the fuck did they name him Darwin?" He said aloud as he gummed a cigarette from the pack and perused the map again.

Billy Wyler was a bitter Englishman with a nose for violence and a wicked tongue. He was a genius photographer and Rooster's mentor. His wife Lydia was a crazy conceptual artist and clairvoyant with regard to Rooster's psyche. She also happened to be a terrible cook who loved to feed everyone. Rooster maneuvered his way down the main road, finally found the street and turned into a little lane and followed the addresses to a one-story brick house with gigantic Dogwood tree in front. A tire swing hung from the right side and a long wood table sat under the left with a chandelier positioned over its center. One of Lydia's art pieces clung to the trunk of the tree, lime green fiberglass loops peaked from underneath its canopy. Rooster parked next to Billy's truck and suddenly wished he'd brought something.

"Momma would kill me," he said slamming the door.

"Ay, who's that then?" Billy walked around the corner cigarette in hand, "Well fuck me, you look like shite. Come on 'ere," Billy threw the cigarette on the ground and wrapped his arms around Rooster like a man just saved from a deserted island.

"You okay?" Rooster asked breaking free from the grasp.

"Let's tell Lid you're here. LID," Billy called out. Lydia came running out yelling "SHUUUUUUUUSH" and then she saw Rooster.

"OH MY GOD, what are you doing here? Oh my God this is surreal. Oh my God, how's your mom? Is she okay?"

"She's okay."

"I'm so sorry about June."

"Thanks."

"WHAT are you doing here? Oh my God, you just made my day." The sound of a baby crying in the distance jarred her.

"I almost forgot I had him for a second and don't look at me, I'm so fat." she said, running toward the house, "Billy's missed you an awful lot," she added, and disappeared inside leaving the men standing awkwardly behind.

"Want a beer, drink? I smuggled a bottle of Absinthe on my last trip to visit me mum. We can pretend we're back in Paris."

Their home, like all of their others, was a mish mash of items from their world travels but all of their houses, no matter the city, were exactly the same in spirit. Lydia rounded the corner with a little blue bundle over her shoulder.

"Wow, so small."

"Wanna hold him?" she asked.

"Uh okay." Rooster sank into the couch and Lydia nestled the baby into his arms.

"So, who is she?" Lydia asked squeezing in next to Rooster.

"Who is who?"

"The girl?"

"What girl?" Rooster questioned.

"The girl on the swing... on your announcement."

"Jupiter."

"You love her." Lydia pronounced.

"What?"

"I told Billy you're in love." She said smiling.

"How can you tell that?" Rooster asked.

"Because."

"Because why?" Rooster asked.

"Not why, but what." She said.

"Okay, so... what?"

"You took a picture," Lydia paused, "of all of her."

Rooster ran his hand through his hair.

"Damn Lid," Rooster blushed.

Lydia called toward the kitchen, "I was right, he's in love."

Billy returned with two glasses of Absinthe, two flat spoons and sugar cubes. "Who is she?" Billy asked, putting the glasses down.

"Oh Bill, really?" Lydia said starring at the full glasses.

"It's a special occasion, love."

"I have to go check on the chicken," Lydia said standing.

Billy hushed his tone, "She's gotten quite good, compared to Paris."

"Remember when she tried to make coq au vin?" Rooster said, laughing, "Got all Julia Child on us."

"And we were all violently ill after," Billy pointed out.

"I hear you talking about my coq au vin," Lydia yelled from the kitchen.

"How did the show go?" Billy changed the subject without comment.

"Good, I guess," Rooster said.

"What do you mean you guess?" Billy pressed.

"Left half way through."

"Why?"

"June Bug, not just that... a lot of stuff... goes with the rest of the story."

"Then you can't tell it yet," Lydia said, setting down a platter with salami and cheeses.

"Do you want help?" Rooster asked starting to get up.

"No, you guys catch up." She put her hand on Rooster's shoulder, pressed him back into his seat and went back to the kitchen.

"She says she doesn't want help but I'll pay later. You alright there?" Billy said eyeing the baby lying content in Rooster's arms.

Rooster nodded and stared at the glass of Absinthe that he could see but could not reach. Rooster looked at his namesake attempting to see the parts of his parents in this little whole but he couldn't. Maybe Jupiter was right, he thought. Maybe his theory about bits was wrong; maybe it was more important to see the whole and then the parts.

"What do you think, Darwin? Who's right? Is she right or am I?"

The baby grinned, ear-to-ear and then laughed. Rooster laughed in spite of himself.

"What is so funny out here?" Lydia said, on her way to set the table, "You got my boy laughing already. Can you work your magic on the other one?" She turned her back to Rooster as she said it.

"How's the Absinthe? Doesn't it bring you straight back to that little café in Montmartre? God, I loved that place. We did great work there, didn't we?" Billy set a perfectly roasted rosemary chicken down at the head of the table. "Wine?"

"Sure." Rooster looked back at Darwin as Billy walked back into the kitchen. Billy went to a turntable and flicked on a vinyl record of Billie Holiday.

"Will you carve?" Lydia yelled from the kitchen.

"Come a long way since Paris," Rooster said, laughing at both of them. Lydia took the baby. Rooster swallowed down the creamy liquid in one gulp.

"Alright Boudreaux, spill it. Don't leave anything out." Lydia said.

Rooster took a deep breath. "Don't I get to eat first?"

"No,"

"Alright fine," he said sitting down opposite her, "You remember Preston?" they nodded.

"Crazy, if I remember correctly?" Lydia said stealing a crispy piece of skin off of the chicken.

"Hey, hey none of that," Billy said poking the fork in her direction.

"Preston paid me to take his best cock to Connecticut to a fight. He had some vendetta against a guy whose bird was fighting up there. He couldn't go so begged me to do it."

"A cockfight?" Lydia asked quizzically, as she served the chicken with mashed potatoes and gravy and beautiful French green beans with slivers of almonds. She set a plate in front of Rooster.

"Lid, this is beautiful," Rooster said, happy to devour a home-cooked meal.

Lydia smiled, "Keep going,"

"Where was I?"

"Cockfight," Billy said with a mouthful of food.

"So I'm at the fight and the guy's a cheater. Put some illegal thing on his bird. The bird went crazy, basically killed our bird. I'm the last one there, sitting with this bird gushing blood and this girl walks in wearing all white. I was like *what the fuck?* She sat down in the dirt next to me and had these green eyes. Anyway she said it was suffering and then she leaned over and broke the fucking bird's neck."

"Really?" Billy asked intrigued.

"Yeah. So I told her she had to come home with me to tell Preston that she killed our bird and she came. Then she made me stop at her parent's house in New Canaan. Her mom died a couple years ago, the dad hasn't talked since her mother died."

"What was she doing at a cockfight?" Billy asked.

"I don't know." Rooster answered.

"You didn't ask her why she was there?" Lydia asked.

"Hot bird shows up to a cockfight alone, strikes me as slightly peculiar," Billy said.

"Was she there to meet a guy?" Lydia asked.

"No idea." Rooster thought about the bloody bird in Jupiter's father's lap, "So we saw her dad and then her black nanny, Willy,"

"She has a black nanny?" Lydia said with a bit of disdain.

"Her dad's some famous scientist invented something, super rich. House looks like the Met. Anyway, Willy asked me to take her home with me."

"Rooster, the black nanny who you'd never met asked you to take a girl who you didn't know home with you?" Lydia looked at Billy. "This doesn't sound like you," she finished shaking her head.

"Felt like I was supposed to do it, Lid. We spent twenty-four-seven together. She's cool. We took her to a cockfight and Preston did the blood sucking thing."

"Oh gross. Roo, he's so weird. That must have freaked her out," Lydia looked ill.

"Yeah, but she handled it and my family. Dealt with all the sisters, no problem."

"Even Delilah?"

"Delilah was nice."

"No way."

"Yeah, June Bug was the one."

"Why?" Billy asked.

"No idea,"

"Oh, I have an idea," Lydia said.

"What?" Rooster asked.

"You're in love Rooster Boudreaux. June Bug saw it. She was just being territorial."

Rooster took a belt off of his wine glass.

"I guess. Momma and I went to look at this home for June. Momma gave her a sleeping pill and we left her there with Jupiter."

"Oh no," Lydia put her hand over her mouth.

"Yeah, we got home, and…" Rooster stopped and put his head down, "Fuck."

"What did she do?" Billy asked.

"She was gone."

"What?" Lydia said, flabbergasted, "she just left?"

"Bailed, departed, no note, nothing. Lost her and June in one fell swoop."

"What kind of person leaves? Who does that?" Lydia demanded.

Rooster didn't answer, gulped his wine and looked at Darwin.

"It gets worse," Rooster said quietly.

"How could it possibly get worse?" Lydia said.

"I was pretty fucked up. Had to bury June Bug then deal with my show. So I hung it and holed up in the studio. Left in the middle of the opening and didn't tell anyone. That really fucked everyone up. Preston and Momma came by and I was shit housed. I told them to go away. Day after Preston got a key and waltzed right in. He started callin' me a pussy and sayin' what an awful bitch Jupiter was and that I needed to forget her… I told him he wasn't helping. Then he said she came to his house and he fucked her."

Rooster took a sip of wine. He looked into the burgundy liquid and tried to focus on the color.

"So I'm going to find her," he said, the anger rising in his voice.

"I don't get it," Billy said.

"He's a liar." Rooster said.

"He says he fucked her…" Billy wouldn't let his gaze go, "Why would he lie?"

"I would have decked him," Lydia said.

"Got a good right hook in and started driving north. I was driving through Northern Louisiana and I thought of you guys—"

"Roo, I don't know," Lydia said wringing her hands. Then she got up from the table and started pacing.

"Bad sign," Billy observed.

"What kind of person leaves the scene of a crime?" Lydia said to no one.

"It wasn't a crime," Rooster said quietly.

"It was a death, a life was lost. I would never have left a dead woman," Lydia said defiantly.

"Not the point." Billy added.

"Yes, it is the point," Lydia yelled, waking the baby, who started to cry, "Oh, sweetie, I'm sorry." She picked up the baby and rocked him back and forth in her arms, "I should probably go put him down and we're not finished here, Mr. Boudreaux."

"Great," Rooster finished off his wine and Billy refilled the glass.

"Fucking women," Billy said under his breath. "I need a fag, let's go outside."

They stood with their wine glasses, smoking, quiet.

"I had to turn down the grant I got to finish the Paris project, because of the kid."

"I thought you wanted this job."

"Fucking hate it."

"I had no idea."

"And she's a freak, feel quite like my head is going to pop off or explode."

"Sorry man."

"Just make quite sure you don't have a kid by mistake, it will monumentally fuck up your life."

"What will fuck up your life?" Lydia said from behind them.

"Nothing, darling, nothing."

"Fuck you, Billy."

"Hey, relax. We're all friends here," Rooster said attempting to keep the peace.

"You have no idea what he's been like," Lydia said with teeth clenched fighting off tears.

"What I've been like, you're a fucking mad woman."

"Come on, don't do this."

"Too late Roo." Lydia turned and went back into the house.

"It's not as bad as it looks," Billy said finally.

"Go take care of your wife, you're being a prick."

Rooster walked back inside and looked for a room to sleep in. The only other room was Darwin's. The baby was on his back with his arms behind his head, peacefully asleep in his crib. Rooster couldn't help but smile. Rooster removed his clothes and got into the little bed. The pillow smelled like Lid. They were his couple, his ideal, what the fuck happened? He rolled on his back and thought about Jupiter curling her skinny body into the back of his. Her fingers running down the side of his leg, her hand holding his hip bone and then moving to find his hand and her fingers tracing his. Rooster closed his eyes and for the first night since Jupiter left, Rooster slept.

47 men

ONE (1) DAY

(1) Days
The duration of the marriage of Eva Braun to
Adolf Hitler hours prior to their double suicide.

(1) Days
Amount of time spent in jail for driving
under the influence (DUI) arrest.

(1) Days
Death resulting from Septicemic Plague.

(1) Days
Jupiter Campbell must be hoping for a
miracle, time to throw the Hail Mary.

CARLYLE HOTEL
35 East 76th St.

Jupiter was jarred awake by a ringing phone, which she did not answer, and then looked at the clock. One in the afternoon. It was her last day. She was sad. She tried to think of somewhere she could go that would boost her spirits.

"Le Bilboquet," she stated aloud.

Le Bilboquet was a jaunty little establishment always enticing a tony French clientele as well as wealthy tourists. The tiny haven of decadence provided the perfect spot for an afternoon perk up. Jupiter put on Marcel's daytime creation, a navy spliced dress by Hervé Léger, a beige embellished Joie cardigan, and patent pumps. She completed the look with new Gucci sunglasses and felt surprisingly better as she strode down Madison Avenue surveying the ladies who lunch, the yummy mummies with babies in tow and the throngs of nannies dragging uncooperative children down the sidewalk away from Central Park. Out front she saw two groups huddled under the green awning sipping their glasses of rose and smoking as they waited patiently for their tables. Jupiter popped her head in and the wonderfully handsome proprietor greeted her.

"Just a few minutes, would you like a glass of Rosé?" Music and increased body temperatures thumped inside.

"That would be lovely," Jupiter answered.

She quickly scanned the room, two older men, dining together well into their second bottle of wine, and table of five younger French boys, all quite darling, tucked in the corner. She smiled in their general direction and ducked her head back out. The encounter with Teddy had bolstered her confidence, even though the deal was not sealed. The table of five could get her to fifty in one fell swoop giving her one to spare, she thought.

A perky Asian waiter delivered her glass. "Your table is ready."

"Merci," she smiled.

She sipped the crisp pink liquid and was led to a table adjacent to the boys, perfect, she thought. She gingerly sat, perched almost. Put her glasses on top of her head and batted her lashes at the crowd.

"Are you alone?" one of the dashing sport-coat wearing French-accented men asked.

"Just for now." She smiled.

"Would you like to join us?" another chimed in.

"Oh I couldn't."

"*S'il vous plait*," another begged.

Jupiter waited another few minutes before pulling her chair up alongside theirs. They cheered her arrival and the room seemed to be transformed into a fête prepared just for her. She nibbled at steak tartare and an entire plate of perfectly crisp French fries. Bottle after bottle of rose came and went from the table; the boys came and went with the smoking of cigarettes and chatting with *amis*.

Another girl joined the party. She was the girlfriend of one of the French boys. Her name was Iris and she was lovely. She had that Parisian *je ne sais quoi* cool, a pair of baggy jeans rolled up to her mid-calf, high heeled Mary Jane's in black satin, a little gray T-shirt and a perfectly aged short leather motorcycle jacket. Her hair, long and dark brown, was parted on the side and tucked behind her right ear. She had full lips painted with crimson and light blue eyes. She smelled of lilacs at their peak. Iris actually smiled at Jupiter as she gazed across the table and delicately sipped her rose. Jupiter could not remember the last time she felt delicate. Iris rose to go to the ladies room and Jupiter followed her, a minute or so behind. She longed to watch Iris wash her hands and reapply her lipstick.

195

47 men

"You are very sweet," Iris said with a thick French accent, "Where you are coming from?"

She rubbed the soap over each of her hands creating a creamy lather.

"Connecticut, not too far."

"Oh, that's nice there, I have been to Greenwitch."

Jupiter smiled. "Your boyfriend is very nice; he was talking about you at lunch."

"He cheats on me," Iris stated matter-of-factly and shrugged her shoulders.

"Why? You're so beautiful."

"I don't really know; the French way *je pense*." She winked at Jupiter and removed the lipstick and began to apply with such dexterous femininity Jupiter was entranced.

"Do you ever cheat on him?"

Iris's face turned crimson and then she laughed "Yes, *avec* Etienne who is out there just now. Uh... it's horr-i-ble, every times, they are drinking; I think Etienne is going to tell Claude. I have to tell him myself I sink, I feel so guilty, like I am a terrible person."

"You aren't terrible. I have that covered."

"Did you cheat?"

"Mine will make you feel better."

"*S'il vous plait*."

Jupiter began to wash her own hands and watched her face in the mirror as she began telling her tale to an almost perfect stranger.

"I have had sex with forty-six men this year, trying to get to fifty. Then I met this guy that I thought was going to be forty-seven. He was amazing, a photographer and sexy and he listened to me. He wouldn't have sex with me because his friend was there. He said it wasn't right... then this other thing happened and I had to leave. I came to New York thinking it would be easier but I can't stop thinking about him. I've tried but he just keeps popping into my head at the most inopportune times. It gets me all off track.

And what if this whole sex thing doesn't even work on my dad, what if I tell him and nothing happens and I have done this all for nothing. What you did... a minor indiscretion... but just for the record... if Claude is cheating on you, Iris, get rid of him."

Iris watched the Jupiter show in the mirror and understanding only a fraction of Jupiter's confession, nodded her head in agreement.

"I don't even know you, but I think you're amazing and Claude is kind of a dick." Iris started to laugh.

"You're right, he is a deeeick."

They stood, watching themselves and each other in the mirror, laughing and relieved at the expression of their secrets. Jupiter then turned to Iris and hugged her.

"Thank you so much."

Iris hugged her back and Jupiter could think only of Ruth Ann and the ache for her mother returned.

"I think your best one chance out there will be Michel. But I think the photographer, he is your one. *Allons-y*, you better go, Oh wait... lipsteek."

Iris retrieved the lipstick from her purse. "He likes the red lips and also he will makes you show something in yourself."

Jupiter obliged with the lipstick and the words, though jumbled, stuck in her craw. What did that mean? Show something, her mind drifted to Rooster. A bubble of emotion rose through her as they returned to the table of men with matching bright red lips. Jupiter took a deep breath and honed in on Michel. A few sips of rose later and his leg curled around hers under the table. There was talk of meeting that night to go to the clubs and suddenly much to Jupiter's dismay, the party began to disburse. Iris came and kissed both of Jupiter's cheeks.

"*Bonne chance.*"

"*Merci,*" Jupiter said and gave her a knowing smile.

With Claude and Iris gone, Jupiter's anxiety mounted.

"What are you doing now, Michel?" her voice cracked.

"No-sing. What do you 'ave in mind?"

"A nap?" Jupiter asked coyly.

"My flat is close; would you like to go zhere?" Michel offered.

"*Mais oui,*" and she stood a little too abruptly; everyone starred at her.

"Not just yet."

Jupiter blushed and sank back down to the edge of her seat... waiting impatiently.

The remainder of the group spat around some French and Jupiter tried to follow for a while but eventually sank into her own thoughts of imminent failure and the loss of Rooster.

"You ready?" Michel tapped her hand.

"Oh, yeah... *oui.*"

"We can walk?" he asked.

"Of course," she said very much off her game and purpose.

There was a note written in cobalt-blue felt tip pen on a brown paper lunch bag, a homemade chocolate croissant and an empty coffee mug with an arrow drawn on another lunch bag, pointing to the coffee maker. The house was filled with sunlight and Rooster scratched his head wondering how he had slept though the family's morning rituals. He poured coffee into the cup, picked up the note and plate and went outside to sit at the long wood table with Lid's art climbing up the tree next to him. The air smelled like dewy grass and little cottony flecks of spores danced around him. The croissant was crispy and flaky and the twinge of bittersweet chocolate hitting his tongue made him shake his head in disbelief.

Rooster picked up the note and unfolded the bag, Lydia's small precise artistic words bled across the surface.

> *Sorry you had to see all that. Be careful, Roo.*
> *Love Lid*

Rooster closed the note, pondered the neon tendrils crawling up the trunk of the tree and then jumped up. He stuffed the note into his pocket, jammed the rest of the croissant into his mouth and ran back to the house. He found his wallet and searched through it. Another scrap of paper, this one written in perfect script; *Wilhelmina* and then a phone number. Rooster lifted the lemon yellow phone off the wall in the kitchen and dialed. There were eight rings and then an answering machine picked up. A "you have reached" and then Willy's voice blurting her name in the center of the mechanized voices and then the beep that came a bit too soon.

"Uh, hi, this is Rooster Boudreaux, I hope you remember me. I'm coming up there to see Jupiter, don't tell her though. I just didn't want to come unannounced and scare y'all. Okay, um, thank you, ma'am."

Rooster hung the receiver back on the wall, ripped a sheet of paper off of the pad hanging by the phone. *Thanks for dinner, please take care of each other. Love you all, Darwin B.* He grabbed another croissant and with renewed vigor circled onto US-29 N ready to face Jupiter.

UPPER WEST SIDE
Manhattan

J upiter trailed behind Michel as they meandered through the streets of the upper west side. Michel greeted a few people on the street, which surprised her. Then he stuck his head into a small antique shop and yelled a greeting in French.

Jupiter stood back assessing Michel. Handsome, very typical New York society French; rail thin, tight jeans, blazer, bright shirt, bad teeth, smoker and more in love with his friends than he could ever be with any woman.

The frontal lobe of her brain began to thump, the buzz of the afternoon was beginning to wear off and a headache was swiftly following in its place. Michel grabbed Jupiter's hand and began to skip down the sidewalk, which she found amusing, and a welcome distraction. They ended up in front of a townhouse, a smashing little building with shiny walnut doors; he sprinted up the flight of stairs and turned at the top flashing a beaming smile. Jupiter lagged behind a bit, perplexed with her lackluster attitude for the task at hand. Michel swung open the door to reveal a meticulously appointed and perfectly tidy apartment.

"Wow... so clean," slipped out of Jupiter's mouth.

"Ah, zee maid."

Michel seized Jupiter's hand and led her straight to the bedroom. He began to undress her, removed her sweater, and unzipped her dress, pulling the top of it down exposing her breasts. He then pulled the dress all the way down to her feet until she was standing in front of him completely naked. He traveled to the edge of the bed and pulled the sheets back. She followed and lay down, watching him as he removed his own clothes. He positioned himself at the foot of the bed, kneeled down and put one of her toes into his mouth. He spent what felt like twenty minutes on her toes. She made a number of futile attempts to grab at his uncircumcised penis, each time thwarted by a skinny limb. He traveled up her legs, kissing, touching, his arms exploring upward to the inside of her thighs but he took his sweet time. He resisted her every advance, not allowing her to move him an inch. Her struggle became slightly more ambitious, and with his head moving toward her crotch, she squeezed her thighs together, held his head and tried again with her arms to bring him to her. He fought with stunning resilience but this time instead of resuming, he turned his cheek and bit into the fleshy part of her inner thigh.

"OWWW," she screamed out. Michel looked up at her.

"That hurt," Jupiter said.

"You musts be patient."

Her head pounded and she wanted nothing more than to just be done with this. Her impatience got the best of her as she tugged at him once more. He bit into the flesh of the other thigh.

"Why are you doing that?" she said angrily.

"You want it too much."

"No... I—" Jupiter started to say.

"Even in casual sex, you have to have your hearts in it." He pounded his chest in demonstration.

"I do," she said unconvincingly.

Michel stood up quickly, "You can go," he said over his shoulder as he walked to the bathroom. He pulled a steel-colored robe off of a hook slipped it over his naked body.

"What?" Jupiter asked.

"Pa-the-tique, go." He said simultaneously pointing toward the door and puncturing her soul.

Michel walked into the living room and Jupiter could hear him speaking on the phone. She stood up from the bed and slowly dressed herself. She put her hand to her heart and felt it pulse. The empty gaping hole inside her chest seemed to be growing larger by the moment.

Jupiter slipped out the front door unnoticed.

The frigid air hit her face and tears began to cascade down her cheeks. She took off her heels and walked barefoot on the cold dirty pavement, her inner thighs throbbing and her mind spinning. People stared as they passed the crying, barefoot, oblivious Jupiter. She finally hailed a cab and her tears continued to flow all the way back to the Carlyle. George opened the door of the cab, as Jupiter handed cash to the driver.

"Oh honey, what is it?" George tried to stop her but she maintained her forward momentum, up the elevator and to the corner window of the apartment where she crouched alone in her small corner of the world. What the fuck was she doing?

47 men

OENOKE RIDGE ROAD
New Canaan

W illy pressed the play button on her answering machine. Rooster's voice filled the air of her bedroom. Willy fell heavily to the edge of her bed. She listened to the message a second time. "You poor sweet boy, she ain't here," Willy said, aloud. She rose up from the bed and trudged into the kitchen and began to make cinnamon rolls for Russell. At least there would be something warm and sweet for him to eat, she thought. She kneaded the dough and prayed, "Dear Lord, protect my Jupiter and bring her back home to me. And please take care of that poor boy I got wrangled into this mess. Praise the Lord Jesus Christ, Amen." Willy crossed herself and began twirling the dough into spheres. She arranged them handily into the baking dish.

"Praise Jesus," she said again and put the pan of rolls into the oven.

maguire

TWELVE (12) HOURS

(12) Hours
Twelve hours of vigorous sex will burn off a
McDonald's 9-piece Chicken McNugget.

(12) Hours
Amount of time it took George W. Bush to address
the nation after the 9-11 terrorist attacks

(12) Hours
Average amount of time couples spend
weekly on their marriages.

(12) Hours
Jupiter Campbell, the sands of time are pouring through the
hourglass... a half of a day was all that was left for old Jup...

TWENTY-SIXTH-FLOOR APARTMENT

"HOUSEKEEPING," bam bam bam against the door.

"Not now, please come back later," Jupiter called toward the door.

The room was a dull gray, the light of the sun held hostage by the thick Manhattan gloom. Jupiter picked herself up slowly from the floor, still wearing her clothes from the day before. She searched for her evening bag and removed James's card from the inside pocket. Jupiter settled down purposefully at the desk and reached for the telephone.

"A club sandwich and French fries and a Shirley Temple please. Just for one."

She dialed the number on the card, "Hi James, it's Jupiter, I was hoping you might be able to take me to New Canaan at," she paused, looking for a clock "Um, around six tonight, if you can. I am at the Carlyle; you already know that, uhhh, okay, thanks, James."

Jupiter returned the phone to its cradle. She turned on the TV and searched for a CSI, settling in as the close up of a scalpel slicing through the gray flesh of a cadaver filled the screen. The assured sound of their voices soothed her in some strange way. She showered, combed her hair back into a slick ponytail and covered the diminishing bruise with beige make-up. She put on the third of Marcel's outfits, jeans, a navy blazer, crisp white shirt and loafers. She carefully placed the pile of clothing into one of the black shopping bags and retrieved her toiletries adding them as well. She greeted the room service man and gave him gratuity on top of the already added eighteen percent. She returned to the desk her father normally helmed and prepared to eat, slowly, purposefully, for nutrition not for hunger or desire. She would need sustenance to face Russell.

Russell… why couldn't she have had a normal father? Father-daughter dances and math tutoring and deb balls and hugs when you needed them. Russell was not a hugger, he didn't pick people up at play dates or attend sporting events, that had been her mother's duty, he said.

Sometimes he was home for dinner but mostly not. Russell's father had never told Russell that he loved him. At least Russell had said it… eleven times in her life. The last time was right before their trip; Jupiter was home for the weekend. Ruth Ann was in the city for the evening and Willy made chicken potpies and served them in Russell's study. Jupiter sat on the floor in worn green Dartmouth shorts cross-legged in front of the roaring fire. Russell sat on the leather footstool of his reading chair, looking down at her. He sipped a bourbon, straight up in a crystal glass and Jupiter had both a tall glass of milk and a root beer side by side. She would eat a bite of the chicken pie and take a gulp out of each of the glasses.

"What on earth are you doing there?" Russell said noticing the edge of the familiar shorts.

"Kind of a root beer float, only not as sweet."

Russell chuckled, "Those are my shorts from college, you know."

"That's why I wear 'em, Pops." she said.

"I rowed in those trousers."

"I can definitely say I have never done such a thing."

"What do you want to do, Jupiter? Passion is an important thing to find in your life."

"Passion?" she said smiling up at him.

"About your work, Jupiter."

"I know Daddy; I'm just playing with you. I don't know. I wish I were like you. I wish I had a crystal-clear picture of what I want to be. I know you wish you had a boy. He would have been a rowing, Swedish-speaking doctor or lawyer by now. You would have been so happy."

Russell looked his daughter straight in the eye, "Jupiter, I love you, I wouldn't trade you for anything." He paused, "You know, you're not so different from me."

"What do you mean?"

"You don't need people; you forge ahead once you find your goal. That's why your mother is so good for us. She makes us live in real time. You're going to have to watch that. People like to be noticed."

"I notice people."

"But you don't engage."

"I—" she stopped and looked at her father. He was addressing their peculiar similarity and though she didn't want this to be true, it was.

She scooped the Hellman's mayonnaise out of the tiny jar, and focused on spreading the white goo inside the top of each of the triangles, then cracked pepper from the miniature silver pepper mill and finally took her first bite. The bacon was all her taste buds would register and then the ketchup but nothing else tasted like much of anything. She chewed the second triangle and the phone rang. She jumped.

"Hello?"

"Jupiter?"

"Yes."

"James here."

"Oh hi James, how are you?"

"Well, just fine thanks. I can take you this evening if you still need a ride."

"That would be great. I need to go home."

"Where ever you want to go, that was the deal."

"I'll be down in front at six."

"Looking forward to it."

It felt like it had been three years since her date with Teddy, Jupiter thought, but she was grateful for James's companionship on this, her walk of shame. Jupiter had failed in every aspect of her endeavor and it was time to concede defeat. She sipped the Shirley Temple and chewed on the cherry.

She visited her corner for the final time, picked the fur coat up off the floor where she'd slept with it and hung it back in the closet. She buried her face in the creamy dark fur once more before her return home.

I-95 NORTH
just outside Philadelphia, PA

R ooster bit into the last of a hot gooey Philly cheesesteak, wiped his mouth with his sleeve and jumped out of the cab of the truck. He crumpled up his trash and shot it into the garbage can. A pay phone attached to the far wall beckoned him. *Call your mother,* it said. He made his way to the phone, dialed the number and then listened to the coins jingle through the innards of the phone. The call connected and rang twelve times before the archaic answer machine picked up.

"Hey y'all, I would just love to chat so leave me a message and I'll call ya right back... chk... chk... chk... beeeeeeeeeep."

"Hi Momma, it's me. Just wanted to say hey. Went and saw Billy and Lid and their baby. Sorry about bein' a horse's ass. I'll call ya soon. Love you."

Rooster put the receiver into the cradle and returned to the truck, feeling very unsure and a little achy for his mom.

TWO (2) HOURS

(2) Hours
Two hours and forty-seven minutes for the Titanic to sink into the Atlantic Ocean - Southeast of Newfoundland.

(2) Hours
Lockheed Martin's Skunk Works designed a twelve-seat passenger jet-with speeds up to 1,200 mph (Mach 1.8) that would go from LAX to JFK in just over two hours.

(2) Hours
Become "An Expert on Anything in Two Hours" with the help of Gregory Harley, a highly decorated former military interrogator.

(2) Hours
Amount of time Jupiter Campbell had to prepare her acknowledgement of failure for the aforementioned task to be presented to Mr Russell Campbell upon her arrival at the parental residence.

I-87
toward Maj Deegan Expressway/Albany

James stood dutifully next to the passenger door of Teddy's Mercedes in the rain.

"Jupiter," he smiled and gave her a slight head tip. George grabbed the bags from her hands and placed them in the now open trunk. George stepped in a little too close and whispered too loudly.

"Are you okay? I worried about you all night, like my own daughter."

"Oh George, thank you, I'll be fine." She patted his shoulder and slid into the back seat. Jupiter handed James a piece of ecru Carlyle stationery with her parents' address on it.

"Did you know your guardian angel is always on your right side?"

"Nope." He said.

James looked at the address and nodded his head.

"I can guide you when we get close," Jupiter said.

"Sounds good. Would you like some music?"

"Sure."

And they were off, cruising through the glistening streets of the Upper East Side. Jupiter watched the colors of light bouncing off of the wet pavement; she had ceased noticing the people. A bizarre mix of tunes played, Billy Joel's "Uptown Girl", to which Jupiter smiled, then Bishop Allen's "Cue the Elephants", Carly Simon's "You're So Vain" made Jupiter laugh aloud.

"That Ted is a funny bird."

"Eclectic taste in music," James said, "So how was the rest of your stay?"

"Fine," she said quickly.

I walk into his office in total darkness. I flip on the lights, including the lamp by his head. I stand in front of him, my father the renowned scientist who is a deaf mute.

"Dad, I couldn't do it. I have failed; the days are up, 365 of them. I had sex with forty- six men. I was trying to get to fifty but I have failed."

My father clears his throat. "What you have done is beyond repugnant. You are no longer my problem. You never were the child I wanted and now... I don't have to pretend to love you anymore. I will tell your mother that you said goodbye. Now go." His voice firm as he stands and points toward the door, "GO," he says calmly.

"She's dead," I whisper it into my armpit and I get up and leave.

"Have you lived in Connecticut your whole life?" James asked.

"Huh... oh yeah... except for college in New Hampshire."

"Cool."

"I guess."

"Running on Empty" blazed through the car speakers.

"Ted, Ted, Ted," Jupiter admonished and then Johnny Cash took the mike, "Nice."

"Jupiter, Teddy asked again about getting your information?"

"Answer's still no."

"That's what I thought you'd say."

She smiled at his eyes in the rear-view mirror.

"You're too good for him anyway. You deserve a great man, a great man for a great woman."

"Thank you, James."

Great woman, ha, she thought. Her mind raced, she was standing above her father in a white municipal hospital hallway, flooded with florescent green light, not another soul, sound, or breath, no sign of human life.

"Dad, she's dead. We have to go home." Jupiter's words echoed off the walls.

Russell's head slumped forward, unresponsive.

"Dad, I need you. They need to know what to do with Mom." Jupiter paused, "I don't know what to do."

Russell remained motionless.

"Daddy, please," Jupiter said pleading.

Russell's tropical shirt seemed to be the focus of his rapt attention. Jupiter thrust his head back harder than she anticipated. His skull smashed against the wall with a resounding thud. She searched into his dull blank eyes and found nothing. Fear rose through her, her hand cocked back and she slapped him as hard as she could across the face. Zip, zero, zilch, nada, save for the guilt and the red finger welts marks striped across his face.

"Sorry, what was that?" James asked.

"Nothing, just thinking."

"In my experience, too much thinking tends to cause more harm than good. My motto is 'keep it simple'."

"Easier said than done."

James laughed, "Too true."

"You can turn left up there, just past the green fence." Jupiter said.

"Got it."

The car wound around the curves, the last time Jupiter ventured down this road she had been with Rooster. The sound of his camera clicking pictures played in her mind. Rooster made her feel part of something, part of a family, part of him. The way he touched her, so simply, so quietly confident. He was like... like... your most comfortable pair of shoes, she thought. When your feet just slide right in and wriggle around, completely content.

"James, what is your favorite pair of shoes?"

"Funny question, well let's see... for looks or comfort?"

"Definitely comfort, looks fade... right?"

James laughed.

"Well, let's see, can it be a pair from a long time ago?"

"Sure."

"When I was fifteen, I had these boots; they were brown and had some furry stuff at the top. I used to wear 'em without socks in the dead of winter. Feet just molded right in."

"Did you out grow them?"

"No, they smelled so bad my Ma wouldn't let 'em in the house, she finally threw 'em out."

"That's sad."

"For me yeah, for her... no."

"Do you have a good relationship with your mom?"

"Yes, I did, very much so. She died a few years back."

"How old were you?"

"Fifty-one."

"How'd she die?"

"Cancer, terrible thing to watch."

"My mom died too." Jupiter said listening to the sound of her words as they hit the air.

"I'm sorry for your loss, when did she pass?"

"Two years ago."

"Rough, isn't it?"

Rough, yes, she thought, I need to look that word up in Merriam-Webster's when I get home. On so many levels, this one word was the most accurate assessment of the entire death experience.

"It gets easier," James said to her lack of response.

"It's up there on the left."

James turned into the driveway of Jupiter's home. Rooster driving her away flashed again through her head. Why did he do that? Why did he take me with him; he didn't even know me and yet he brought me home.

"God, I screwed up," Jupiter said under her breath.

"What's that?" James asked, pulling up to the front door in the darkness.

"Nothing."

"Thinking?"

"Yep," she laughed.

"Is anyone home? Looks pretty dark."

"It always looks like this. James, thank you, for everything."

Jupiter leaned forward into the front seat and kissed him on the cheek. She could see in the rear-view mirror that he was smiling. James hopped out, grabbed her bags and walked them up to the massive front door. He placed them carefully on the top step.

"Well, Miss Jupiter, it has truly been a pleasure." Then he bowed a bit and offered her his hand.

"Goodbye, James." Jupiter said, properly shaking his hand.

Jupiter labored up the steps like a prisoner about to walk the plank. She pressed the doorbell and watched the black Mercedes pull away into the darkness. She heard footsteps coming toward her. The door opened, it was Willy.

"Oh praise Jesus... praise Jesus," Willy repeated, "Child, you are a sight for sore eyes."

Willy snatched Jupiter up and held her, rocking her back and forth in her big black arms.

"Where have you been?" she pulled Jupiter away and looked at her. "You look awful. When was the last time you ate a proper meal?"

"Today."

"Come on," Willy said ignoring her, "let's fix you something."

Willy scooped up the bags, wrapped her arm around Jupiter's waist and clomped down the hall in her slippers and bathrobe to the only cozy room in the house, Willy's kitchen. Jupiter plopped down on a stool up against the marble counter top. Willy checked the three huge cooper pots she had percolating on the stove, all bubbly and delicious. The smells wafted up and around Jupiter.

"I have some beef stew and then there's a brisket and mashed potatoes. How does that sound? I have a chicken roasting too but it's not quite ready yet."

"Perfect, whatever is easy."

Jupiter wasn't ready to talk and Willy knew it. This exchange would be a slow meandering process and if handled improperly, Willy knew Jupiter might bolt again. She needed to keep Jupiter here until Rooster arrived. Willy set the brimming bowl of beef stew in front of Jupiter with a homemade sourdough roll and the butter dish. She poured a glass of milk, which Jupiter drank all the way down.

"Thirsty?"

"Yeah, guess I was."

Jupiter tasted the first few bites of the stew and watched Wilhelmina trying with every inch of her being, to tread lightly. The meat fell to pieces in her mouth, and then the warm potatoes and carrots, she chewed slowly, allowing the flood of childhood food memories overtake her with each bite.

"Willy, what are your favorite shoes?" Jupiter asked chewing on a carrot.

"These fuzzy slippers," Willy held her foot up in the air for Jupiter to see, "Your momma bought these for me for Christmas in…. Well let's see, I think it was 1989. They're positively ancient but my toes fit right into their little furry spots." Willy checked a pot on the stove and turned back to Jupiter,

"That's a funny question."

Jupiter smiled and finished eating her stew.

"Noreen called," Willy said quietly.

"What'd she say?"

"She said," Willy paused, "That you left your momma's car in her driveway with a letter sayin' she should have it. Oh sweet girl, I thought you were gonna kill yourself." Willy started to cry.

Jupiter had never seen Wilhelmina cry. She was terrified.

"I'm sorry, Willy." June Bug's purple feet flashed through Jupiter's mind.

217
47 men

"Oh sugar, don't mind these old tears. Just happy to see you; it's just a little relief is all, just a little relief."

Willy wiped the tears from her face with her apron and picked up Jupiter's bowl.

"Now, let's get you something that'll stick to those ribs."

Willy put the dish in the sink and continued to wipe the tears from her face with her back to Jupiter. Then she padded over to the stove and placed her hands wide against it, like she hoped the stove would hold her up under the weight of it all. Something about her gesture made Jupiter move to her and wrap her arms as far around Willy as she could get them. Willy patted the outside of Jupiter's hands, humming and swaying the way she did when Jupiter was little. Jupiter never knew the song exactly but she figured it must have been a hymn from Willy's childhood.

After a long time, Willy said, "Thank you sugar." And she began to shuffle about the kitchen in her usual fashion. Jupiter returned to her stool and then Willy began her interrogation.

"Child, where on God's earth have you been?"

Jupiter tipped her head down and answered dutifully, "New Orleans, Alpharetta and Manhattan."

"What were you doin'?"

"I'm not sure."

"What happened to that sweet boy you brought 'round here?" Willy asked hoping to get a head start on the situation she would soon have on her hands.

"He's... well... I don't know. In New Orleans still... I think."

"That one was a keeper. You know, he didn't even flinch when you were doing all of that craziness."

Jupiter wanted to change the subject desperately and the only other place she could think to go was to ask about her father.

"How's Daddy?"

"Not too good, sweetie. While back, I thought he might be getting a little better but now... he seems like he slipped further underneath it all. Dr. Hart comes by once a week. Every time, he leaves shaking his head sayin' 'Nothing physically wrong Willy, damnedest thing I have ever seen.' Then he leaves and your daddy and I are all alone in this big empty house."

Jupiter said nothing but her disappointment was palpable.

"Did you think you were gonna come back and find him sittin' at his desk working?"

"No... I guess... I hoped."

"Hope springs eternal, guess that's what keeps us all goin'."

Willy delivered the next plate of food to Jupiter. She devoured every morsel, the mashed potatoes buttery and smooth going down her throat, the savory meat electrifying her taste buds.

"I feel like I haven't tasted anything for such a long time," Jupiter said, to no one in particular.

"Mr. Johnson, from the mortuary, has been calling here... every day."

"I know, I know." Jupiter said, cutting her off. "Where is Daddy?"

"He's in bed already."

Jupiter regarded Willy thoughtfully as she stirred the pots, then opened and closed the oven.

"How do you do it?"

"Do what?" Willy asked not looking at her.

"Take care of him like that, with no responses, no feedback."

"Jupiter," Willy turned around and said very seriously, "Your daddy saved my life. It's the least I can do to repay him."

"What do you mean? You never told me that."

"Time wasn't right."

Willy took a deep breath and sat heavily on the stool next to Jupiter.

"Your daddy was at MIT, he was workin' for a man that... Well this man, the professor, he called himself, had my momma as a slave, really. Never paid her, I mean he fed her and gave her a roof over her head. He was a

219

47 men

gray-headed white man, lived in a four-story townhouse in the back bay of Boston. He was real smart, famous I think and he had had a wife but she died somewhere along the way. So he started havin' his way with my momma. That's how I was born, it was all fine until, well, I guess I was about fifteen and he wanted to have his way with me. My momma tried to stop him but he beat her. So this one time, your daddy was comin' to drop off some papers for the professor and he heard me screamin', because if he was gonna be doin' that to me I was gonna be screamin'. Your daddy came upstairs to find out what all the screaming was about and he saw what the professor was doin' to me. Your daddy knocked the professor out cold. He told me to go get my momma and pack my things. My momma wouldn't leave because she was afraid but I got my things and kissed her goodbye. Your daddy brought me home to the little house where he and your momma lived. Mrs. Ruth Ann was about to have you, so he asked if I wanted to have a job cleaning and working as a nanny for you. Your Daddy quit working for the professor and ended up switching universities. He saved me, gave me a good life and a beautiful little girl to raise like my own."

Jupiter's eyes were filled with tears, "That's so awful."

"What's so awful about it? I have a good life. I have my friends and you and your daddy to take care of and someday you're gonna give me some grandbabies."

"Didn't you ever want a family of your own?"

"No ma'am. That man did rotten things that made my insides all messed up. Didn't need to explain that to nobody."

"Oh, Willy..."

"Now hush up and forget I ever told you. You should get on up to bed now, look like you could use a good night's sleep."

Jupiter stood up and wanted to hug Willy but did not.

"Goodnight Willy, thank you." Jupiter started to clear her plate.

"Just leave it. I'm gonna stay up and make your daddy some more sweet rolls, seems like it's the only thing he likes to eat. I keep tryin' all my old recipes but he just won't eat a thing."

Jupiter nodded, hence the stew, the brisket and the chicken.

"Sweet dreams baby." Willy's voice followed her up the stairs.

Jupiter tiptoed past the closed door of her parents' bedroom. She flipped the lights on in her room and the reality of her little girl room glared at her. She felt old and sordid as she sat down on her white canopy bed. She removed her clothes and piled them carefully on a chair. She went to her dresser and pulled open the nightie drawer and her favorite Posey pink nightgown lay perfectly folded on top of the pile. She respected all of her childhood rituals, brushed her teeth, washed her face, said a simple prayer and wished for a moment that she had brought the fur coat then dutifully put herself to bed.

OENOKE RIDGE ROAD
New Canaan

6:47 a.m. – Rooster Boudreaux arrived at the Campbell home.

6:55 a.m. – Willy greeted Rooster & showed him to the guestroom.

7:15 a.m. – Rooster sipped a cup of freshly brewed black coffee.

7:22 a.m. – Willy served Rooster a warm gooey cinnamon bun.

7:35 a.m. – Rooster asked for a second cup of coffee.

7:42 a.m. – Willy asked Roster what happened.

7:45 a.m. – Rooster Boudreaux spilled his guts.

"Me and Jupiter were all good, Miss Willy. Spent every minute together. Something incredible happened, not like anything I have ever known. But my aunt... she was sick, real sick, mentally ill," Rooster stopped.

"With what, sugar?" Willy asked.

"Manic depressive. The doctors told us she needed to go to an inpatient treatment program and my momma needed me to go look at it with her. Her husband just couldn't handle it. Momma gave June Bug the pills the Doctor told us to give her and she was supposed to sleep. She didn't take the pills and instead she killed herself. Jupiter was at the house alone and..."

"Oh Lord no," Willy's hand covered her mouth.

"I think she must have gotten scared and left."

"What do you mean she left?" Willy asked.

"She left the house."

"For good?"

"Yes ma'am."

"Now, what kinda person does such a thing?" Willy stood up wringing her hands together and Rooster sat mesmerized watching almost the exact same reaction as Lydia had.

"It was another dead woman," Rooster said finally, "But that's not the bad part."

"There's more?" Willy crossed herself.

Rooster nodded trying to gear up for another recanting of the tale. Noticing his discomfort and feeling her own, Willy stood up and went to the liquor cabinet. She removed an unlabeled bottle of dark brown liquid. She poured two small glasses, brought them back to the table and handed one to Rooster.

"It's my momma's recipe; it'll help us get through."

Willy put the glass to her lips and drank it down. Rooster followed suit and then inhaled deeply.

"Thank you," he said, "Then, she drove to my best friend's house," he paused, "and he said that she offered herself up to him like a prostitute and they had sex."

Willy crossed herself again.

"I came here to look her in the eye and see for myself if she really did it."

Willy placed her hand on top of Rooster's and just left it there. His head hung low, his eyes burned from the hours of driving and he wanted nothing more than to crawl into a bed and sleep. But his fury was reignited and a terrible fire burned inside his stomach, growling for an answer.

"She's upstairs," Willy said, "Came home last night. When I got your message, I hadn't heard a word from her since the two of you were here. She left her momma's car in Atlanta with her momma's friend, Noreen. There was a note and I thought... well, it doesn't matter, she's here now."

8:32 a.m. – Willy and Rooster sat quietly at the kitchen table.

8:35 a.m. – Jupiter woke up.

223

47 men

Sunshine woke Jupiter. She bolted upright and went straight to the bookshelf to retrieve her enormous volume of Merriam-Webster's Dictionary. She took it to her bed, flopped on her stomach and went to R. Ra, re, ri, ro....

> **ROUGH** 1 a : marked by inequalities, ridges, or projections on the surface **: coarse b :** covered with or made up of coarse and often shaggy hair <*rough*-coated collie> — compare **smooth, wirehaired c** (1) **:** having a broken, uneven, or bumpy surface <rough terrain> (2) **:** difficult to travel through or penetrate **: wild** <into the rough woods — P. B. Shelley> **2 a : turbulent, tempestuous** <rough seas> **b** (1) **:** characterized by harshness, violence, or force (2) **:** presenting a challenge **: difficult** <rough to deal with — R. M. McAlmon> **3 :** coarse or rugged in character or appearance: as **a :** harsh to the ear **b :** crude in style or expression **c : indelicate d :** marked by a lack of refinement or grace **: uncouth 4 a : crude, unfinished** <rough carpentry> **b :** executed or ventured hastily, tentatively, or imperfectly <a rough draft> <rough estimate>; *also* **: approximate** <a rough idea>

Yes, rough, she thought. All of it accurate and her conversation with Russell promised to be just that. Jupiter rummaged for some slippers in the bottom of the closet.

8:47 a.m. – Jupiter began her descent of the stairs.

Jupiter tramped down the stairs to the kitchen. Sunlight poured through every inch of glass, like it was trying to burst through the panes. Jupiter stopped half way down the stairs; she heard voices, maybe Dr. Hart? She could only see the top of Willy's head sitting at the kitchen table. Willy never sat at the kitchen table. Willy turned and caught Jupiter in her tracks.

"Well, look who's awake."

Something in Willy's voice made Jupiter feel uneasy, something was up. She tentatively took another step toward the kitchen. Jupiter caught Willy's stern gaze and wanted to flee.

"Look who's here, been telling me some fascinating things."

Jupiter peered into the kitchen like a dog that's been caught with a raw steak in its mouth.

Rooster Boudreaux sat with his arms folded across his chest, an empty coffee cup in front of him and a plate with only the crust of a sweet roll left.

"Seems as if you have some explaining to do," Willy stated her voice dripping with contempt.

"Can I go change?" Jupiter answered meekly.

"No ma'am, you're gonna come down here right now."

Jupiter stepped forward. Rooster's eyes drilled a hole through the center of her.

"Rooster, here, has few questions he'd like answers to. Based on what I've heard child, I think you owe him at least that."

Willy stood and brushed her hands down her apron. Then she shook her head slightly and as she passed Jupiter she whispered,

"You tell the truth Jupiter June, you hear?"

"Yes ma'am," Jupiter blushed.

"I'll be upstairs with your daddy."

Jupiter stepped to the edge of the table looking like an over-grown child in her pink nightie. She watched Rooster, his hair disheveled and crazy, his white T-shirt wrinkled, as he crossed his arms and waited for her to speak. She had to look away. Her brain felt like a blender, all of the questions and answers chopped into fragments and then liquefying into one. He waited, with an expression on his face Jupiter had never seen before, which only added fuel to her preexisting condition.

"Is it okay if I sit down?" she asked.

Rooster tipped his head a fraction of an inch to the affirmative. Jupiter skidded the chair leg against the dark wood floor and it shrieked, causing her to flinch. Rooster remained perfectly still. Her body lowered onto one haunch and she leaned uncomfortably on the edge of the chair, its ladder-back stabbing into her shoulder blade. He watched her carefully as if her every movement were giving up some tidbit of salacious information.

"Hi," she said.

He said nothing.

"Why are you here?" she said very quietly without looking at him.

He unfolded his arms and pressed the thumb and forefinger of each hand into the glossy wood finish of the table. He remained mute, but his body was beginning to exhibit signs of rage. Jupiter felt the mounting anger leaking from his person but kept her gaze on the floor.

"I guess I should start at the beginning."

Rooster's head motion signaled to the affirmative again.

Jupiter scooted the chair back, arranged herself square in the seat and rested her arms on her knees. The blender had stopped... she thought of rough again; this was beyond anything referenced in the dictionary. She began clearly and quietly.

9:01 a.m. – Jupiter Campbell summoned the courage to finally tell the truth.

"On the twenty-fifth of March at 1:07 p.m., my mother was pronounced dead at the scene. From that moment forward my father has not spoken a coherent sentence. I had and still have no idea what my mother wanted... I didn't know if she wanted to be buried or cremated, I didn't know if she wanted her ashes spread somewhere special. I know nothing. Her body has been on ice for two years. I researched to see how long she could last without cryogenically freezing her; two years seemed to be the absolute maximum before the decomposition was irreparable. Mr. Johnson from the mortuary calls me once a week to find out what my plans are for Mrs. Campbell's interment. Then he describes in excruciating detail the decay that is taking place. I figured I would be able to snap my Dad out of it. After a year, I started to have serious doubts. I tried humor, sweetness, empathy, shock but nothing worked. In my research, I found that a severe shock seemed to be the only constant with those afflicted regaining consciousness. My father is Swedish and very puritanical so I devised a plan for the second year of her being on ice," Jupiter paused, eyes down to her feet and continued. "I would have sex with fifty men and tell my father. This knowledge would give him a shock of such a magnitude it would jolt him out of his stupor. I made it to forty-six. I called my friend Guillaume who told me to drive up to the cockfight in New Haven to meet forty-seven. But there was traffic and when I got there it was over. You had the dying bird in your lap and I completely forgot why I was there."

Jupiter's chest heaved up and down with a deep breath. She continued, tempo increased, words flowing off of her knees and onto the floor.

"I killed your bird, because I couldn't stand to watch you feeling so much..." She stopped again and waited for him to bolt or smack her, he did neither so she proceeded.

"When you said I had to come home with you, I figured a little detour to see if the bloody bird might shock my Dad out of it, seemed worth it. The next part... well you saw that... and then you took me home. All I wanted was to stay there with you and your family and then June Bug—" Jupiter paused, "I was there in the kitchen pouring elbow macaroni into a strainer stirring orange powder into it. I ate on the floor with Ed Peterson. Then he freaked out and tore outside. A second later it felt like there was an earth-quake in the house. I didn't know what it was. I looked everywhere and then I saw her hanging from the banister. I wanted to call you, I did, but you don't have a phone. I tried to pull her up, but she was too heavy. I was supposed to be watching her and then your aunt kills herself. I'm so sorry."

"That's not why I am here."

Jupiter's head jerked up at him in surprise.

"What?"

"That's not why I'm here. You had nothing to do with June. Would have happened with or without you."

Jupiter blushed, diverted eyes to the floor again.

"Preston," She said under her breath.

Again, an imperceptible nod.

Jupiter licked her lips and wiped her sweaty palms on her nightgown.

"I didn't know what else to do, he was the only other person I knew. I drove to his house and asked him to come help me. He made me come in. When we got in his room, he locked the door behind me and zip tied my hands behind my back,"

Jupiter stopped and touched her hand to the dark place behind her ear.

"Then he ripped off my clothes and he, you know, tried to rape me but he couldn't get an erection. I was crying but I made fun of him. He got so mad he punched me as hard as he could across the jaw."

She held her hair back and turned her face sideways so he could see the bruise behind her ear.

"When he was off balance from the punch, I broke free and ran. He yelled at me and told me he would tell you I came over to have sex with him. So I left. I didn't think you would ever believe me and then June Bug, and I just, I couldn't face you. I drove to Georgia and then went to Manhattan and the time was up so I came back here to tell my father that I failed."

There was a very long pregnant silence and then Rooster said, "Do not tell your father what you did," then a pause and very quietly, "ever".

Then he continued speaking very deliberately as if trying to process all of the information.

"Preston told me you came over and offered yourself to him."

"I knew he would," she interrupted, fingering her jaw line again.

"I didn't believe him," his voice gravelly.

Jupiter looked over at him and started to cry. She put her head down on the table. Rooster left her there alone; eyes deliberately focused out the window and didn't say a word. She finally picked her head up and smeared snot and tears on her pink flannel sleeve.

"I'm very sorry he did that to you, but the other, well I'm just not sure what to do with that." Rooster said head turned in profile. He put a hand to his temples and squeezed hard on either side of his skull.

"I know..." her voice trailed off.

The room was brimming with sound, the faucet drip-drip-dripping against the stainless sink; a wall clock ticking with metronome precision, the busy hum of the refrigerator, birds presenting a cacophony just outside the glass, the steady whirr of a lawn mower engine. But the sound of a human voice was glaringly absent.

Jupiter stole a glace. His tense arms folded into each other, his breath shallow and rushed, his eyes directed out the window, darted back and forth unable to rest in one place for too long.

"Do you wish you weren't here?" she whispered.

"I wish I didn't know." He said quickly the back of his head all she could see. His hand scratched at the nape of his neck as if trying to scratch off her gaze.

"I thought, guess it doesn't matter."

"What? Please, it matters." Jupiter said perched on the edge of the chair, eyes huge, trying to capture his.

But his gaze was still fixed out the window. Then he stood up and strode to the glass with specific purpose. His shoulders slumped, left hand shoved down into his pocket. But the right touched a steady finger to the glass like he was tracing the outline of something he wanted to draw.

"I thought you were different," he paused, laughed a single ironic laugh "I guess that's true."

Jupiter blushed and sweat beaded on her top lip and in the caves of her armpits. She scratched at the dry skin on her elbow and then tucked her hair behind her good ear. Rooster was now standing with his legs apart, arms out to the sides, hands pressed into the top of the wainscoting. The muscles in his shoulders flinched, the anger-like sparks firing across his torso. She bit into the edge of her lip and touched the bruise behind her other ear, pressed on it and felt the twinge of pain.

"I don't know how to explain it. When I say it out loud, it sounds crazy. I know that but I was alone and..."

"You need to bury your mother." He interrupted.

Jupiter eyes swung in his direction, hopeful but his body remained in the same aggressive stance.

"I don't know what she wanted," she said flatly.

"Where are her parents?" Rooster asked his voice also free of intonation.

"Dead."

"Were they buried or cremated?" continuing in his toneless manner.

"Buried," She returned.

"Did she visit their graves?"

"Yes, she brought flowers to them every year on both of their birthdays and a cream puff for her father. He loved them."

"Where are they buried?" he asked.

"In Massachusetts; she would drive there." Jupiter said, not grasping where this line of questioning was going.

"Did you ever go?"

"No, she always went alone because my father thought it was stupid."

"She wanted to be buried." Rooster pronounced, arms pulled up and crossed in front of him.

"How do you know?" Jupiter looked at him, waiting for him to face her.

"You just told me."

He did not turn.

"I did?"

"Yes and your father might not have done what she wanted if he were awake." Rooster said finally turning to her.

Jupiter was shocked both by this revelation and his sudden movement. She wiped her upper lip on her sleeve.

"I need to call Mr. Johnson." She said with sudden urgency.

"And pick out a casket." Rooster said eyes directly at her.

"I did that." Jupiter blushed uncontrollably.

"Why are you blushing?" Rooster asked.

"Forty-six."

Rooster turned away without a word. Jupiter rose from the table and started in the direction of Rooster who was now shellacked to the windows. He resembled a bird trapped in the house, determined no human hand would ever make contact. Jupiter retreated and moved instead to the kitchen counter where the pan of warm cinnamon rolls sat. She pulled a hunk off of one and snuck a look in Rooster's direction. He was watching her reflection in the window, calculating her every movement as if she were the Siamese cat to his sparrow. She opened the refrigerator and removed the orange juice container, flipped off the lid and brought the spout to her lips.

"What ON EARTH do you think you are doing?" Wilhelmina yelled down from the top of the stairs.

Jupiter almost spilled the entire container down the front of her but somehow managed recovery with just a few drops on her nightgown.

"What am I doing?" Jupiter asked. "Were you listening the whole time?"

"I was making sure you told the truth," Willy said quietly as she descended the staircase.

Jupiter found a glass and poured the juice, her hand shaking as she did, trying to catalog the purge information that had just been vomited from her person.

"How 'bout a little more coffee?" Willy asked in Rooster's direction.

Rooster turned and nodded. Willy poured a fresh cup and set it down at the head of the table.

"It looks like we've got ourselves a funeral to plan." Willy said.

Rooster looked at her parked by the stove and moved to pick up the coffee cup.

"Jupiter, you need to call Mr. Johnson first thing." Willy said.

"What do I say?" she asked, the shrill pain of humiliation permeating through her.

"Ask what his availability is and what else needs to be done on our end," Willy offered.

"Okay." Jupiter's legs obeyed and trudged up the stairs.

Once Jupiter was safely out of earshot, Rooster finally spoke.

"I couldn't have done this without you." He whispered.

"Me either," she whispered back and continued to the sink with Jupiter's half-full glass. "I don't know what to say sugar. There's just..." and Willy stopped speaking.

"I know." He said and sat back down at the table.

"Do you need any help with Mr. Campbell?" he said finally.

"I have a friend's son who I can call." Willy said.

"Is there anyone else to call for the service?" Rooster asked.

"So many people at first and now, just doesn't seem so important."

Jupiter came down the stairs still in her nightgown.

"Is there anyone you would like to call about the memorial?" Willy asked Jupiter.

"Mr. Johnson said he can do the service this Friday if we go to the cemetery today and get everything taken care of."

"Is there anyone?" Rooster asked.

"Noreen," Jupiter said softly.

"Want me to call her?" Willy asked.

"Please," Jupiter replied.

"Do you have a cemetery picked out?" Rooster pressed.

"Uh, yeah," Jupiter replied, still a little shell-shocked.

"Well, alright, let's get this show on the road." Rooster pointed to her jammies.

Jupiter retreated upstairs again.

"Willy, can you pick out something pretty for Mrs. Campbell to be buried in?"

Willy watched Rooster watching Jupiter and didn't answer the question but plainly stated, "You love my girl…"

"Miss Willy, contrary to my good sense…"

"Well that's just fine," she said with a hint of a smile and removed his empty coffee cup. "Yes, I will pick out something pretty."

Jupiter descended a few minutes later in one of Marcel's outfits looking positively adult like.

"What do you want me to make for the supper after?" Willy asked Jupiter.

Jupiter froze; the food, why was it always the food that got her? Rooster watched Jupiter tumbling into some vortex that might require hours to recover from.

"Miss Willy, just make all her favorites," Rooster finally answered.

CEDAR HILL CEMETERY
Hartford, Connecticut

Rooster walked toward his truck. He opened her door and Jupiter climbed onto the bench seat. Sticking out of the empty ashtray was the announcement, with the picture of her flying off of the swing.

"Hey, that's me." She held it up in front of her face almost as if she couldn't believe it.

"What's it for?"

"My show."

"Did it already happen?"

"Yep."

"How'd it go?"

"Not sure."

"What do you mean?"

"Left early."

"Why?" Jupiter looked at him incredulous.

"Wasn't in the mood."

"It's beautiful."

"It sold out."

"The whole show?"

"Yep."

"So it went well."

He shrugged.

Rooster turned on the ignition and turned to her.

"Where to?"

"Cedar Hill Cemetery."

"Directions?"

"Oh, sorry, turn right at the end of the driveway and left at the first signal which won't be for a while, it's about an hour and a half drive."

Rooster turned right and Jupiter still held up the card. They traveled in silence with the exception of her directional advisements. Jupiter stared at the person on the card, wishing she could navigate her way back to that place. They curved through wooded glens and country roads and finally arrived at Cedar Hill. It was ancient with gravestones from the eighteen hundreds; there were enormous trees naked from the recent loss of foliage, they pulled up to a quaint building adjacent to a parking lot.

"Here we are," Jupiter said stating the obvious.

Rooster parked the car and turned off the engine and looked at her.

"I'm really sorry for what Preston did to you and I'm sorry that he lied to me. But I probably wouldn't be here if he hadn't."

Rooster then quite abruptly hopped out of the truck and went around to let her out. He walked five paces ahead and yanked opened the heavy black door, which led Jupiter into the vacuum-sealed room where no sound produced any lasting effect. It was empty, save for the lineup of coffins in an anteroom to the right.

"Hello?" Rooster called out, "Anybody here?"

A Goth creature in a demure black suit crept out from an office and began to greet them in his customary cemetery manner, then stopped.

"Oh, hello Jupiter."

"Benedict."

"You know each other?" Rooster looked at Jupiter.

Jupiter could only nod; the Goth creature actually formed a blush on his deathlike pallor. Rooster stared at Jupiter incredulous. Jupiter iced him, gave him nothing. A painful awkward silence followed so Rooster finally stepped in and took the reins.

"Alright, what have we done so far?" he asked Benedict trying to maintain his composure.

"Jupiter selected a casket and I believe she was going to speak to her father about the plot and the type of monument she would like."

"Do you have any family plots?"

"Of course."

"Can you give us a map with the locations?"

"Why of course, I can accompany you if you wish."

"Nope, don't think that'll be necessary." Rooster said, "We'd like to have the burial Friday, would you be able to accommodate that?"

"I'll have to check, sir. Let me get the map and look at the reservation book."

"Thank you."

Benedict left them alone.

Rooster looked at her with disapproval.

"It was gross, please don't."

"I can only imagine."

Benedict reappeared like an aberration.

"Alright, you lucked out; we had a cancellation in the afternoon, three-thirty on Friday. Also, I have marked the best ones, that's what you wanted, correct? You talked about that cemetery in Paris."

"Père Lachaise," Rooster and Jupiter said in unison and then looked at each other in shock.

Jupiter clutched the map. "Thanks, we'll be back."

"Take your time; it is a very important decision. The burial site is crucial because it gives mourners a place to pay homage to the departed. Whether gathering for the funeral or simply visiting to show their devotion, a picturesque and accessible burial site will make this trying time easier."

"Thanks," Rooster said as they started to walk out.

"They don't like me to tell people this, but," Benedict paused looking over his shoulder and then whispered, "There was a family who selected a lovely spot and had the mausoleum erected and placed on the site. It has an exceptional view of our lake. They were unable to complete it due to... a reversal of fortune. The façade was never carved. It is a Palladian monument, superb architecturally with stunning bronze doors, complete with a beautiful stained- glass window which replicates the Dove of the Holy Spirit in the Throne of St. Peter at the Vatican, done by Gian Lorenzo Bernini," Benedict droned on.

Jupiter nodded her head, "My mother loved the Vatican."

"Let's take a look." Rooster said.

"I will have to accompany you as I have to unlock it." Benedict skittered to the office and returned with jingling keys.

"You just can't tell anyone that I told you about it. You have to say you found it on your own and inquired, alright?" Benedict said, again in a whisper.

"Of course," Rooster said.

"We will drive there."

Benedict led them to a black limousine and they piled in the back. Benedict traveled through the cemetery pointing out the other available plots but as they came over the crest of a knoll overlooking a magical valley packed with treetops for Russell and a perfect little lake in the immediate foreground for Ruth Ann; it was actually the perfect spot to be laid to rest. Benedict explained that the magnificent chestnut tree was the reason the previous family had selected this location. The three of them walked purposefully toward the mausoleum, Benedict unbolted the enormous bronze doors and a beam of light shone directly through the dove and onto Jupiter.

"I wish I had my camera," Rooster said very quietly. It was as if some small religious experience were occurring in their midst.

"It's perfect." Jupiter did not step inside, instead basked in the beam of light.

"We'll take it," she whispered.

"Would you like to..." Benedict started to say.

"No," Jupiter stepped out of the light and returned to the insane view of the state she had, up to this moment, virtually ignored.

Benedict locked the doors and walked solemnly to the car, as was his way.

"We'll be right there to do the paper work," Rooster called after him. He nodded and silently pulled away.

Jupiter and Rooster sat down on the top step of the limestone mausoleum and inhaled the view.

"I would come back here," Jupiter said.

"Yes."

"She would have loved this."

"It's a good place."

He patted her hand.

"You didn't do it in the coffin did you?"

Jupiter yanked her hand away.

"Stop it," Jupiter spat the words at him, "It's not funny."

Rooster paused, didn't say a word and stood up with his back to her.

"No," he stopped, "it's not funny at all, it's fucking tragic," he paused again. "You know, in the South, that's what we do; we laugh in the face of tragedy. You're gonna have to move on, sister. Bury your momma, stop wishin' that your daddy's gonna wake up. And you're going to have to deal with the fact that you fucked almost fifty men and you can't tell your daddy because it's disgusting." He looked her square in the eyes.

Jupiter blushed hard and her eyes welled up, the humiliation crushed down like a building imploding on top of her.

"And here's the other thing," he continued, "If you want me to stick around, which I'm not even sure I can stomach, you're gonna have to learn to laugh about it."

Rooster hopped down off of the mausoleum steps on to the grass and kept walking toward the road. He didn't turn around just continued his forward momentum. He fished a pack of cigarettes out of his pocket and lit one. She helplessly watched his body moving away from her, smoke hitting the frigid air and she suddenly felt stone cold. She stood up wrapping her arms around herself.

Rooster was no longer in her sights. She thought of the postcard again and of sailing through the air. She started down the steps toward the road. She watched as Rooster's truck cut a white thread across the verdant landscape and he was gone.

47 men

OENOKE RIDGE ROAD
New Canaan

upiter paid the taxi driver and noted the white truck parked in the driveway. Her heart sunk.

She felt like the proverbial dog with her tail between her legs as she skulked her way to the front door. She opened it carefully and stepped silently into the dark foyer. She shut the door with quiet precision in an effort to go unnoticed. She stood in the dark and listened... nothing.

Jupiter then readied herself for her father, stood up straight, tucked her shirt in and smoothed her hair back into a ponytail. Resolute, she mounted the stairs to her father's study. She registered the millions of scenarios concocted in her mind and then Rooster's directive; do not tell your daddy because it's disgusting. The blush flew violently across her face and humiliation dripped all the way down to her toes.

Quiet was all she could get from the crack of light between the door and the wall. Her toe caught the edge of the door and she nudged it further open. Her heart felt like there was a rabbit inside, kicking its two feet against her sternum. She stepped in; Russell was slumped in a human heap in his enormous wing-backed leather chair. Jupiter wondered how he didn't just slide right out of it. The lamplight accentuated the deep crevices in his face. She walked to him and kneeled down by his feet, attempting to replicate the circumstances of the story Mrs. Boudreaux had shared with Jupiter about her uncle and the kitten.

"Hi Daddy, it's me."

She dipped her head down and cocked it sideways attempting to look him in the eye. His eyes, glazed over and watery, made her despondent. She jumped up and paced in circles frustrated. What difference would any of this make, she thought but then refocused to finish what she had come here to do. She lowered back down to the forest-green carpet and looked at him.

"Dad, I figured out what to do with Mom. We picked a nice place. There is a lake right next to it that she would love and a treetop view, like Central Park, for you. I went to the apartment and it really made me miss both of you. We are having the funeral on Friday and then burying her afterward. I think Noreen is coming for the funeral and Miss Willy's going to make Mommy's favorite food for supper. She's taking really good care of you and she told me what you did. You saved her life, Dad." Jupiter patted his hand closest to her.

"I really can't believe it's been two years since she died. I miss her at the weirdest times... like in line at the grocery store or in the back seat of a car or if I see a swimming pool." Jupiter stopped for a moment, "God, do you know I haven't been in a pool since she died." She paused again.

"I have been terrible, Dad."

She looked up at him.

"I met this guy and I love him, but... I really don't know how to love him. It's a weird realization to have. It seems like something you should just be born with but I guess it's not."

Jupiter rose after waiting a minute to see if any of this might have roused him. Then she leaned in with her hand on his shoulder.

"We're going to bury Mom, put her in the ground and lay her to rest." Jupiter patted him three times. "Maybe that's what you've been waiting for. I love you, Dad."

Jupiter kissed him on the cheek and started toward the door and stopped. She grabbed a chair and pulled it over next to her father.

"Do you remember the time we fed the geese in Atlanta? You told me that geese mate for life and that they fly in family groups. You said if there is an available habitat, the young females nest in the same area that they were raised in. All of that to say, I think I'm going to hang out here for a while, be a part of your sub flock."

Russell did not move, speak or react in any way. He just sat. Jupiter brushed off her legs in an incredibly Willy-like manner. She strode to the door confidently and turned to him.

"I really wish I watched you and Mommy love each other better."

Jupiter stepped into the hallway and she could now hear Rooster and Willy's voices echoing though the foyer. Then she heard Willy laugh, really truly laugh. Jupiter stopped and listened. She had never heard this before; she wondered what they were talking about. She tiptoed to her room, took off her clothes and without completing any of her childhood rituals crawled into bed. Jupiter lay, looking up at the canopy. She was finally home, she was giving her mother a proper burial and Rooster Boudreaux was one floor below her and she had no idea what to do about it.

BOUDREAUX HOME
Coliseum Street, New Orleans

The phone rang. Rosie Boudreaux eyeballed it, every bone in her body not wanting to pick it up. She was cozy, sitting in her pale pink velvet chair reading the *Times-Picayune*, dog at her feet, cocktail by her side. It rang a few more times, guilt finally made her reach for it.

"Hello." She said, minus the upward lilt.

"Hey Momma, it's me." Rooster said into the faux old-fashioned phone in the opulent downstairs guest suite.

"Oh Roo, it's so good to hear your voice."

"You too." He could hear her relief and feel his own hearing the warmth of her voice.

"I almost didn't answer, good thing I did. Where are you?" She said scooching up in her chair and removing the cotton-candy-colored glasses from the bridge of her nose.

"In Connecticut."

"So you found her."

"Yeah, but I'm coming back after the funeral tomorrow."

"Whose funeral?" she asked shifting again in her chair

"Her momma's." he wrapped his chunky fingers through the coils in the vanilla-colored cord.

"She's not buried yet? Christ almighty, those Yankees have no respect for the dead."

"That's why she's been trying so hard to wake her daddy up. Her momma died so suddenly and they never talked about what she wanted." Rooster paused, "So what do you want Momma?"

She laughed softly, settling back into the down-filled cushions.

"Well sugar, in spite of everything he did, I want to be buried right next to your daddy."

"What do you mean what he did?" he asked pulling the coils taught.

"Aw sugar, we don't need to pretend anymore. Y'all have lives to get on with."

Rooster looked at his feet lying straight out in front of him on a bed that was so high in the air you needed a ladder to get to it. He imagined this was what his feet might look like in a coffin. He searched the room for his camera. It was in the truck.

"What are you talkin' about?" he asked staring at his feet, lost in his own thoughts.

"Rooster, your daddy told me you saw him in Baton Rouge and you were going to tell me if he didn't. He said he was real sorry, that the whole thing just got away from him. He said he didn't mean me any harm, wished I never had to know. He did say something about me bein' like his favorite old shoes and she was a shiny penny in the street, caught your eye for a glint but when you picked it up, you realized it wasn't worth anything. Said he still loved me like the day is long."

Rooster was dead silent, fixated on his outstretched feet and legs, having somewhat of an out-of-body experience.

"Rooster? Are you there?" Rosie scooted up a little in the chair as if trying to get closer to him.

"Um..." his voice cracked, he cleared his throat. "I thought he died because of me, because I threatened him."

"Oh sugar..."

"Why didn't you tell me this before now?" Rooster inspected his white socks, then his dirty boots on the floor.

"I don't right know. He was gone... I wanted y'all to have a good memory of him." She brushed her hand through her hair.

Rooster did not respond. Rosie, uncomfortable, filled the silence.

"Your daddy made a mistake but he wasn't going anywhere, he loved me. Rooster, we all make mistakes, it's what you do with them that counts."

Rooster said nothing.

"I'm sorry. I really thought you knew that I knew. I just didn't want the girls to know. I didn't want to ruin it for them." She now sat up straight with her feet on the floor.

"What about me?" Rooster said finally.

"He didn't mean as much to you, Roo."

"How do you know that?"

"Because sugar, you have me." Rosie stood and began to pace around the room. A picture of the happy family stared out at her from the bookshelf. She inhaled deeply then walked back to her chair, picked up her gin and tonic and took a sip.

Rooster wanted to be mad and lash out at her but he couldn't. She was correct on every front. He loved his father but did not particularly like him. His mother was his. She let the silence be there, knowing he had to work through it in his head, then finally as she sat back down she spoke.

"Why are you giving up?"

"On what?" he tugged at the phone cord again.

"Come on Roo."

"She's crazy." He wiggled his toes in his socks.

"You like crazy."

"No, Momma this is different."

"I know it." She said smiling into the phone.

"That's not what I meant."

"But it's what you said."

"I..."

"We all make mistakes Rooster, don't let this be yours."

There was a long silence and then finally he spoke.

47 men

"Okay, Momma." He scrutinized his hands that were so like his father's that his momma sometimes had to look away.

"I love you more than molasses, Rooster Boudreaux. You be brave."

The phone clicked into his ear. He looked into the receiver surprised she hung up first; it was not generally her way. He rooted into the pillows on what had become, in his mind, the bed for his funeral pyre. The back of his head crushed into the down pillow and his arms curled up around him. The fire blazed, the warmth womb like, and he thought about Ruth Ann making this room warm and cozy for guests who never came. His appreciation of her skills was marked. His body was sort of buzzing, experiencing a visceral reaction of relief. He felt his heart slow, the crease in his brow unfurrow, his breathing smooth out, his limbs loosen, his brain at long last cloudless and tranquil.

Darwin Francis Harlan Boudreaux had not, in fact, been culpable in any way, shape or form for the untimely death of his father.

CAMPBELL PLOT
Cedar Hill Cemetery

Mr. Johnson, in his well-worn dark suit, led the service himself. Jupiter thought he must be so grateful to be finally rid of Ruth Ann's decaying corpse he wanted to see her placed in the ground himself. Jupiter wore her one black dress and her mother's pearls. She stood next to Russell who was propped up in his wheelchair. Willy dressed Russell in a dark suit and a sunny yellow tie. She marveled at how Willy was able to maneuver him around. Jupiter rested her hand on his charcoal shoulder and Willy nestled in beside her. Noreen who looked uncharacteristically dour in her black ensemble was positioned next to Willy. Rooster stood at the back uncomfortable in his borrowed dark suit. Willy and Noreen cried steadily through the entire service. Jupiter did not. They each placed a French Lace Rose on top of the Angel Wing casket. Mr. Johnson awkwardly hugged Jupiter after the ceremony.

"Thank you," Mr. Johnson said.

"For what?" she asked.

Mr. Johnson tipped his head and said nothing. He patted Russell on the hand and hugged Willy. They had a hushed conversation, which Rooster watched.

Rooster brought his camera.

He documented the paltry group of attendees with the lake in the background.

He photographed Jupiter, fidgeting with the pearl strand around her neck, next to Mr. Johnson.

He snuck a picture of Goth Benedict with his nose in a rose.

He captured Willy and Jupiter with Russell in the center, sporting his French Lace Rose boutonniere on his gray cashmere lapel.

He chronicled Noreen's black dress hiking up past her cottage cheesy thigh as she attempted to hug Jupiter and Jupiter resisting the comfort, her shoulders caved in toward each other, chin down, and eyes directed at her feet.

He caught Noreen animated, trying to talk to Russell and when failing to get a response, bursting into tears.

He photographed Willy in her snug black dress, her bosom heaving and her arms constrained by the cap sleeves, trying to console Noreen as a handsome young African American man in a black suit, too short at the ankle and tie too thin, wheeled Russell toward a black limousine with the lake in the background.

He snapped Willy's silhouette from behind with the sun dipping into the trees and the salmon-colored light reflecting on the surface of the lake.

He documented the top of the pearlized white casket with the white roses.

He shot Jupiter standing uncomfortably, ankles bent in slightly on her high heels and arm resting heavily on her hip in the doorway of the mausoleum. The once brilliant now dim, stained glass dove behind her head. He longed for the picture of the day before.

He took the view from the top step of the mausoleum in all available directions to remind him of the place he walked away from.

"Do you think you could give me a ride home? They have to take Noreen to JFK." Surprised to hear a voice directed at him, Rooster turned, the lens of his camera smack in Jupiter's face. She flinched and retreated backward as if being assaulted. He wasn't sure which but he pressed his finger down on the shutter. The sound drilled a hole into the silence.

"I was going to leave from here." He said finally, still holding the body of the camera in front of his face.

"Oh," Jupiter replied the weight of his words like a sock to the stomach. She began to walk in the direction of the limo. The crest of her head trying to hold itself high but the slightest tilt belying her noble intentions. She deserved this, she thought.

He sat down on the top step and watched her walk away. He didn't want this.

Or her.

He was right.

She was crazy.

He had done his duty.

It was over.

His momma's words thumped in his brain.

His mistake.

He didn't take risks; you have to take a risk to make a mistake.

She took risks.

His eyes followed her slogging away from him, her ankles bending in toward each other as her black patent heels struggled to navigate through the grass. The bones of her ankles were too skinny to fill the backs of her shoes and her calves seemed to be struggling to hold up the rest of her body. Her knee bones looked like they were going to bang into each other and the thought of them colliding made him cringe. The bottom of her dress swung too far from side to side as she stepped because it was a little too big. Her shiny black purse banged against her hip, popping out to the right. Her hair fell in a blonde fountain over her shoulders, bouncing in sync with her gait. He thought about touching her hair. He thought about her in the attic asleep on the floor in a sea of his images; all of them specific, solitary, lonely pieces of things. What was that about? No striking panoramas, no packs of humanity, no sweeping vistas except for today, a view from a grave. Her mistakes were all over the place, he thought, looking out at the lake reflecting the pink ball of sunset on its surface and then to Jupiter. He had missed a million of his own mistakes.

He suddenly felt like a pussy and stood up.

47 men

She had reached the road; her feet teetered from grass to pavement.

He watched the angle of her body straighten with resolve.

He regarded Willy, who turned and looked back up the hill at him, the questions physically filing into her brain.

He shook his head, thinking somehow this might jar the pussy wrench from his gut.

He saw Willy disappear into the limo without looking back.

He observed Jupiter and something about the line of her body as she curved toward the opening about to disappear, made him shout.

"Wait."

Her head turned back to him.

"I'll take you,"

Jupiter straightened and waited for him to come to her.

He walked slowly wondering why the fuck he had just done that. When he reached her he rubbed his hands on the front of his pants.

"I'll take you but then I have to go." He said looking at his boots coming out of bottom of her father's trousers.

"Thanks." She said quietly, Would you come meet my dad?"

Rooster followed her to the open door of the black limo. Jupiter poked her head in,

"Daddy this is the boy I was telling you about. His name is Rooster Boudreaux. And then she turned her head to Rooster. "Rooster, this is my father, Russell Campbell." Jupiter stepped away from the door and Rooster looked into the back seat. Miss Willy was beaming, a smile so wide it almost made him start to cry. Then he looked at this once formidable man, bent, hunched over, head tilted to the right and eyes fixed straight into nothingness.

"Hello Mr. Campbell. My given name is Darwin, just so y'all don't think my parents were crazy. Then again you did name your daughter Jupiter. So well, it was a beautiful ceremony and I am very sorry for your loss." Then he reached out and patted Russell's knee.

Willy put her soft warm hand over his and with tears in her eyes. "Praise Jesus for a boy like you, you tell your momma I said that. You healed this family up, whether they know it or not. Thank you Rooster."

Rooster squeezed her hand.

"No Miss Willy, you did." He reached out and touched her cheek. Then he ducked back out and let Jupiter say goodbye. He felt suddenly overwhelmed with emotion, he thought about his own father and how he had never been able to forgive him. He began to pace and the "Star- Spangled Banner" hum crested on his lips. But he swallowed it back and looked out at the lake; forgiveness was a tricky bird he thought.

Rooster and Jupiter walked quite separately down the hill as the black limousine cut the same line across the landscape as Rooster's truck had the day before. He opened the door for her but did not wait to close it. She slammed it shut as he hopped on to the bench seat next to her. He turned the key in the ignition and gunned it. The roar of the engine made her jump which she tried to conceal.

Rooster looked out at the road lost in crevasses of his own mind. He clicked on the radio out of habit and static filled the air. He twisted the dial trying to find a clear station. There was none.

"Thanks." She said.

"Yep." He turned the radio off.

He studied his hands on the steering wheel, they made him feel guilty, he thought of his mother not being able to look at them. What kinda love is that? He watched his knuckles turn white with his grip. A love that forgives cheating, he thought. Would she cheat?

Jupiter played with the gold clasp on the top of her purse, procured from her mother's collection. Then she looked inside to see if there were any remnant treasures in the inside zipper pocket. There were not. Her discomfort was palpable but he was completely oblivious to it. She picked at the cuticle on her thumbnail and bit the skin with her teeth, which when she pulled it off made her thumb bleed. She pressed the side of her thumb into the fabric of the black dress to make it stop. She then put it in her mouth and

47 men

sucked on it. It tasted like metal. She wiped it on her dress again and faced the window. The truck bounced along the rural roads, the silence deafening.

Forty-six dudes in a room together, it was the image he couldn't seem to shake. He glanced toward her; the curve of her breast caught his eye, so many hands there before him. He shook his head to knock the vision from his mind. He looked straight out the windshield to the road slicing through a swath of foliage, hatred filled him.

Jupiter pulled a piece of hair from the right underside of her head and braided it into a tiny braid. Then she undid it. "I Love You Just the Way You Are" was on repeat in her head from the Muzac version in the funeral home. She tried to think of another song.

"Do you mind if I try the radio again?" she asked uncomfortably.

"No." his tone revealing his mindset.

She leaned over and twisted the dial and snuck a glance at him. Rooster stared straight out with no expression on his face, though she noticed the crease in his forehead seemed to be more pronounced; she wondered if that was her fault. Static filled the air again, for a few seconds some mariachi music blared through the cab and then it was gone. She turned the dial across the balance of the numbers, nothing else. She gave up, snapped it off and leaned back into the seat. She twisted the pearls around her neck and ran her fingernail across the surface to feel the irregularity. She wished he would say one thing to her. He didn't. She stared at him to see if it would get him to talk. He blinked; she noticed the ends of his eyelashes were almost white. She concentrated on the side of his head, trying to use her mind to will him to speak; she had seen this on late-night television. His eyes focused on the road, his lips parted slightly and she waited for the sound to come out. Instead, his mouth closed and his lips pursed, her will apparently not strong enough to illicit words.

Rooster's dream from this morning swirled in his mind. All forty-six men were milling about in a room with a dirt floor where the cockfights are held. They were in their underwear with no shirts on. Preston was stand- ing in the middle of the circle with red socks on; taking bets that Jupiter would fuck Rooster over. The odds were weighing in heavily that indeed she would. Rooster, dressed in camo hunting gear, pointing a DeMarini Voodoo baseball bat screamed at all of them.

"You don't know, Preston, this is different."

"Did she tell you that Roo? That what she said with her little white panties down around her ankles while you banged her? Or wait was that him?" Preston said pointing to a tall blond guy with his fist full of money, "Or maybe Bill over there," he continued pointing to huge African-American dude, "or you Benny boy, didn't you defile her in a coffin?"

"Shut the fuck up," Rooster yelled at Preston.

"What Roo, you tryin' to pretend this bitch isn't one big whore?"

"Fuck all of you." Rooster yelled. Then he picked up the bat and started swinging, connecting with the temple of the first guy, his skull exploding like a watermelon, the meat in chunks on the ground. He ceremoniously went through the rest until he was knee deep in head meat, his bat crimson, his face covered in blood spatter. There was just Preston left, mouth agape, staring at him.

"Come on man, do it." Preston took a step toward him pushing out his chest. "You're too much of a pussy. You won't hit me."

Rooster stood bat poised, primed to swing, he began the motion and stopped. Preston started to laugh at him. He pulled the bat back into position and unloaded his swing.

He woke himself seconds before impact, sitting upright in a full sweat, heart pounding and hands like they were still gripping onto the bat.

Rooster's truck hit a pothole pulling the steering wheel to the right. Startled, he pulled it back to the left, his heart pounded and he gripped harder.

"How did you know about Père Lachaise?" she asked tentatively, unable to handle the silence any longer.

Her voice surprised him. He cleared his throat and answered welcoming the diversion from his own brain.

"Ah, uh I studied art in Paris. I spent hundreds of hours there."

"Why?" she asked.

"A project for school."

"What was the project?"

"I picked five famous people and camped out at each of their graves, a week for each. I took pictures at different times of day so the light and weather would be a factor as well as the visitors. I made a book out of it." Rooster said like he was giving an oral report in third grade.

"Why?" Jupiter asked pulling the high heels off of her feet and pushing them to the edge by the door.

"Which part?"

"What were you trying to see?"

"Revelations about humanity. The cycle of life, our collective obsession with mortality, the desire to preserve what is unpreservable." Rooster stopped, cutting himself short.

She waited for him to go on. He did not.

"Which five?" she pressed her bare feet into the dashboard.

"Chopin, Delacroix, Oscar Wilde, Jim Morrison and Edith Piaf." He replied looking at her red toenails against the beige vinyl.

"Oscar Wilde's grave was my favorite, with all the lipstick kisses."

She wondered if all of his pictures from there were of pieces or if he had taken any pictures of the wholes. She didn't ask.

"What was the best picture you took there?"

"No idea."

"Come on, a few have to stand out."

Rooster didn't answer. He thought about the pieces again, all of his photographs had been pieces save for a few. Only three pictures were of the whole of anything. The gates to the east, an old French widow he shot everyday so one day he took all of her because there was nothing left to do and the Jim Morrison guy.

Jupiter shifted awkwardly in the seat. She thought she might have broken through but alas, no. She turned toward the window and started to make another braid, looking out at the landscape whizzing by them. She undid the braid very slowly and "Swing Low, Sweet Chariot" filled her head, very low and very deep. She was grateful but had no idea where this one had come from, maybe Willy. She thought about all those tears Noreen and Willy had cried and wondered why not one had fallen from her own eyes.

"I went one morning right as the cemetery opened. It was Jim Morrison's week." Rooster said into the silence. Jupiter turned toward the voice and watched him like a hawk.

"I had a few different vantage points for each of the gravesites. There was a thin white guy wearing a black leather jacket with fringe. He was standing with his guitar singing, "Break on Through" to the headstone and he sucked. But his commitment was total. It's of the back of him, the neck of his guitar, the fringe flying and the sun breaking through clouds in front of him." He paused, "Maybe it's not so much the picture, as it was the experience."

She noticed his eyes light up with the memory of Paris so palpable in his being.

"I'd like to see the book." She said afraid he would stop talking.

"It's at my studio."

Jupiter didn't say anything. She waited to see if he would offer anything else. Again, nothing.

"My father took me there," Jupiter said softly turning her body toward the window.

"That's cool," he imagined his own father in Paris and smiled, "With the exception of their honeymoon; I don't think my father ever left the great state of Louisiana. When I told him I wanted to go to Paris... phew..."

"What did he do?"

"Asked me if I was in fact a homosexual."

"Why?" Jupiter asked.

"I wasn't the son he had in mind."

255
47 men

"I'm familiar with that experience."

"What did your dad want?"

"A boy."

"Tough to get around."

"Yeah."

Rooster shifted in the seat, pulling the striped tie from around his neck. He looked out into the darkness.

"My dad had all those girls and then me. The idea of a boy was good, but the reality wasn't really. He loved the girls much more than he did me." He finished quietly and his momma's face popped into his head.

He scratched his forehead. Jupiter leaned her back up against the door to face him. She put her feet on the seat and wrapped her bare arms around her knees.

"But, you had your mom."

He looked out the side window smiled and then back to the road without the smile.

"Funny, she said that too." He paused. "Yeah, I did. Seems like you did too."

Ruth Ann underwater, flashed into Jupiter's head. Golden hair flowing like a mermaid and tiny bubbles coming from her mouth and then smiling with her pearly white teeth and more bubbles escaping. Then pretending to sip tea from a non-existent china cup and a mass of bubbles erupting in a laugh before her return to the surface for air.

"You're right," Jupiter said.

For the remainder of their drive, they were silent. Jupiter stared out the window still confounded by the fact that she had not shed a tear. She began to get nervous, as they got closer to the house. She started fiddling with her necklace again and pulled her legs and feet up underneath her. When they drove into the driveway, Jupiter turned to him and asked, "Do you want to be buried or cremated?"

"Burned on a funeral pyre."

Jupiter's eyes widened and she started to laugh, "No way."

"Yep," he said turning off the ignition. He remained in the seat like he was waiting for her to get out. Jupiter felt a well of desperation gurgle inside her.

"Willy made food; do you want to eat before you go?" her voice wavering mid-sentence.

Rooster looked at the clock and thought for a moment.

"Sure, I guess."

He put the keys in the center console and got out of the truck. Jupiter finally breathed.

OENOKE RIDGE ROAD
New Canaan

Jupiter held the black patent heels in one hand and her mother's purse in the other; she searched for her keys trying to balance everything and then had difficulty negotiating the lock. Rooster stood three feet away from her not offering any assistance. Finally, the door creaked open, the alarm sounded and she dropped everything on the floor running in her bare feet for the panel. She pressed buttons and the beeping was silenced. It was pitch black.

"God, this house is always so dark."

She walked back to the door, hit all the light switches at once with the butt of her fist and then retrieved her things. Rooster stood by the entrance fully illuminated; wearing suit pants, his work boots, shirtsleeves rolled up and holding a dark gray jacket in one hand with the tie strewn over the top. His hair, which he'd tried to tame, was beginning to release itself back to its comfortable state of disheveled and those blue eyes staring at her. She had forgotten how good-looking he was.

"Come in, Willy made all of my mom's favorites."

They passed the dining room on the way to the kitchen and Jupiter stopped, awestruck. Willy had prepared the table for a group of at least twenty. Every piece of silver had been laid out and polished to within an inch of its life. The special occasion Raynaud Dutchess china pattern was on display and white scalloped linen napkins were expertly pressed, folded and fanned out next to the dishes.

"What was she thinking?" she said under her breath.

Jupiter deposited her things on a chair and walked to the buffet table lined with chafing dishes. She swung around to find Rooster. He was hanging the jacket on a chair back and felt her gaze. His eyes fell in a direct line with hers, this skinny barefoot blonde girl in a too big black dress holding a huge metal lid and her green eyes welling up with tears.

Lobster Thermidor and steak of some sort and tears streaming down Jupiter's face. He walked past creamed spinach, twice-baked potatoes, creamed pearl onions, stuffing, Fettuccine Alfredo, and closed in on more tears. The oyster pan roast and bread pudding with warm butterscotch sauce caught his eye. A key lime pie and a pot of black-eyed peas with corn bread on the side ended the buffet, which from his perspective appeared to be the catalyst for a few heaving sobs.

Jupiter stood frozen at the end of the line of food, still clinging tightly to the first lid she had picked up. Her childhood lay before her in chafing dishes on a buffet line. Rooster watched, unsure of what to do. Finally, recovering a bit but with the tears still streaming down her cheeks Jupiter asked.

"What should we do?" her voice cracked.

"Eat, definitely, eat," he said with a little grin.

Jupiter remained motionless.

"Why did she do this?" she whispered.

"We all honor the dead differently." Rooster offered.

He moved to her, took the lid out of her hand and pulling a chair away from the table, sat her down.

Then, he turned his attention to the alarming array of delicacies. An ice bucket at the end of table with the neck of the bottle poking out derailed him. Might help he thought, he walked over and pulled a bottle of Dom Perignon from its melted ice bath. He quietly popped the cork and poured champagne into two flutes. He set a glass on the table in front of Jupiter. Her head was tipped down; he touched her hand lightly and pointed to the glass. He returned to the buffet and made two plates heaping with a taste of every item Willy made. He brought them to the center of the table next to his champagne glass and the bottle.

She watched him push the place settings out of the way, remove his boots and socks and shove them under the chair with his barefoot.

259

47 men

Rooster climbed onto the Chippendale chair and then onto the ebony surface of the table. The smooth cool finish felt tremendous under his sweaty feet. He sprawled himself out in the dead center of the grand table.

"What are you doing?" Jupiter asked quietly regarding his every movement.

"Celebrating your mother, come on."

Rooster got up and sauntered down the middle of the table to her chair and extended his hand. Jupiter gingerly stood on the chair and griped his hand as she tentatively stepped onto the table surface.

"Grab your glass," He instructed.

She bent over and picked up the flute still holding his hand. She ducked her head under the crystal chandelier as they made their way toward the center. Rooster helped her sit down and then sat across from her. The table bounced as his weight hit the surface. She looked at his feet; there was blond hair on the toes and dirt under the side of the right big toe nail. He shifted his legs, trying to cross them and hit his glass with his knee, it teetered and he caught it. He took a quick sip and set it down out of harm's way.

Jupiter picked up a stiff napkin, wiped her nose on it and sniffed hard. She glanced around the room from her new vantage point. She felt the shiny wood holding her up and pondered the millions of meals she had eaten in this room. The dim light of the chandelier flickered against the crystals still swinging slightly with movement from her brushing against them; the huge window at the end of the room, in the day acting as a framed painting and at night a framed view into darkness. She observed her father's empty seat at the head of the table and then her mother's, neither of which would ever be filled again.

She wanted to hit Rooster, lash out at him. She would never have noticed their profound absence had he not made her get on the damn table.

Rooster raised his glass.

"To your mom..." he stopped and nodded his head up and down with a hint of a smile. "And to June Bug; she woulda gotten a real kick out of this."

Jupiter didn't move; she still wanted to punch him.

"What do you say we try some of this food?" Rooster stuck his fork into a hearty piece of lobster. Jupiter watched him, put her head down and plunged her fork deep into a savory morsel of Steak Diane. The juicy flavor of the meat hit her tongue and filled her mouth with the memory of Russell Campbell.

It was Christmas Eve of her ninth year. He wanted beef, but not roast beef, he said. Ruth Ann laughed at him.

"So picky Mr. Campbell," she said and he touched her cheek ever so gently.

"I want a Christmas tradition, Mrs. Campbell, one that's just ours. So what will it be?"

Her eyes lit up and she started to giggle,

"Ready?" she paused a beat heightening his anticipation, "Steak Diane, from 21, remember the night you sang with the bartender?"

"You can sing, Daddy?"

"Quite well." Ruth Ann said winking at him. He chuckled. Jupiter felt way outside of the inside joke.

"Willy," Russell shouted.

"Grab your coat, we're going to 21."

"Russell? It's Christmas Eve."

"If we're making it our tradition, it needs to be made properly."

They trekked to the city and ate the most delicious steak Jupiter had ever tasted, flambéed, table-side with a Shirley Temple and Miss Willy. Willy had made it every Christmas since.

Jupiter wished she had asked what song her father sang.

"Where'd you go?" Rooster said quietly peeling her from her daydream.

"Christmas Eve, age nine," She said.

Rooster finished his champagne and filled up both of their glasses.

"Steak on Christmas?"

"Our tradition." She sipped her champagne.

Rooster ate a pan-roasted oyster, "Now that is something," he said gleefully.

"Why did you make me sit on the table?" she asked with a scolding tone.

"This house is too serious."

He took another bite of lobster.

"Why did you take me home with you?" she asked.

"What?"

"That first night, when Willy said you had to take me. You could have said no."

"Yep." Rooster looked into his glass.

Jupiter waited for more of an explanation.

"Yep, what?"

"I could have, but I didn't." Rooster deposited his glass on the table and looked directly into her eyes.

"But why."

"You killed our bird." Rooster said.

He waited a minute before answering and took another swig from the champagne glass.

"Because I was supposed to," Rooster said eyes darting away.

"I don't understand."

He shifted uncomfortably as the silence hovered loudly.

"Why did you go with me?" he asked.

"You were supposed to be forty-seven,"

She put her hair behind her bruised ear and looked down at her plate.

"Why did you stay?" he asked, eyes fixed at his feet.

"Because I liked you." She said focused on a pyramid of creamed onions.

Rooster Boudreaux didn't say a word. He ate a spoonful of black-eyed peas.

"We eat these every New Year's day for good luck." He said chewing on a pea. "We have 'em with collard greens and corn bread. Momma throws a dime in the pot and who ever gets it is supposed to get an extra serving of good luck for the year. Delilah has never once gotten the dime, steams her up every year."

Jupiter put a spoonful in her mouth and chewed.

"They taste terrible."

"Delilah hates 'em too, makes her even madder about the dime."

He put another spoonful in his mouth, chewed on the waxy surface and examined her. Her body was nestled on the table in a sort of a z shape, her limbs out at one side and though not totally comfortable, elegant in her repose.

She was the only person in his entire life that he saw the whole of. He didn't pick out a nose or a cheekbone or a rib cage, the teeth or the toes. He saw her entirety. In the light of the chandelier, the reflection shining in her eyes, the white of her form against the black wood of the table, Rooster decided it was time to take his risk.

"You're the only whole thing I've ever wanted to take a picture of." She looked up at him.

"Jumping off the swing. I knew you'd do it. I saw the light and the pieces but all I wanted was the full image of you flying through the air.

His eyes shot toward the table with the release of this information. The enormity of letting his well-honed structure go was proving to be a bit more terrifying than he'd anticipated. Rooster took a sip of his champagne and looked up at her. She smiled.

"Would you go swimming with me?" she asked quietly.

He waited just a beat,

"Sure," He pronounced and flew off the table, spilling his glass and kicking one of the plates of remnant food.

"I haven't been in a pool since my mom died." Jupiter added quietly.

"Shit," he said using his napkin to soak it up and righting the glass.

Jupiter crawled to the edge on all fours and made her way into the chair all discombobulated. She got to her feet and turned her back to him.

"Can you unzip me?"

Rooster did and she slipped out of her too big black dress.

"Don't you need a bathing suit?" he inquired looking at her bare back.

"They won't be back for hours, they had to go all the way to JFK," she said.

Rooster tentatively unbuttoned his dress shirt and stepped out of Russell's borrowed suit pants, unveiling sear-sucker boxers. Jupiter, in her mismatched bra and panties, galloped through the mostly dark house to the door to the outside. She flicked on the swimming pool lights revealing the largest pool Rooster had ever seen. He was pleased to see the plumes of steam coming off the surface. Jupiter flung open the door and ran to the diving board. She did a full summersault in the air, landing in a perfect arrow cutting through the surface of the water. Rooster followed her with a mighty cannon ball, which created awesome waves across the surface of the pool. Their two black heads bobbed on the turquoise surface, their legs glowing in the artificial pool light.

Jupiter was finally home, like a dolphin returned to the sea from captivity. Her body twisted and curled, gliding effortlessly though the water. She relished the water on her skin, the weightlessness of her body.

Jupiter swam to Rooster in the deep end of the pool. Steam rose like fingers off the surface. She came very close to his face, it made him a little uncomfortable, he wanted to pull back but did not.

She held out both of her hands. He watched the alien forms glowing white under the surface of the water. He took her hands as she whispered "take a deep breath." She gently took him under the surface of the water and guided them down deeper until she hovered inches above the bottom of the pool. She released his left hand and held tight to the right. He kept his eyes open watching her body flutter and maneuver to keep them submerged. Her limbs hung off of her core suspended, her head tipped back and her hair moved in the water like the thin tentacles of a moon jellyfish.

Rooster wanted to stay dunked and floating in his personal baptism but was out of air. He pulled at Jupiter's hand, she smiled and he pointed toward the surface. She let go and followed him. She was happy, so happy to be here with him. He took a deep breath, grabbed her hand drawing her back under.

They floated, quiet, holding each other's hand, arms outstretched, listening to the strange high pitched sound of the pool equipment churning and echoing through the water. He again had to return to the surface. Jupiter sank to the very bottom of the pool and sat Indian style. This spot was her station of refuge. Here, she felt impregnable, contained and free all at the same time.

She surveyed her long-familiar surroundings; the rusty discoloration of the plaster by the drain; the rippled glass on the pool light's surface and the vast expanse of water revered from below. She tilted her head back and glanced up, the vista, usually serene, suddenly included legs kicking above her... his legs. The view made her grin. Empty before, she thought, always empty.

She thought about being full. He made her feel full in a way she'd never experienced. He was here for her and the weight of this actually landed. He had come to find her; he helped her lay her mother to rest. He believed her, not Preston, knew what she'd done and still he was here. Realization bred fear, she tried to go back to the feeling of fullness but her lungs began to bark.

Jupiter swam up toward his legs and then to him, curving her body up against his.

Rooster pulled her to him and kissed her.

Then he took her by the hand, climbed up the steps and into the frigid air, his boxers now see-through and clinging to his body. She looked at the outline of his ass through the fabric and wanted to touch it but did not. He turned and she looked away embarrassed. Jupiter, in her own see-through undergarments pink and yellow respectively, ran past him. She grabbed a towel and threw one to him. She wrapped herself up and tipped her head toward the sky, stars... millions of them. Rooster's eyes followed hers as he dried himself off.

"Do you know about them?" He asked.

"More than you'd ever want to know, but I kind of love it, there is an incredible sense of order." She said, looking at him, black against the light blue rectangle of light.

Rooster reached for her hand and slowly made his way to the open door. She suddenly weighed a ton; like pulling a Labrador toward the door to the vet. This was amusing to him as he led her by the arm down the hallway toward the opulent guestroom. She stopped in front of the door and seemed to dig her heels into the marble. He put his arm around her and guided her through the room to the shower. He jacked up the water temperature and left her standing in front of it. He rubbed his head and shook his hair, spraying her in the face like a dog shaking dry. He wrapped the damp towel like a sarong around his waist. He reached in felt the water, pulled the towel off of her and then shoved her in. She slipped off her bra and panties and left them on the shower floor and welcomed the space. She used the soap that smelled like her mom instead of avoiding it. She held it to her nose and inhaled the scent. Suds herself up with the pale purple bar and closed her eyes, letting the smell of lavender flood her nostrils.

"Tell me the how you met story again." Jupiter asked lying cozy in her canopy bed. Her mom looked down and rolled her eyes.

"Please," Jupiter begged.

"Oh okay. Well, you remember Daddy's friend, Adam?"

Jupiter nodded on cue to the routine she and her mother had for her favorite bedtime story.

"Someone had set me up on a date with Adam. He was wickedly funny and we enjoyed ourselves but it was clear we would just be friends. Apparently, he thought I was just the girl for his dear introverted friend Russell. I was modeling in New York at the time and so he arranged for a 'coincidental' meeting. We had a mutual friend who was a musician and happened to be playing at an underground club in the Village. The Village wasn't the way it is now so it was a bit scandalous for me to show up to meet them there alone. I had an event before so I was all dressed up and stood out like a sore thumb.

"What were you wearing?" Jupiter interrupted.

"A black cocktail dress, patent leather pumps and my hair up I think, or maybe I took it down when I got there, trying to tone it down a little. Anyway, Adam was there all smiles and introduced me to Russell. Russell Campbell was a very polite and nice-looking man but a bit of a stiff. He was wearing a dark suit with no tie, which I guess was his version of casual. He had beautiful blue eyes and they kind of twinkled when he was excited about something but he seemed so serious and his work, very specific."

"Boring?"

"Well yes, a little boring, but shush if you want me to finish the story. So our friend finished his set, came and said hello and both he and Adam had to leave. Russell very politely asked if I would like to stay and have another drink with him. Adam nodded his head over Russell's shoulder and then mouthed 'please'. So I smiled and agreed. Another band came up to the stage and they were terrible so we were forced to chat a bit. He was working very hard to make conversation, I felt like he hadn't spoken to another human being for months and was a little rusty at it. But there was something about him that kept me sitting there because I had become quite good at extricating myself from a bad date. He was drinking scotch on the rocks and I was drinking Manhattans, Grand mommy always told me to stick with champagne, but something about this whole night was making me take some uncharacteristic chances. Suddenly, there was a twelve-piece orchestra setting up on the stage. It was salsa music and as they began, a number of people jumped up to dance in the tiny space in front of the band. I watched them longing to join their joyous crew. I guess he saw my eyes glaze over when he started explaining his research and figured he'd better do something quick. He stood up very gallantly and asked if I would like to dance. I was quite surprised; he certainly didn't seem like the dancing type. He removed his jacket and rolled up his sleeves. So I got up and he put his arm around my waist.

The electricity was really quite shocking, I think for both of us. We danced; he was looser somehow and was smiling watching me. You know the grin he gets when he figures something out he's been tooling on for a long time. I whispered in his ear that if he hadn't asked me to dance there wouldn't have been a second date. He laughed at me and whispered back, 'I know you fell madly in love with me the minute you laid eyes on me.' We both laughed at that one. He was funny, kind of shy but completely full of himself at the same time. He was like no one I'd ever met. We stayed at the club until the band was packing up. They invited us to join them for a roof party in the Village. Daddy said no, but thanked them profusely. He said he just wanted a bit more time alone with me. We walked the thirty blocks to my apartment that I shared with Noreen and two other models. Noreen was peeking out the window; I never came home that late. I waved and she ducked back into our room. Your daddy gave me the most special kiss I had ever had in my life. Fireworks practically went off in my head."

"Really?"

"Well no, I guess not but I was quite smitten. I think we fell in love right there and then standing on the stoop of my walk up. It was a warm night, the scent of flowers mingled with the spring air and when he was about to say goodbye. He put his hand on my cheek and looked into my eyes and said 'You are what I have waited for my entire life.'"

Rooster opened the shower door; Jupiter jumped. He held a huge fluffy robe in front of his face so as not to see her nakedness.

"Time to get out." He draped the robe over her shoulders, put a towel on her head and rubbed her hair to dry it off. She smiled under the cloak of terrycloth. She attempted to smooth it out with her fingers as he walked her into the bedroom. The fireplace glowed; Bob Marley provided the vocal stylings and the half full champagne bottle and glasses sat on the bedside table.

"How'd you do this so fast?"

Rooster winked at her. He was sporting a matching fluffy white robe. Jupiter, surveying the room and assessing the situation, began a mouthful of nervous chatter.

"I feel like I should have an outfit. Like Grace Kelly, did you ever see *Rear Window*? She had this tiny dark brown Mark Cross case and she had a negligee, slippers, toothbrush, the whole shebang, all packed in it. Maybe I should go get a nightgown or something?"

Rooster wrapped his arms around her from behind, "Shhhhhh," he whispered into her ear. "You're fine."

"What should I do now?" Jupiter said fidgeting.

"It's customary to get into the bed."

"Okay," her deep breath exposed her level of nervousness. She climbed up the little ladder and pulled back the duvet.

She stripped off the robe and dove under the covers. She flipped over and yanked them up under her chin.

"This is way better than my bed."

Rooster was enjoying her nervousness so he strung her along... "Would you like some champagne?" he said, adjusting the tie on his robe, for effect.

"Um, yeah sure, I guess." She said squirming under the covers. Rooster poured her a glass and handed it to her.

"Thanks," she said reaching only her arm out from underneath the sheets and taking it.

He sauntered over to the other side of the bed, brazenly dropped his robe and climbed under the covers next to her. She wasn't looking. He put his glass to hers, they both sipped. He was up on one arm with the sheet only barely covering his groin. Jupiter stared into the fire. She felt butterflies in her stomach that seemed to be turning into bats.

"I'm so nervous," she whispered.

"I know," he whispered back and laughed.

She took a huge swig of champagne and then flashed him a smile. He returned the favor and then Jupiter, beyond her control, let out a monstrous belch. It ricocheted off all available surfaces including Rooster. Jupiter fell backwards in a heap of giggles, spilling champagne everywhere. Rooster rescued the glass, averting further disaster.

"Oh my GOD, that was so gross," she said, choking on her words. "I'm so sorry."

"Oh my God, it's okay," Rooster said imitating her, also enjoying the comic relief.

He laid back, beside her, both of them with the flavor of laughter on their lips.

Rooster leaned over her and switched off the bedside lamp.

"Come here," Rooster planted a juicy kiss on her lips and held the side of her face in his hand.

Jupiter came up for a moment of air, her brain and body trying to reconcile the overwhelming mass of electricity pumping through her. Rooster very gently leaned over and kissed her nipple in the firelight. The rush of nerve endings shot through her body and she shuddered. He smiled at the response and took her nipple completely in his mouth and sucked harder. She felt the wetness rush between her legs and was surprised how easily he had elicited this response. She arched her back up and pressed her right thigh against him. She stopped herself from reaching for him, finally wanting every moment of this experience to last. He moved up to her mouth, stuck his fingers between her lips and she sucked on them. They tasted like chlorine. She felt him get harder against her thigh. He pulled his fingers out of her mouth and replaced them with his tongue, it was dizzying. Soft and warm, his tongue had this gentle but firm way about it. He tasted sweet, like he had just eaten a strawberry and a hint of it lingered.

His hand cupped her breast, his fingers lightly playing with her nipple as his tongue worked its magic in her mouth. His fingers dappled down across her stomach, her heart tumbled though her chest, as he reached inside her. She gasped, his fingers moved back and forth on her with a delicacy she had never experienced. It was like all of the love and care he had in his body was coming out through his hand. She let herself go, relaxed and allowed him to take her. Her brain quieted, her body responded to his touch, her hips arching up, he moved his hand faster and harder and she held onto the edge as long as she could finally letting go, she screamed out so loud she surprised herself. Her body hummed from the inside out. He let her rest for a minute.

She opened her eyes and he was watching her.

"What are you looking at?" she whispered.

"You." He whispered back.

He nuzzled into her neck gently biting her flesh and rolled over on top of her. His weight felt good against her body. He dipped his head down and put his mouth to hers, his body firm and heavy. She ran her fingers over his soft skin to his downy covered ass; she had a flash of her dream and grabbed handfuls of him and pulling him against her.

"I dreamed this." She said into his mouth.

He nodded and then closed his eyes, wrapped his arms around her and flipped her over on top of him. She laughed, wanting him, but again she stopped herself.

"Come here," he said.

She lay her body down on the length of him and hugged him, pressing her pelvis into him. Her heart felt like it was vibrating through her skin into his. Then she straddled his legs and held herself up above him, lowering herself down slowly and back up again. In and out and finally he couldn't take it, he thrust himself hard inside of her. It was like when you find the missing piece of the puzzle and you put it in its place and the picture is complete. Up and down, their bodies sweaty and juicy, slipping on and off of each other, skin on skin sliding, pushing, pulling and thrusting. She suddenly stopped at looked down at him.

"Can you believe this?"

"What?" he said his breathing heavy.

"That this is actually happening." She said with a beaming smile.

He smiled back and then flipped her back over, mounting her. His girth and length hitting all points of sensation, she wanted to scream but didn't.

He was looking into her eyes with such clarity it made her feel that for the first time in her life she was actually being seen. His eyes did not move off of her, his hair falling into them. She brushed it out of his face and put her hand to his cheek as he had done to her. He started to move faster. She watched his body begin to stiffen as he reached orgasm. He yelled out, a guttural utterance straight up from his groin and then he fell heavily on top of her. She wrapped her arms and legs around him and held him, rocking slightly. He kissed her neck and sent shivers through her. They lay there quiet until she could feel his heart beat slow.

"Wow," Jupiter whispered in his ear.

She put her arms back around him squeezing him tight. He kissed her neck. She pulled him close, her breathing hot and slow in his ear. She opened her mouth and sucked on the tip of his ear lobe, he shuddered, still inside of her. She continued to suck and she could feel him getting hard again. Good Lord, she thought to herself, some recovery time. She blew on his wet earlobe and he shivered. She giggled and began to move her hips underneath him. He groaned softly and reached his hands under the cheeks of her ass and pulled himself further inside of her. Her hips began a circular motion and he bit into the flesh of her neck, "Ahhhhhhh" and then nuzzled his head up against hers. She wrapped her legs around his waist and tipped her pelvis up toward him. His body slammed into her, so different than the first time. She dug her fingers into the flesh of ass and he began to pump himself back and forth into her.

"Oh my God," she called out and then he sort of growled, low like a big grizzly bear and fell on top of her with all of his weight, his body spent. Her hands traveled up and down his back, he didn't move. She reached down to his hand and laced her fingers between his. They grasped onto hers and he squeezed her hand. She smiled into his shoulder and squeezed back.

"I love you, Rooster Boudreaux," Jupiter whispered into his ear. She waited for a reply.

When she didn't get one she took a deep breath and continued.

"Would you stay here with me for a bit?"

He rolled over on his back and looked up at the ceiling. He crossed his arms against his bare chest and smiled.

Yeah was all he said.

Jupiter put her head on his shoulder and after a little while he whispered, "I love you" into the top of her head.

Then Rooster waited patiently until the full weight of her body landed on him, asleep – the head, the skull, the feeling of her lower lip falling open on his skin. The photograph was so clear in his mind. He gingerly moved out from underneath her, letting her heavy head fall softly onto the pillow. He crossed the room naked, his body lanky somehow, lighter than it had been earlier. He pulled the camera from his grandfather's bag. The Leica in his hand felt like her breast had moments before, natural, meant to be there. He put his eye to the viewfinder to see her through his lens. He moved the body of the camera, stretching from one end to the other of her lithe naked form. She was curled into a "c" in the center of the bed. He put his index finger on the shutter release button and abruptly stopped, pulling the camera away from his face. He looked at her, the shape of her form, the rise and fall of her breath, the expression resting on her beautiful face. He felt arousal stir in him and looked down to see himself, to feel himself, noting the instinctual reaction of his body to the whole of her. Separate from his mind, his body had the facility and courage to experience her. He felt a hollowness and fear flooded into his brain.

"Stop," he whispered it aloud. Preston flashed in his mind, then June Bug. Finally his momma's voice saying, "Be brave" hit him like a slap across the face. He looked at the camera in his hand.

Rooster moved as far away from her as he could. He held the camera high above his head and pressed down. The sound of the shutter echoed off of the walls, the familiarity and solace the sound gave him from behind the body of the camera was marked. In this moment he not only heard it but saw the enormity of it.

47 men

The lemon colored hair wrapped around her head in a halo
Her part, peaking through the tangle of flaxen strands
The eyebrows that changed color half way across her eye
The curl of her dark lashes back toward her eyelid
The little blonde fuzz that covered her face
The high curve of her cheekbone
Her nose, small, straight and perfectly aligned on her face
The swell of her lower lip, pale pink and shiny
White, slightly rounded teeth
The perfect ball of her chin
The pearly white skin along the back of her neck underneath her hair
One skinny arm curled up around her head and the other lying heavy
across her torso
The oblong freckle at the inside corner of her arm pit
The gentle curve of her breast into the line of her stomach
The small cave of her belly button
The outline of a bikini made by the sun on her body
Her hip falling into the line of her pelvis
A tiny honey-colored patch of pubic hair
The cheek of her butt, white and round Legs, long and thin, without mus-
cle tone
Her ankles, delicate, small, incongruous
Toes, painted with red, little in relation to the foot.

Rooster pressed down three more times, cradled the camera in his arm
and savored the view. After a few minutes, he replaced the camera in his
bag and climbed into the bed beside her. Her body was magnetically drawn
to his, the fit uncanny, her smell oddly like his own. She curled her head
into the space between his shoulder and chest and held him.

Click

Whole.

ONE FIFTH OF A SECOND
(.02) SECONDS

(.02) Seconds
Shutter speed of Rooster Boudreaux's Leica M4 used
with 35mm Ilford Delta 3200 Professional black and
white camera film, negative #23 of woman sleeping.

(.02) Seconds
Syracuse University. "Falling in love only takes a fifth of a
second, research reveals." Science Daily, 25 October 2010.

ACKNOWLEDGEMENTS

I would like to thank Joan Tewkesbury, my mother, for her brilliance, love, superior editing skills and for being an exceptional role model to writers everywhere. Chiwan Choi for his genius and the Finishing School for their honest opinions. Ramey Arnold for all things southern. My kids, Hailey, Piper, Gracie and Ramsey for growing up to be incredible people and most of all to my fiancé Marc Schaberg, without whom this book never would have happened. I am eternally grateful for his undying support, guidance, persistence and most importantly, love.

www.ingramcontent.com/pod-product-compliance
Lightning Source LLC
Chambersburg PA
CBHW061949170626
46813CB00006B/2581